'How dare you take advantage of me, sir?'

Nicholas stepped back. She thought she saw a glimmer of laughter in his eyes, then it had gone and his expression became harsh, withdrawn.

'I am sworn to one purpose, Mistress Stirling—to avenge the dishonour and murder of a gentle lady. Until then I can promise nothing.'

'I want no promises from you, sir,' Deborah replied. 'I am already promised to Miguel Cortes.'

Nicholas stared at her. 'You are a stubborn wench, mistress. I pray you will change your mind, lest I make you a widow before ever you are a wife.'

'You are a wicked rogue, sir!'

'I warn you, lady. If you set sail for Spain with this intent you will never reach its shores. I take anything I can that rightly belongs to the Cortes family—and Miguel's bride is no exception.'

Anne Herries lives in Cambridge but spends part of the winter in Spain, where she and her husband stay in a pretty resort nestled amid the hills that run from Malaga to Gibraltar. Gazing over a sparkling blue ocean, watching the sunbeams dance like silver confetti on the restless waves, Anne loves to dream up her stories of laughter, tears and romantic lovers. She is the author of over thirty published novels, thirteen of them for Harlequin Mills & Boon®.

Recent titles by the same author:

ROSALYN AND THE SCOUNDREL
A MATTER OF HONOUR
SATAN'S MARK

and in Medical Romance™:

THE MOST PRECIOUS GIFT
SARA'S SECRET

and in Mills & Boon®'s *The Steepwood Scandal*:

LORD RAVENSDEN'S MARRIAGE

THE ABDUCTED BRIDE

Anne Herries

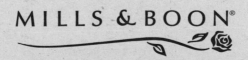

First published in Great Britain 2001
Harlequin Mills & Boon Limited,
Eton House, 18-24 Paradise Road, Richmond, Surrey TW9 1SR

© Anne Herries 2001

ISBN 0 263 82737 2

Set in Times Roman 10½ on 12 pt.
04-0701-82636

Printed and bound in Spain
by Litografia Rosés S.A., Barcelona

Chapter One

'Pray look over there! Now, is he not a fine figure of a man?' Mistress Sarah Palmer whispered to her cousin and giggled. She clutched at the other girl's arm in her excitement. 'Were he to offer for either of us, we should make haste to accept. Would you not agree?'

Deborah Ann, daughter of Sir Edward Stirling, glanced across the crowded gallery of the palace at Whitehall and frowned. The gentleman at whom her cousin had been gazing was indeed handsome, but to her mind he looked proud and arrogant, his dark brown eyes holding a haughty stare as they swept over the assembled courtiers.

'Oh, Sarah,' she said, a hint of laughter in her voice. 'How can you speak so? I vow I should not be comfortable married to such a man. His countenance is so harsh. He looks as if he might be...' Words failed her. 'Why, marry, he might be anything. I do not know.'

'I think he is a sea captain,' Sarah replied, giving the object of her admiration a roguish smile. 'He has a brownish look about his skin, as if he were often exposed to wind and weather.'

Deborah glanced again in the direction of the gentle-

man who had so captured her cousin's interest. He was
looking directly at Deborah and his dark eyes held a
distinct gleam of mockery. She turned her head away at
once. The wretched man! He need not imagine she was
interested in him, for she was not—not one whit!

She cooled her cheeks with the large fan she carried,
which was made out of chicken skin and painted with
pastoral scenes. Her embroidered satin shoes were new
and pinched her toes a little, and the elaborate dress she
was wearing had begun to feel heavy and over-warm,
for all she had thought it so fine when she chose it.
Indeed, her pleasure in being at the Court of King James
I was fast waning.

Deborah turned away from the mocking gaze of the
stranger, glancing about her with feigned interest. Here,
in the older wing of the palace, the gallery walls were
thick stone, which kept out both the cold and the heat
of the summer day. At night torches flared from iron
sconces set at intervals about the large room, but for now
the only light was from narrow windows in the thick
walls. Here and there a silk tapestry covered the rough
surface of the walls, lending colour and warmth to the
sparsely furnished chamber, but the floor was flagged
with thick stone tiles of black and white, its icy coldness
sending a chill through her body.

How she wished they were back in her father's pleasant manor house, with its wooden floors and the fresh
scent of herbs replaced daily to keep the air sweet. Deborah would not have wasted such a lovely day inside,
for her herb garden would have tempted her out into the
sunshine.

She spied her father in conversation with a tall, thin
gentleman; the other man had pale, pinched features and
wore clothes of black and silver, his body hunched as if

he felt the chill of the palace in his very bones. Seeing Sir Edward nod his head at her, Deborah began to make her way towards them, here and there exchanging a pleasant word with various acquaintances as she passed.

She was fond of her father, and proud of his air of distinction, which marked him out as a man to be reckoned with. He, too, was thin but upright in his stance: a handsome man, though past his prime, his hair streaked with silver at the temples and his eyes a faded blue that held memories of his private sorrow.

Sir Edward had brought his daughter and her cousin to Court this very week, and this was their second attendance at His Majesty's promenade. Deborah had been a little disappointed at how swiftly the King had passed through the assembled ladies and gentlemen, noticing only a few and passing on without speaking to more than one or two favoured courtiers.

She had heard much talk of the King before she came to Court, and a great deal of it was not good; people spoke disparagingly of his temper, his obsession with witchcraft, his lifestyle and his love of hunting, but Deborah had thought him merely sad and a little ugly.

Sir Edward's purpose in bringing the two young women to Court was to find husbands for them both if possible, but Sarah Palmer in particular. Sarah had some three years earlier lost both parents to the plague. Fortunately, she had been from home at the time and thus escaped taking the terrible illness. When he had been informed of the terrible tragedy of his sister and brother-in-law's deaths, Sir Edward had gone immediately to fetch Sarah to his home, where she had since resided as friend and companion to his daughter.

Deborah Ann and Sarah were much of an age, being close to seventeen years and therefore well ready to be

married. Sarah's parents had died before the arrange-
ments could be made for her marriage, and Deborah's
betrothed husband had been taken by a dread fever when
but seventeen years himself.

Since the death of a young man of whom both he and
Deborah had been fond, Sir Edward had been in no hurry
to see his only child wed. Nor did he wish to have her
marry out of her faith, for he and his dear lost wife had
been devout Catholics. However, during the reign of the
present king it had proved wise not to flaunt this fact to
the world.

When Queen Bess was on the throne Sir Edward had
been a frequent visitor to Court, for Gloriana tolerated
those she liked no matter what their faith, and after her
death he had retired to his home in the north of England.

James I was a man with whom it was possible to find
favour if one was prepared to court it—and most were
more than willing for the wealth such favours could
bring.

Sir Edward did not court the King's favour, neither
did he speak against him, preferring to mind his own
business, living quietly on his estate and tending his
land. He would not have come now to London had not
the matter of his ward's marriage begun to weigh on his
conscience. It was time both girls were wed, and if he
found his house too empty after they had gone, he must
look about him for a pleasant widow to warm his bed
and tend his comforts. Yet he could not imagine his life
without Deborah. He smiled as she approached.

'Father,' Deborah said, reaching his side at last. 'I
grow weary. May we not go to our lodgings?'

'Ah, daughter.' Sir Edward looked at her with affection mingled with approval. She was without doubt a
beauty, though perhaps a little too slender. Her cousin

was more comely, but her fair English rose looks were not as striking as Deborah's dark chestnut curls and green eyes. 'This is well met, my dear. I wished to introduce you to this gentleman. He asked if he might speak with you himself.'

'Mistress Stirling—your servant.' The gentleman spoke English with a heavy foreign accent as he bowed gracefully to her. 'I am the ambassador of Don Manola Cortes, a gentleman of high rank and the owner of fine vineyards in Spain.'

'I have done business with Señor Juan Sanchez for many years,' Sir Edward said to his daughter. 'Some twenty years ago I had the honour to call Don Manola my friend, and Señor Sanchez has brought me much good wine from his vineyards.'

'My master is a wealthy man,' Señor Sanchez went on with a smile for Deborah. 'He has a son, Mistress Stirling. A fine young man of just five and twenty. It has long been the Don's hope to see his son wed to a worthy young woman. I believe I may at last have found the lady he seeks—a lady of both birth and beauty.'

'Not so fast, señor,' Sir Edward interrupted with a smile of caution. 'My daughter and myself will listen to your flattering proposal. You shall be given a fair hearing, but I must know more of Don Manola's son. You will furnish us with a likeness of the gentleman if you please, and if my daughter favours the young man—and he her, of course—we may then discuss the details of a marriage contract.'

'You indulge Mistress Stirling,' Señor Sanchez replied. He seemed surprised and not altogether pleased. 'Our ways are more direct, I think. In Spain a father's wishes are paramount.'

'Many an Englishman would agree with you,' Sir Edward said, his eyes meeting the Spaniard's steadily. 'It is, of course, accepted that a daughter should marry where her father pleases, but Deborah Ann is precious to me. I shall not lightly give her to any man—no matter how wealthy or virtuous. Her happiness is also mine.'

'My father does truly indulge me,' Deborah said, her mouth soft with love as she looked at him. 'Yet my respect for his wishes is all the greater because of it, sir. I am confident that he wishes only my good, therefore my pleasure is to obey him in all things.'

'Not quite all,' Sir Edward murmured. 'You manage to have your way in many things, daughter.'

Deborah laughed, tossing her head and gazing mischievously up at him. 'But that is because you are so very kind to me, sir.'

Father and daughter smiled in perfect understanding. Both knew that the girl was capable of twisting the man around her little finger, but both also knew that their love and respect was mutual: neither would willingly distress or hurt the other.

'Your willingness to oblige your father is most pleasing, Mistress Stirling,' said Señor Sanchez. 'I return to Spain on the evening tide tomorrow and will carry news of your beauty and good character to my master.' He bowed low before Deborah and her father. 'If you wish it, I shall carry a letter from you to my master, sir. With fair winds I shall return in three weeks. I shall then be able to bring greetings from my master's son.'

'The letter will be ready in the morning. We wish you a safe voyage, señor. Do not neglect to bring Don Miguel's likeness,' warned Sir Edward with a smile for his daughter. 'All the ladies like a well-favoured man. Is that not so, Deborah?'

Señor Sanchez bowed once more and walked away.

'He has always been honest with me in business,' Sir Edward said to his daughter when the Spaniard had disappeared amongst the press of courtiers. 'I have settled nothing, Deborah. If you should meet a suitable admirer you truly like and respect before Sanchez returns, I shall not force you to this marriage—nor yet if you should form a dislike for the idea. I would have you content in this as in all things, Deborah.'

'You are always so good to me, dearest father,' Deborah said, her hand on his arm. 'I shall be guided by you. I know you wish only that I might be as happy with my husband as you and my mother were together.'

Sir Edward's faded blue eyes clouded with sorrow. 'Would that my dear Beth were here with us now. How proud she would be of her daughter.' He sighed and touched Deborah's cheek. 'It cannot be. Now—did you say you wished to return to our lodgings?'

'Yes, Father. May we, please? We have seen His Majesty's procession. There is no reason to linger—and my shoes pinch.' She did not add that she thought the King so ill favoured with his large eyes, thin beard and ungainly stature that she had found the sight of him progressing through his fawning courtiers less than inspiring.

Sir Edward laughed. 'Uncomfortable shoes! A better reason could not be found. Where is your cousin?'

'I left her in conversation with Mistress Goodleigh, but…oh, there she is. She seems to be talking to a gentleman.'

'No gentleman, if rumour be truth,' Sir Edward replied with a frown of disapproval. 'That is the Marquis de Vere, a Frenchman by birth though his mother was an English gentlewoman—and he himself a privateer by all accounts. He preys on Spanish ships. Sanchez has complained of his actions to the King, but apparently his words fell upon deaf ears. His Majesty promised only that he would consider the matter.'

'Surely His Majesty must listen to the Don's complaints,' Deborah Ann said. 'We are not at war with Spain. Are not the prince and my lord Buckingham in Spain to treat for a marriage between the Spanish King's daughter and Prince Charles?'

'Indeed, it is so,' Sir Edward agreed. It was the news that the negotiations for the Catholic marriage had seemed to go well that had encouraged him to venture to Court once more. 'One would think His Majesty would rather hang de Vere than welcome him to Court—but it seems the rogue finds favour in the royal eyes.'

'Why would that be, Father? The marquis is little better than the Algerian pirates who prey on our ships.'

'Queen Elizabeth was wont to smile on such men,' Sir Edward said with a little frown. 'One could not blame her so much, for the might of Spain could have snatched the crown from her had our brave sailors not beaten off the great Armada the Spanish sent against her—but our present king should have no need to fear Spain.'

'Then one must suppose His Majesty to have other reasons for his leniency.'

'With a king it is always best to suppose nothing and be ever on one's guard,' Sir Edward replied. 'Your cousin is alone now. Go to her and tell her we are almost ready to leave. There is someone else I must speak to for a moment and then we shall go.'

'Yes, Father.'

Deborah began to walk towards the spot where she had last seen her cousin. Where was Sarah? Oh, there she was! She had moved to the other side of the gallery.

Changing her direction to catch up with her, Deborah was startled when a man stepped directly into her path.

'Whither so fast?' a deep, husky voice asked. Deborah caught the faint accent, which she realized must come from his having spent much of his life in France. 'Why are you in such a hurry, mistress? You were like to knock me down in your haste.'

That was most unlikely! Deborah stared up into the wicked dark eyes of the Marquis de Vere and drew in her breath sharply. Close to, he was even larger than he had seemed from a distance. A powerful man with broad shoulders and strong thighs, his nearness was intimidating. His court dress was fashioned of black velvet slashed through with dusky gold braid, his doublet heavily sewn with jet bugles.

Unusually in these times he wore no beard, though a slight shadow could be discerned on his chin as if it were some hours since he had shaved. His hair was dark brown and waved thickly back from his brow, and he wore only a small ruff about his neck. Even in court clothes, which taken to excess could appear ridiculous on some, this man had the look of an adventurer.

'It was you who impeded my progress, sir,' Deborah replied, her head high, two spots of colour in her cheeks. 'I pray you, allow me to pass. I wish to speak with my cousin.'

'Ah, yes, the pretty Mistress Palmer,' Nicholas Trevern, Marquis de Vere, murmured throatily. 'A bold wench that one, and no better than she ought to be, I'll vow.'

'How dare you impugn the honour of my family?' Deborah's eyes flashed with anger. 'If I were a man I would demand satisfaction, sir!'

'I could afford you a deeper satisfaction as a wench, Mistress Stirling.'

The expression in his eyes coupled with the mockery in his voice shocked her. She knew that men were freer in their speech in town than she was accustomed to hearing in her father's house, where she was always accorded the deepest respect, but this was outrageous. How dare he make such a ribald suggestion to her!

'You are unwise to insult me, sir. My father has powerful friends.'

'Indeed?' Laughter danced in Nicholas's eyes. 'Would you have me hanged drawn and quartered for daring to tease you, mistress?'

'I have no wish to listen to your teasing, sir.'

'Have you not? Your cousin seemed amused.'

'My cousin is young and perhaps something foolish.'

'Of your own age, methinks?' He made her an elegant leg. 'Forgive me, mistress. I bow to your superior wisdom.'

'You are pleased to mock me, sir.'

It was all Deborah could do not to stamp her foot. Oh, if she were but the son her father had hoped for and never-had! She would teach this devil a lesson he would not soon forget.

'One must mock at life,' Nicholas went on before she could make up her mind how to deliver her set-down. 'Too oft life plays its cruel jests on both the godly and ungodly alike. 'Tis as well to laugh in the face of fate as lie down beneath it. Yet I meant not to offend you, mistress. Go on your way in peace.'

He stood aside. Deborah swept past, the wide skirts of her sumptuous gown swaying with indignation. It was as well for her peace of mind that she did not turn her head to look back, for the sheer delight and mischief in

Nicholas's eyes would have added to her sense of frustration. How many times had she longed to be free of all the restrictions placed on a woman? How often she had wished herself a man, and never more so than now. Oh, that dreadful man should suffer if she but had a sword to run him through!

Deborah was no stranger to swordplay, or to a man's costume. Her father had indulged her in whims others might find strange. He had been amused to see her strut and playact in her role as a youth, and had delighted in her skill with the rapier.

'I vow I could wish for no finer son,' he had told her once when they had practised the art of fencing together and he found himself disarmed. 'But this must be our secret, Deborah, for the old tabbies would speak you ill if it were known you had behaved so immodestly.'

'I care naught for the spite of tabbies,' Deborah had replied confidently. 'But as you ask it, Father, I shall be discreet. What we enjoy in private shall remain so.'

'You are always my good daughter,' her father had teased, a smile curving his mouth. 'I must be on my guard for 'tis certain you will want something—a new gown, perhaps?'

'How should I want a new gown when I already have so many?' Deborah asked, then a little smile flickered in her green eyes—eyes that had caused many a young village lad to dream of her in vain. 'But there is one thing you might do for me—if you wish?'

'Of course, daughter. What is it now? Would you have me give more of my gold to master parson—or open my kitchens to every beggar in the whole of Northumbria?'

'It is just Mistress Donovan. She is a widow now, Father, with three small children. All I ask is that she may remain in her cottage until she can find a man to take her husband's place.'

'Of course, child. She is a comely good woman. I dare say a man can be found to wed her before I am entirely ruined by lack of rent or labour.'

'Oh, Father!'

Deborah had laughed at his gentle mockery of her good works. Yet she was not moved to laughter by the wicked teasing of the Marquis de Vere, though in her heart she could not find him guilty of malice. When he smiled he did not look so very harsh, but there was mettle in him. She thought that he might make a fearsome enemy, and a little chill ran down her spine. For a moment it was as if a dark cloud had passed over her and she was afraid of something, but of what she could not be sure. It was just a sense that her life of sweet content was about to change forever.

She shook her head as if to clear it of such thoughts. Sarah had turned her way and she lifted her hand to beckon her to her side.

'It is time we were leaving,' she said as her cousin came up to her. 'I have had enough of the Court for one day.'

'Oh, must we go?' Sarah dimpled as a young man smiled at her from across the crowded gallery. 'I have found our visit vastly amusing, have you not, cousin?'

'It is interesting to see so many gathered here in the hope of a smile or some notice from His Majesty,' Deborah replied. 'Though his appearance was so brief that most must have been disappointed.'

'Oh, the King…' Sarah pulled a laughing face. She was well aware that she had aroused the interest of more than one gentleman that day. 'It is not His Majesty's attentions that I care for, cousin.'

Deborah noticed the young man who was staring so hard in their direction and smiled inwardly as she saw the flush in Sarah's cheeks.

'Come, Sarah,' she urged. 'Master Henderson will find his way to our lodgings if he wishes to further his acquaintance with our family.' So saying, she took her cousin's arm and began firmly to steer her towards Sir Edward, who was now waiting for them.

The bold-eyed marquis seemed to have disappeared and Deborah was relieved that there would be no more encounters with such a wicked rogue. She wondered that he even dared to appear at Court, for if there were any justice His Majesty would surely hang the fellow.

'What would ye have of me now, rogue?' James I of England and VI of Scotland eyed the younger man with amusement. Disfigured by childhood weaknesses and birth defects, he liked to see charming, handsome faces about him and his partiality led to many complaints about his favourites.

'Why, nothing, sir,' replied Nicholas. The son of an English gentlewoman and a French nobleman, only a genuine liking for this man some called fool kept him at court. He had estates in France that needed his attention, but James had asked for him and he had come in answer to the summons. 'I believe you had some need of me?'

'Mayhap.' The King frowned. He had to look up to this giant, who towered above most men at Court, and he disliked the crick in his neck it gave him. 'Sit on that stool by me, laddie. I give ye the royal permission. Aye, I might have need of your services. This foolish venture of my son has cost me dearly, and I do not know what will become of it all in the end.'

'You mean Prince Charles's marriage to the Infanta of Spain? I thought it was Your Majesty's own wish?'

'Aye, I have thought it for the best. You know I do not want war. These miserly Englishmen will vote me no money for peace, let alone war. The marriage might have brought a lasting peace between our two countries, one that would go on when I am dead—yet I confess I am uneasy. Buckingham and my son went incognito to Spain, thereby placing themselves too securely in the hands of the Spaniards. 'Twas foolishness and against my orders—though you will keep that to yourself, Nicholas. I will not have *Baby* criticised by others. You hear me?'

'Yes, sire. Nothing you confide in me goes beyond this chamber.'

'Aye, I know it. I trust ye. The negotiations for the marriage go apace and all seems well—but I fear that I do not hear all that goes on in the council chambers of Spain. I have been forced to make concessions, though I do not like them—nor do they please these stiff-necked Englishmen. There are rumblings, laddie…rumblings. I cannot grant too much favour to Catholics or my crown may fall, but Spain would suck the last drop of blood from my poor old body.'

Nicholas nodded. He had heard rumours of the way Buckingham had conducted himself at the Spanish court, preening his feathers and generally giving himself airs. The Duke believed he was secure as James's favourite, but there had been murmurs against him and it was plain the King was anxious about what was happening behind the scenes.

'Buckingham has perhaps been a little unwise,' Nicholas said carefully. 'Yet the good that may come of this marriage is perhaps worth the expenditure of your jewels, Majesty…which reminds me. I have a gift for you somewhere, sire—silver and gold from the New World.'

'Treasure you stole from Don Manola, I'll warrant.' Humour sparkled in James's eyes, a humour seldom seen by any outside the few he favoured with his confidence.

'His ship was over-heavy in the water and like to sink,' Nicholas replied, an answering gleam in his own eyes. 'I did but relieve the captain of his burden and send him safe on his way. Besides, he had stolen the treasure from its rightful owners. I see no crime in robbing thieves, sire.'

'The Don's emissary would have me hang you,' said James. 'But though some would have it otherwise, I am not a fool.'

'The wisest fool in Christendom,' Nicholas murmured beneath his breath.

'Your grandfather, Sir Nicholas Trevern, was a good friend to me at a time when it seemed my life might lie in the balance. During those dark days I was forced to suffer indignity and oppression, but a puppet in the hands of those who would rule in my stead—and though a young child, your mother was like a sister in her kindness to me,' James went on. 'For their sakes I would spare you did I not love you for your own.'

'You are generous, sire.'

'Whist, no such thing! At times I love too well and some take advantage of me, but never you. I want your loyalty, Nicholas. Few have your knowledge of the Spanish and their ships. I pray for peace, but this business troubles me and I sleep little. I suspect Spain of demanding too much and I fear some misunderstanding that will lead to war between us. They have long coveted our crown.'

'I think you are wise to be cautious, sire. Queen Bess gave Spain a bloody nose and it has not been forgot.'

'I know it,' James sighed. 'I would have *Baby* back home safely, Nicholas. I must take care and seem to acquiesce in all things until he returns—with or without his bride.'

James was a man who loved good company, feasting and hunting. Nicholas thought he might have lived content had he been born a country gentleman. The flattery of others had exploited a weakness in the King, but the man was sound.

'You know you have my loyalty. I choose to live in France, but the land of my mother's birth is dear to me— and I would serve you if I can.'

'Bring me word,' James said, 'if you hear anything of importance. I would be warned of any ill news before it is too late.'

'My ship is being provisioned and made ready,' Nicholas replied. 'I sail for Spanish waters within three days and will return ere long. Be assured that I shall glean what news I can—but is it certain that things go ill with the contracts?'

'I have no firm confirmation yet, merely whispers and innuendo,' James replied. 'But I feel something dark and heavy in my heart. Now, away with you, laddie. The night is young. Have you no wench waiting for you?'

Nicholas laughed. 'Why should I have but one when there are so many beautiful young women in London?'

'They say you have only to glance at a wench to have her itching to warm your bed,' said James, chuckling. 'I vow it would be a shame to disappoint the lasses. Away now and do your duty.'

Nicholas bowed and walked respectfully from the King's apartments. His smile faded as he left the palace and began to make his way towards the river, where he intended to summon a boatman. He was lodging at an inn down river and had promised to meet with Henri Moreau, his friend and able lieutenant. They had much to discuss before they put to sea once more.

Attacking Don Manola's ships afforded Nicholas little satisfaction these days. After the death of Isabella Rodrigues, to whom Nicholas had been betrothed, his first thought had been to take revenge on her murderer. Now, almost two years on, he still had not managed to take Miguel Cortes prisoner. He had been told that the Don's son cowered at home, afraid to put to sea lest *Le Diable* should take his ship and his miserable life be forfeit.

Nicholas had cursed the man who had raped and killed the beautiful young woman because she had refused him in favour of another. What woman would willingly become the bride of that monster?

Miguel Cortes might have the face of an angel, but his soul was twisted and evil, as black as hell. Nicholas knew that the Don's men called him *Le Diable*, because he outran and out-fought their ships with ease, but he had never taken life wantonly, never tortured men or animals for pleasure, sparing his enemies whenever possible: there was only one man he wished to kill!

Nicholas had never taken an unwilling woman, though there had been wenches enough to warm his bed. Of late, though, Nicholas had found little satisfaction in pleasuring tavern wenches. His feelings for the lovely Isabella had been those of a gentleman for a woman he admired and respected. He had liked and cared for her, believing that such a virtuous woman would teach him the gentle ways of love.

It was Isabella's very vulnerability that hurt Nicholas so much—that such a sweet child should have suffered

so terribly at the hands of a monster! He had been told
that she had screamed and begged for mercy on her
knees before she died, but none had been granted.

Miguel Cortes deserved to die. Justice demanded that
he pay the penalty for his dread crime! And die he
should. Nicholas had sworn it and he would find a
way—even if he had to pry the sniveling coward from
his hiding place. Isabella's pleas should not go unanswered.

Unbidden, on the scent of summer flowers, the memory of a young woman's face came to Nicholas's mind.
He smiled as he recalled the spirited way she had parried
his teasing. It had been obvious that she was unused to
Court manners, which could be coarse and bawdy, for
most women attending that day would have responded
very differently to his flirting.

The King had spoken truly when he said Nicholas had
only to look at the ladies of the Court to have them
panting for his loving.

He was not sure why he had found Mistress Deborah
Stirling so intriguing. She was beautiful, but so was her
cousin Sarah Palmer. It was the obliging Mistress Palmer
who had furnished him with the details of her cousin's
name and person.

Mistress Stirling was in the market for a husband. Her
father was a gentleman of whom little was known at
Court, though it was said he owned a goodly estate in
the north—and that he was Catholic. Not something he
flaunted at Court, being more discreet than many of his
kind who screeched of betrayal and broken promises and
made their position all the worse.

Nicholas too had been raised a Catholic, yet he had
denied his faith these many months. What kind of a god

would let scum like Miguel Cortes flourish when poor Isabella lay in her grave unavenged?

Not for much longer! Somehow Nicholas would find a way to tempt that monster from his lair—and then he would kill him with his own hands.

Dismissing his wayward thoughts of a girl with fire in her eyes, Nicholas put his mind to the task ahead. Henri had news for him. Perhaps at last the means to take his revenge had come within his grasp.

Perhaps Miguel Cortes had at last been driven back to sea by his frustration at having been cooped up for so long. If that were not the case, then some plan must be found to make him leave the shores of Spain.

Chapter Two

The girl was lost in a mist...running from something that terrified her. She glanced over her shoulder, but could not see anything. Yet she knew if she stopped running it would catch her and then...

Deborah woke from her dream, shivering with fright. What could she have been thinking of to make her have such a nightmare? She usually slept peacefully and woke refreshed, but that morning the unease the dream had created seemed to stay with her as she dressed and went downstairs.

Was it that strange meeting with the Marquis de Vere the previous evening, that had prompted such dreams? No, how could it be? She laughed at herself. She had met the man but once and he could mean nothing to her. She would think of him no more.

They had come to London to enjoy themselves, and she meant to make the most of her visit. It was very unlikely that they would come again. Nor did she particularly wish for it. Oh, it was amusing at Court, and she liked to see the courtiers parading in their fine gowns, but there was too much backbiting and spite amongst them to please her.

She thought that, if she were to marry, she would like to live in the country with her friends about her. She tried to picture the man she might wed, but the only face that came to her mind was the Marquis de Vere's. How very vexing! She was sure she did not wish to meet the rogue again.

'Ah, there you are, daughter,' Sir Edward said, coming out of the parlour as she reached the hall of the house where they were lodging. It was a fine house, sturdily built of brick and wood in the Tudor style, and situated near the river. Like most other houses in the street it had wooden shutters, which were firmly closed at night, and the windows were so tiny and so dark that they let little light inside. 'I have been composing a letter to Don Manola. Señor Sanchez is to call for it this morning. Would you care to see what I have written?'

'Thank you, Father.' She took the letter and glanced through the elegantly phrased words. 'I think it will do very well, sir.'

'I shall send the small portrait I had done of you on your last birthday as a gift for Don Miguel,' her father said, smiling at her with affection. 'I have others and it is my intention to ask the artist to make another portrait of you when we return home. I shall want some keepsake when you leave me for your husband's home, Deborah.'

'Oh, Father,' she said, her heart aching for the look of sadness in his eyes. 'You know you will always be welcome in my home. I could not bear to part from you forever.'

'Ah, my sweet child,' Sir Edward replied. 'I must not seek to hold you. You must be allowed to find happiness in a home of your own—but I admit that I shall miss you sorely.'

'I am not married yet,' she reminded him. She linked her arm in his, smiling up at him. 'Now, dearest Father—pray tell me what you have planned for today?'

'I thought we might take a little trip on the river,' Sir Edward replied. 'And then, after we have supped—a visit to the theatre?'

'Oh, yes.' Deborah smiled at him in delight, the remnants of her headache disappearing as she thought of the pleasures to come. 'Yes, my dear Father. I think I should enjoy that above all things.'

She would forget the marquis and his impudence and she would forget her foolish dream. The next few weeks would fly by and then they would go home—whether or not they had found husbands.

'Prithee tarry a little longer,' Sarah begged as she poured over the fabulous wares of the silk merchant in Cheapside. 'I cannot decide between the rose damask and the green brocade—which do you prefer, Debs?'

'They would both suit you very well,' Deborah replied with an indulgent smile at her cousin. 'Why do you not order a length of each?'

'But they are so expensive.' Sarah stroked the soft materials under the indulgent eye of the silk merchant. 'And I have already overspent my allowance. I do not like to ask my uncle for more.'

'I have sufficient monies left to lend you some. Besides, my father would not think of denying you. Order both and let us away to the glovemaker. The hour grows late and I have bespoke a pair of gauntlets for Father.'

Sarah dimpled with pleasure, for in her heart she had wanted both silks. She gave her order to the merchant, who promised to deliver it within the hour to their lodgings, and, tucking her arm into Deborah's, she willingly accompanied her cousin from the shop. The two girls walked farther down the street, then turned into another where the sign of the glovemaker swung to and fro in the breeze.

'Mistress Palmer—Mistress Stirling. Stay a moment, I beg you.'

Deborah glanced at her cousin and, seeing the blush in her cheeks as Master Will Henderson hurried up to them, understood why her cousin had lingered so long over the purchase of the materials. This meeting had not happened by chance.

'Oh, how pleasant to see you, sir.' Sarah dimpled up at her young and handsome suitor. 'We are on our way to the glovemaker.'

'Why do you not wait here a moment or two?' Deborah suggested as she caught the longing in the young man's eyes. 'The shop I need is but a step away and I have our footman to watch over me. Bide here while I see to my business, Sarah. I shall not be long and you will be safe enough with Master Henderson.'

'That she will,' he declared, 'for I would defend her with my life—and you, of course, Mistress Stirling.'

'I do not doubt it, sir.' Deborah smiled and left them together. Sarah had other admirers, but only one made her blush so prettily. She was certain that her cousin would soon be wed. As for her…Deborah sighed. They had been in London for more than three weeks now and she had met no one she could think of as a husband.

She had not lacked for suitors, but none appealed to her. Some were too old, some too foolish—but most were greedy. They wanted her for her father's fortune, not her person. She saw no reason to exchange her happy companionship with her father for something that could afford her no pleasure or benefit.

As yet no news had come from Spain. Deborah was not certain how she felt about the prospect of marrying a man she had never met, but the negotiations were only just beginning. Until the contracts were signed, it would be a simple matter for either side to draw back. Besides, Don Miguel might not be pleased with her likeness.

When she thought about it, she was not at all sure she wished to wed anyone. Perhaps she would do better to remain at home and care for her beloved father?

For a moment the memory of a pair of mocking eyes came to haunt her, but she dismissed it instantly. The Marquis de Vere had been no more to Court—at least, he had not on the days when she and Sarah had attended. Why should she care whether he came or not? Besides, she did not like him. He was arrogant, insulting and rude!

There was to be a masked ball at Court on the morrow. It would be their last visit for the time being, for Sir Edward was minded to go home. He did not care to neglect his estates too long, and Deborah was tired of the long, tedious appearances at Whitehall, which for her were neither pleasurable nor useful.

'Your cousin is in a fair way to be settled,' Sir Edward had told his daughter a day or so earlier. 'As for you, Deborah, I have seen no sign of any preference on your part?'

'I have none, Father. I would as soon go home unpromised.'

'I expect word from Señor Sanchez any day now. We shall hear what my old friend Don Manola has to say—and then we shall go home and discuss the matter. I am duty bound to find Sarah a husband, but there is no haste to arrange your own marriage, my dear.'

Deborah knew that her father was secretly glad of a

reprieve. In his heart he dreaded the moment of their parting yet felt he would be failing in his duty if he did not see her safely wed. Deborah would be an heiress of some substance. Sir Edward had no male heir or any relatives to speak of, and his estate was not entailed. There was a distant cousin on her mother's side—Mistress Berkshire—but she and her husband were old and lived quietly in the country, and would not be deemed fit guardians.

If anything should happen to Sir Edward before her marriage—God forbid!—Deborah's estate would be overseen by the King's council and she become his ward. A marriage deemed suitable by His Majesty would be arranged, unless James coveted her estate. She might then be left to live a solitary life or sent to a nunnery, never to fulfill the bright promise of her youth.

Sir Edward knew he must see her safe one day, but he was still only in his middle years and a strong, healthy man. A few more months, even a year or so, could not harm her and would afford him joy.

Deborah completed the purchase of the gauntlets for her father. They were fashioned of soft grey leather and studded with pearls at the cuffs. She thought he would be very pleased with the gift and was smiling as she left the merchant's shop. A startled cry left her lips as she walked into a man who was about to enter, stepping heavily on his foot and dropping her package.

'Forgive me, sir! I was not aware of...' The words died on her lips as she found herself staring into the mocking eyes that had haunted her dreams these past three weeks. Her heart began to beat wildly. 'Oh, it is you...'

'You seem determined to injure me, mistress,' said Nicholas and bent to recover her package.

'Indeed, I do not!' Deborah gave him a speaking look, but despite her annoyance a smile quivered at the corners of her mouth, which had she but known it was quite delectable and extremely tempting. Face to face, she had to acknowledge that her cousin had been right from the start—he was a fine figure of a man! She had seen none to rival him at Court.

'Your purchase, mistress.'

'Thank you. I apologise if I injured your foot.'

Nicholas grinned. God's body! She was a beauty—and such spirit! It was no wonder the memory of their brief encounter had lingered in his mind despite all attempts to dismiss it. Perhaps it was in part why he had returned to London sooner than he had intended, though he also brought news for King James.

'You have no doubt made a cripple of me, mistress—but I shall struggle to bear the pain with dignity.'

His taunt was so outrageous that Deborah laughed. 'You are a wicked tease, sir. I cannot think what I have done that you should mock me so.'

'Nor I, come to think on it,' he replied, his bold eyes challenging her. 'Unless it is that your eyes are more lovely than the brightest star in the heavens—your lips as sweet as a rose dew kissed.'

'You would rival Master Shakespeare,' Deborah replied with a toss of her head. She had been to the theatre several times now, and found the performance entrancing, though the audience was noisy and often shouted at the actors whenever they disagreed with something that was happening on stage. 'I shall listen to no more of this nonsense, sir. My cousin awaits me in the street and I must go to her.'

'I believe she is pleasantly engaged,' Nicholas said, a faint smile on his mouth. 'You will allow me to delay you a little, mistress. May I be of service to you? Perhaps I could call chairs for you and Mistress Palmer?'

'Thank you, sir, but I believe Master Henderson will escort us should we wish it—and my footman is close by.' Deborah avoided looking at him. He was too sure of himself and her heart would not behave itself when she saw the way his eyes danced with laughter.

'If Master Henderson puts his claim above mine I have no love for the rogue. I believe I shall call him out!'

'Pray be serious, my lord.' Deborah was beginning to remember this man's reputation. She had been warned that he was not to be trusted. She ought to walk away at once, but her feet would not obey her. 'Your levity does not become you.'

'I fear you would like me even less if I were to show you my other side, lady.'

'Yes, I do think you have a darkness in you,' Deborah said with a considering look. There were two sides to this man, one charming and pleasant, the other dark and threatening. 'I sensed it when we first met.'

'Is that why you disliked me?' Nicholas frowned. 'You have no need to fear me, Mistress Stirling. I have never harmed a wench. It is true that I have a devil inside me, but it is for others to fear—not you.'

'Do you speak of a Spanish gentleman, perchance?'

'What have you heard of that accursed rogue?' Nicholas's eyes glittered with sudden anger, startling her. 'I swear you will hear nothing to his good from me.'

'They say you attack Don Manola's ships—that you are little more than a pirate.' Deborah tipped her head to gaze up at him defiantly. She did not know why she was pressing him like this, unless it was a perverse need in her to see his reaction. She would be a fool to let his charm sway her judgement of him. He was both a scoundrel and a thief.

'Some would call me a privateer,' Nicholas muttered, his mouth hard, features set into the harsh lines she had noticed before. 'Know this of me, Mistress Stirling—I may be *Le Diable* to the Spaniard I attack, but I have never killed for pleasure.' He touched his hat to her. 'I bid you *adieu*, mistress.'

For a moment Deborah was quite unable to speak. She wanted to cry out, to beg him to wait and explain his meaning, yet could not force the words from her lips.

What could he have meant? Who killed for pleasure— Don Manola? It was what he had implied, yet it could not be. He was her father's friend and Deborah would trust Sir Edward's judgement above any other. He was considering a marriage between her and Don Miguel Cortes. Never would he think of entrusting her to the son of a man he did not admire or trust.

Was it merely spite on the marquis's part, then? She would not have thought it of the man. Surely a powerful man like that would have no need of petty lies and innuendo? His weapons would be sharper and more deadly.

There was clearly some quarrel between Don Manola and the marquis. She imagined that the marquis truly believed his cause was just. Was it not always thus when men quarrelled? For herself she abhorred violence of any kind. It was surely wrong to attack another man's ships? Men must be wounded or killed during the action. Yet seemingly the marquis believed he was behaving fairly. Why should that be?

'Know this of me...I have never killed for pleasure.'

Once again Deborah shivered as she felt the chill go through her. She sensed a dark shadow hanging over her, as she had after their first meeting at Whitehall. Yet what had she to fear from him? Her destiny was not to run with his. Sir Edward would never contemplate such a match—nor did she wish it!

Deborah denied the prompting of an imp within her— a wicked voice that whispered she had never felt so challenged, so alive as when in the presence of the marquis. It was but a wayward thought that told her life had been almost too safe, too comfortable, that her true fulfilment as a woman would only come if she were brave enough to snatch at the burning brand this man offered.

For there had been fire in her when she gazed into his eyes. She had known a restless longing for something— but she knew not what. It was surely not to be in the arms of that wicked rogue!

Deborah shook her head. She was foolish to let him into her head. The Marquis de Vere was nothing to her, nor ever could be.

Sarah turned to her as she approached, her eyes glowing with excitement. 'Dearest Deborah,' she cried. 'You will never guess what has happened since you were gone.'

'What is it, cousin?'

Deborah was already certain that she knew. Master Henderson had spoken of his intentions. She smiled but held her peace. Let Sarah enjoy her moment of triumph to the full.

'Master Henderson has gone to summon chairs for us, Debs—but that is not my news. I told him we were to leave London soon and he was devastated. He returns with us to the house and will beg my uncle for my hand in marriage.' Sarah looked at her anxiously. 'Do you think Sir Edward will look favourably on the match?'

'Is it what you truly desire, Sarah?'

'Yes, with all my heart.'

'Then I am sure my father will consent. Master Henderson is of good family and, though not wealthy, will come into an estate on his father's death. Besides, you have money lodged with the goldsmiths of London. Father placed it in safe keeping when your father's house was sold. You will not go to your husband with empty coffers.'

'Both you and my uncle have been so good to me,' Sarah declared. 'I shall be sad to leave you, Deborah—though I cannot wait to be Master Henderson's true wife. He loves me with all his heart and I love him.'

'Then you are fortunate, cousin.'

'Yes, indeed I am.' Sarah smiled as she saw her gallant returning with two sedan chairs and their bearers in tow. 'Is he not handsome, Debs?'

'Very handsome,' Deborah agreed, though privately she thought the young man's features a little weak. For herself she preferred stronger men like her father…and the marquis. 'All I wish for is your happiness, cousin.'

'And I yours,' Sarah replied, her eyes curious as she looked at Deborah. 'Have you found no one at Court who stirs your heart, Debs?'

'No one,' Deborah answered at once. She did not meet her cousin's open gaze for she knew that she lied, and Sarah would see it in her face. One man had stirred forbidden feelings in her, but she would not admit it to anyone. 'I have not been as fortunate as you, sweet Sarah.'

'Mistress Stirling…' Arriving breathless and anxious at that moment, the young man looked at her and then his beloved. 'Mistress Palmer has spoken to you of my hopes?'

'She has, sir—and I approve. I am certain Sir Edward

can have no objection, though of course I may not speak for him.'

'No, no, of course not. It was just that Sarah said he always does as you wish…' Master Henderson flushed and looked awkward. 'Forgive me. I did not mean to imply anything…'

'I have taken no offence, sir. It is well known that my father indulges me. I am in favour of my cousin's marriage to you—and I ask only that you treat her with kindness.'

'I shall spend my life serving her,' he avowed, a flush in his cheeks. 'I live only for her.'

'Then I may ask no more.'

Deborah was thoughtful as she was handed into her chair. Master Henderson was truly a gentleman and it was thoughtful of him to escort her and Sarah back to their lodgings, though they were safe enough with her father's servant to walk a little distance behind. There were parts of London she would not have dared to venture to, even in broad day, but here in this busy street with honest folk going about their business, they had never been in danger.

She smiled as she saw the young man's hand upon his sword. He was prepared to defend his beloved with his life—yet she wondered how capable he would be should beggars or footpads attack them. If that were to happen she would rather trust her stout footman—or perhaps the Marquis de Vere.

Deborah thought it would be a brave footpad who attacked a lady escorted by the marquis. She imagined that he was skilled with the weapon he had worn at his side that morning. If she were ever in a dangerous situation, she would be glad of his company.

Such foolish thoughts! She was more like to need protecting from the Marquis de Vere. He was charming but a rogue and she had best remember that and put him out of her head once and for all.

Deborah tried valiantly to dismiss the pictures, which would keep popping into her head. Soon she would be returning to her home in the country, and then she would never see the rogue again.

Perhaps she would be married within the year—to the son of the man who was the marquis's sworn enemy.

'Well, Deborah, I am glad to see your cousin settled,' Sir Edward remarked to his daughter when they were alone later that day. 'We shall remain in London for her betrothal and we can all travel home together when Master Henderson takes Sarah to meet his family.'

'Yes, Father. It is fortunate that Master Henderson lives no more than fifty leagues from us. His family will not have so very far to travel for the wedding. We must do our best for her, see that she leaves us well endowed with linens and goods.'

'Yes, yes, of course,' Sir Edward agreed. 'All that will be seen to. Now it is of you and your marriage I wish to speak, Deborah. Señor Sanchez has returned. He called on me while you were out this morning, bringing letters for us both and a gift for you.'

He handed her a small object wrapped in blue velvet. When she opened it, Deborah gasped in surprise and pleasure. It was a miniature portrait of a young and handsome man painted on a shell background and framed in gold set with garnets and pearls.

'Oh,' she said. 'He is beautiful, Father. I have never seen such a countenance on any man. Do you think it can be a true likeness? Can anyone have hair that colour—like spun silver—and eyes so very blue?'

'If you look at the back you will find a compartment that opens,' her father said. 'Within it there is a lock of hair just that colour.' Sir Edward smiled as he saw the wonder in her face. 'So if the hair be true we must suppose the artist has not lied and it is a faithful likeness.'

'And this is Miguel Cortes?'

'I am assured of it, Deborah.' Her father arched his brows at her. 'Does his gift please you, my child?'

Deborah stared at the portrait in her hand for a while before answering. She seemed to see another, darker image—a man with laughing eyes and a roguish manner— but she resolutely shut it out. The Marquis de Vere was a man of mystery and shadows, of light and dark: Miguel Cortes had the face of an angel, his mouth curved in a smile of great sweetness.

'It pleases me very well, Father,' she replied at last. 'If Miguel Cortes is as pleasant as his likeness would indicate, I think he would make any woman a fine husband.'

'I believe it could be a good match for you, Deborah.' Sir Edward was clearly excited about something. 'Don Manola's letter was writ in the warmest terms. He says it would give him great pleasure if our families could be joined in marriage—and he has asked that we visit him. If I find the life suits me, I am invited to join with the Don in a new business venture.'

'Oh, Father!' Deborah gazed at him in delight. 'Does that mean that I should see you sometimes?'

'Often,' her father assured her with a smile. He seemed to have shed all his inhibitions about her marriage. 'I must admit that I wondered how I should bring myself to part from you, daughter—but now it may not be necessary. Don Manola offers me the hospitality of his home whenever I care to visit—and to help me build a villa on his own land if I should wish to settle in Spain. He has told me of a place where sweet oranges grow…'

'Then I have nothing more to ask.' Deborah flew to embrace him. 'To have you near me always—it would give me the greatest happiness in life, my dear father.'

'It is more than I could ever have hoped for had you married here,' her father confessed. 'We might have met occasionally, but your home would have been with your husband. This is great consideration from a man I know and trust, Deborah. I must admit it has greatly relieved my mind. Shall I write to the Don and say you agree to the betrothal in principle? Naturally, you will need some time to get to know one another, but if things go well I think this a good match for you. We must see your cousin wed before we leave England, of course, and I have business that must be settled, but after that there is naught to keep us here.'

Deborah glanced once more at the miniature in her hand. She could not but admire the beautiful image. Surely he would be as welcome to her as any man she had met? At least he did not desire her for her fortune, for the Don was wealthier than Sir Edward. And it meant that she would be able to see her father often in the future.

'Yes, Father,' she said. 'Please write at once so that everything may be made ready for a betrothal, and then, when we have had a little time to become accustomed to each other, a wedding.'

'What a beautiful thing,' Sarah said, looking at the miniature. 'Shall you wear it to the masque this evening? It has a loop whereby you might hang it from a ribbon about your neck.'

Deborah held the ornament against her throat. Indeed,

it was a vastly pretty piece of jewellery and her cousin's suggestion found favour, especially as the gown she had selected was of cream silk sewn with garnets and pearls on the falling sleeves.

'Yes, why not?' she replied, looking through her collection of fal-lals for a ribbon to match her gown. 'After all, we must look our best this evening, cousin, for it is our last at Court before we leave for the country.'

'Yes.' Sarah smiled dreamily. 'We have both been fortunate to find handsome husbands. It is not always so, Debs. Mistress Anne Goodleigh has been promised to a man twice her age and as ugly as sin. I vow I would rather die an old maid than submit to such as he!'

'We are both lucky,' Deborah agreed. She leaned forward to kiss her cousin's cheek. 'You look so pretty this evening, Sarah, that shade of blue becomes you very well.'

'Thank you,' Sarah said and dimpled. 'I think I am pretty—but you are beautiful, Debs. I do not think I have ever seen you look so well as you do this evening.'

'Beautiful?' Deborah glanced at herself in her hand mirror of silver and Venetian glass. The glass was dark and showed only a hazy image of her face. 'I have never thought so, but I dare say I am well enough. Father has commissioned a portrait as a gift for Don Miguel…I hope he will be as pleased with it as I was with his.'

'He would be addled in his wits if he were not,' Sarah said and giggled as her excitement overcame her. 'Are you ready, Debs? I cannot wait for the evening to begin. Master Henderson has said he will give me a ring to seal the promise he made me, and tomorrow we shall be betrothed.'

'And the day after we go home.' Deborah took her cousin's arm. 'I am quite ready, dearest cousin. Let us go down and see if the chairs have been summoned.'

Chapter Three

The masked dancers were in merry mood, twirling in reckless abandon to the music. This was no sedate country dance but a wild romp that brought each couple close in what was almost an embrace, and many gentlemen had seized the chance to behave immodestly towards their partners. Their behaviour was quite shocking, and Deborah did not care to join them.

She could see her cousin dancing with her betrothed, her cheeks flushed and excited. She herself had already refused two partners who seemed to be intoxicated from too much wine, preferring to watch rather than participate.

'Not dancing, fair one?'

The man seemed to have come from nowhere, or perhaps she had been too preoccupied to notice his approach. He was masked, as was everyone present, but his size marked him out. He could only be the Marquis de Vere. Deborah drew a sharp breath as he grasped her hand and pulled her into the throng of carefree dancers. She would have resisted had he asked her permission, but his grip was firm and strong and she felt it would be useless to try to free herself. He was determined to have his way.

'This is madness,' she breathed as he placed his hands about her waist to toss her into the air and then catch her to him.

It was as if she weighed no more than a feather. Her heart raced furiously as he held her crushed against him for a brief moment before setting her on her feet to whirl her round and round the room. Again and again, she was caught, tossed and held, the madness of the dance infecting her so that her natural caution was all but lost.

Deborah gazed down into the handsome face of her captor, for that in truth was what he had become. He had daringly made a prisoner of both her body and her mind. She seemed to have no will of her own and was seized by a strange desire as she met the fire in his dark eyes, a longing that was so strange and wanton she was suddenly afraid. Was this man truly a devil? How else could he have made her so far forget herself?

The music was ending at last after what had seemed an eternity. Deborah was finally set upon her feet by the marquis, and his hold on her released so that she was able to breathe freely once more. Slowly, her senses returned to normal and she stood staring at the mocking set of her partner's mouth. He was laughing at her! She drew herself up to her full height, which came no farther than the top of his shoulder. Her expression became proud and withdrawn, her eyes cold.

'I shall not thank you for the dance, sir. Had you had the courtesy to ask, I should have refused.'

'Yet I would swear there was delight in your eyes while we danced, sweet mistress.'

'More like fear,' she answered waspishly. 'I thought myself in the clutches of a madman.'

'Aye, mayhap we were both a little mad for a moment.' His eyes had narrowed beneath the slits of his velvet mask, the colour of them so intense and dark that a shiver went through her. His hand reached out to touch the pendant she wore about her slender throat. 'You wear a fine jewel this night, Mistress Stirling.'

Deborah lifted her head, anger making her speak as she did without truly thinking of what she said. 'It is the gift of the man to whom I shall soon be betrothed. Don Miguel Cortes…'

'God's breath!' Nicholas ejaculated and tore off his mask. His features were contorted with a terrible anger, making Deborah recoil in genuine fear this time. 'You lie! I beg you, Mistress Stirling—tell me this is some wrong-headed jest to punish me for my behaviour towards you. You cannot wish to be the wife of such a man. It would be sacrilege.'

Deborah was trembling inside as she saw the strange, almost haunted look in his eyes, but determined not to let him see that she was so affected by his words.

'His likeness pleases me.' She faced him with a steady gaze, though she was near ready to faint. 'I am aware that you and he have some quarrel between you, but…'

'You think my disgust is because of a petty quarrel?' Nicholas gripped her wrist, his fingers digging so deeply into her flesh that she almost cried out in pain. 'That man is a monster—a murderer! Were I to tell you of his hideous crimes you would never again sleep in peace. Do not give yourself to such a man, Mistress Stirling. If you value your self-respect—or your life!—you will step back now, before it is too late.'

Deborah saw hatred and a chilling horror in his eyes. His words terrified her. There was a sickness in her stomach and she felt as though she would swoon.

'Please let me go,' she whispered. 'I must…I need air.'

Nicholas saw the distress in her eyes and cursed himself for a fool.

'Forgive me, you are unwell.' He took her arm, feeling her tremble beneath his hand. 'I am a brute indeed, sweet lady. You are not to blame for that monster's crimes. Do not fear me. I would kill Cortes if I could but you are safe with me. I swear it by my honour.'

Deborah had no strength to break free of him as he led her from the hall, which was crowded with flushed and sweating dancers, into a quiet chamber nearby. A single torch flared here and the air was cooler, fresher. She sank onto an oak settle near a window and drew in a deep shuddering breath to steady her nerves. It was dark outside with hardly a star in the night sky. An omen, perhaps, of what the future held for her if she were to believe this man—but could she believe him?

'Are you feeling better?' Nicholas asked after a few moments. 'I should not have shocked you so, though I spoke only the truth. It would have been better had I gone to your father. He has been deceived in this matter. I cannot think he would allow the marriage if he understood what kind of a man this Spaniard truly is. No father would give his only child to such a monster.'

'Don Manola is my father's friend. He offers us much kindness…'

'The Don seeks to trap you with honeyed words,' Nicholas replied harshly. 'No Spanish woman of gentle birth would wed with his son, for his reputation is known beyond his own province. Why do you imagine he has sought a bride abroad? Listen to me, Mistress Stirling, I entreat you. Draw back now. There are a score of true, honest men present here this evening. Any one of them would make you a fitter husband than Cortes.'

'*You* perhaps?' Deborah's eyes flashed with scorn as she looked up at him.

'No, not I, mistress,' Nicholas replied. 'I shall take no woman for wife while Isabella lies unavenged in her grave. I have sworn it and I do not lightly break my vow.'

'Well, I am glad that was not your reason for trying to poison my mind with falsehoods,' Deborah replied coldly, 'for I should never have consented to such a match. I have listened to your words, sir, and I find them less than convincing.' She was feeling better and more in control as she rose to her feet. Her eyes gazed up at him steadily. 'I thank you for escorting me here, sir. I was in need of some respite after that dance. Now I ask that you leave me. I shall make my own way back when I am ready.'

'You hate me for my plain speaking? You are perverse in refusing to accept my warning, lady. I fear you will come to regret it ere long.'

'You have no power to arouse an emotion of any kind in me, sir,' she replied haughtily and tossed her head. He took too much on himself! How dare he dictate to her? 'Your warning has been made. I give you leave to go.'

To her surprise and chagrin, her regal manner did not provoke the response she imagined.

'I see that you are feeling better.' Nicholas grinned at her, clearly much amused. 'Then I shall leave you as you request, my lady.' He made her an elegant leg. 'I regret that I was the cause of distress to you—yet I am minded to prove that you lied when you said I had no power to arouse any emotion in you.'

Before Deborah could guess what was in his mind, he reached out and caught her to him, his eyes seeming to burn into her, setting a flame leaping within her body. Then his head bent towards hers and his mouth sought hers, caressing her with a softness that took her unawares. Had his kiss been demanding or greedy she would have fought him, but its very sweetness drew an instinctive response from her. The flame his gaze had ignited became a fire roaring up from the centre of her femininity. Without realizing what she did, Deborah slid her arms up his chest to clutch at the fine fabric of his doublet, clinging to him as if she feared he might leave her.

She felt as if she were swooning, drowning in the sensations of pleasure that washed over her, and her body seemed to meld with his as if she were being absorbed into his very flesh. Never had she imagined a man's kiss could arouse such wild longing within her, or that she would yearn for it to go on and on endlessly. She was like a leaf in a stream, wrapped about by swirling waters, carried on regardless of her will to submerge in the tide of passion he had aroused in her.

It was Nicholas who drew away at last, not Deborah. He stood staring at her for some seconds after he had let her go and the expression in his eyes was so strange—so bleak—that her heart jerked. Why did he look so—as if he were in Hell? As if some tormenting demon tore at his soul with sharp claws, making him suffer terrible pain?

For a moment she wanted to reach out to him, to comfort him, to beg him not to leave her. Then she remembered his kiss had been meant as a jest, to prove that she was a weak and foolish female he could dominate at will. He had meant to punish her, not thrill her.

Her cheeks flamed and she was humiliated. How could she have been so foolish?

'How dare you take advantage of me, sir?'

Nicholas stepped back. She thought she saw a glimmer of laughter in his eyes, then it had gone and his expression became harsh, withdrawn.

'I should not have kissed you thus, Mistress Stirling. It was wrong and I do humbly ask your pardon.'

'You are not forgiven, sir.' Her eyes flashed with pride mixed with anger. 'Please go away. I do not wish to see you or speak to you ever again.'

Nicholas knew he should go, yet still he hesitated.

'I might persuade you to change your mind,' he murmured, the harsh look fading as swiftly as it had come. 'But I have not the right. I am sworn to one purpose, Mistress Stirling—to avenge the dishonour and murder of a gentle lady. Until then I can promise nothing. No matter what my mind or heart might dictate, my honour demands no less than I have sworn.'

'I want no promises from you, sir,' Deborah replied spiritedly. 'I am already promised to Miguel Cortes, in honour if not yet in law. My father has given his consent to a betrothal when we reach Spain. Nothing you can say will change that. We shall leave as soon as my cousin's wedding has taken place.'

Nicholas stared at her. 'You are a stubborn wench, mistress. I pray you will change your mind, lest I make you a widow before ever you are a wife.'

'You are a wicked rogue, sir!'

'I warn you, lady. If you set sail for Spain with this intent you will never reach its shores. I take anything I can that rightly belongs to the Cortes family—and Miguel's bride is no exception.'

With that he turned and strode away, leaving Deborah

to tremble at the harshness of his last words. She stared into the shadows around her, her mind in turmoil. She felt as if she were being torn apart by conflicting emotions—anger, outrage and something more. A feeling she did not understand but which gave her much pain.

Surely the marquis had lied concerning Miguel Cortes? The man whose portrait she wore about her neck could not be the monster he had described—an evil man who tortured and killed for sheer pleasure?

No! She would not believe it. She touched the jewel at her throat with shaking fingers. Never had she seen such an angelic countenance on a man. The artist had painted a true likeness, and it was said a man's soul could not be hid from the artist's inner eye.

The Marquis de Vere had lied for his own personal advantage. It must be so! Perhaps, despite his denials, he wanted her for himself—for her father's wealth. Was that not what so many at Court had seen in her, a chance for personal gain? No doubt the marquis had covetous eyes for Sir Edward's gold. Yes, that must be it.

If it were not so, why had he forced himself on her in the dance? Why had he brought her here and kissed her in such a way that she…? A fierce heat flooded through her as she remembered her instinctive response. She had acted like a wanton, a tavern wench, willing and eager to be bedded. Shame washed over her. How could she so far have forgotten who and what she was? To let a stranger bring her to the point of surrender…

'Deborah—are you there?'

She turned at the sound of her cousin's voice. 'Sarah?'

The other girl came towards her, her manner anxious as if she had been concerned. 'So here you are…alone. Master Henderson saw you leave with…he thought you might be with the Marquis de Vere?'

'As you see, I *am* alone. I was a little faint from the heat in the hall. The marquis was considerate. He brought me here and then left me to recover in peace so that I might compose myself.' What a liar she was! Yet she could not have confessed her shame to anyone.

'Are you ill, cousin?'

'No, not at all.' Deborah had recovered a measure of calmness at last. 'It was merely the heat. I should never have danced with the marquis.'

'Your father is almost ready to leave,' Sarah said, her eyes curious. 'He asked me to tell you.'

'Yes, of course. I shall come at once. I should not have left the hall.'

'Oh, the King left an age ago,' Sarah replied carelessly. 'There was no discourtesy on your part, Debs. Several ladies were near to swooning. You were not the only to take the opportunity for cooler air—though I would dare swear some had another purpose quite in mind.' She gave Deborah a wicked look.

'I hope you do not suspect me of seeking an assignation?'

'The marquis is very handsome,' Sarah replied, her eyes twinkling. 'I should not blame you if you had taken the chance to dally a little with him.'

'Well, you may disabuse your mind of such thoughts. It was no such thing,' Deborah lied, not quite meeting her cousin's candid gaze. 'I do not particularly like the marquis. Nor would I wish to be alone with him.'

Sarah glanced at her oddly. 'I think he likes you, Debs.'

'What makes you say that?' She was curious despite herself.

Sarah smiled confidently. 'Oh, it was just the way he looked at you—when we first saw him at Court. He asked me who you were and seemed most interested in all I had to tell him concerning you.'

'It would have been better had you told him nothing,' Deborah replied, her tone perhaps sharper than she intended because she was upset. 'Such a man can hold no interest for me or I for him. I dare say it was my father's estate that appealed to him.'

'You are harsh, cousin. I have not often heard you speak so unkindly of anyone. What has the marquis done to upset you?'

'Nothing. Nothing at all.'

Oh, but he had. He had! He had kissed her and made her lose all sense of right and wrong—and he had told her terrible, unspeakable things about Don Miguel Cortes. She wished he had not! She did not believe his lies, of course, and yet she had become aware of a deep unease within her mind. Just suppose the marquis had been telling her the truth?

Nicholas faced his friend across the inn table, his expression one of such bleak despair that Henri Moreau was shocked. Around them, the noise of raucous laughter seemed to fade into a dulled echo, the stench of the river on a warm night forgotten and unnoticed.

'What ails you, Nico?' he asked. 'I have not seen you in this mood since…for many a day. Is it that you fear for this wench?'

'She knows not what she plans,' Nicholas replied, his dark eyes beginning to glitter with anger as he remembered the way Deborah had rejected his warning so proudly. 'She is little more than a child and yet…' She had felt warm and willing in his arms, a passionate woman awakened to desire. Something had stirred within him, arousing feelings he had believed dead.

'As Isabella was when that monster destroyed her innocence and then killed her.' Henri watched his friend intently. 'For that he is cursed, Nico. He will be punished, his death is certain. We have both sworn it.'

'Would that I had been there that day to protect Isabella!' Nicholas struck the table with his clenched fist so hard that ale spilt from his tankard. 'I shall never rest until I have avenged her death with his, Henri.'

'We shall trap him,' Henri replied soothingly. 'Never fear, *mon ami*. One of these days he will grow weary of skulking in his lair—and then we shall have him.'

Nicholas took a drink of the warm ale; it tasted sour in his mouth, giving him no pleasure. His expression was harsh, angry, as if terrible thoughts gathered in his head, tormenting him.

He could not let Deborah marry that devil! It must be stopped at all costs. He turned the alternatives over in his mind, considering first one and then another. Would Sir Edward listen to him if he went to him, told him what he knew? It was doubtful that he would even grant an interview to the man who was the enemy of his friend. He must trust Cortes or he would not be contemplating this marriage—to give his precious daughter to such a man! It was more than flesh could stand!

Would Deborah listen to him? She was wilful, proud, impatient—and he had already tried to tell her that Miguel Cortes was an evil beast. She had laughed in his face, and her defiance had made him want to ravish her there and then—but he had contented himself with a kiss. A kiss that lingered still, and would torment his dreams if he believed her at the mercy of that Spanish dog!

There was a way... It was wrong and might cause grief to her father and fear to her, yet he knew her to be brave. She would not be afraid for long. It was a desperate act—but one that must be carried out for her own sake…and perhaps for his.

No, he would not let himself think of her in that way! If he carried out this bold, dangerous mission, let it be for her sake alone.

'Perhaps there is a way to tempt the beast from his den, Henri. Something so irresistible to him—to his pride—that he will forget what a cowardly cur he is and seek an honourable end to the affair.'

'You mean the wench?' Henri stared at him, frowning as he nodded assent. 'No, Nico! That is not the way. *Mon Dieu*. You cannot use an innocent girl so wickedly. It would make you almost as bad as that dog of a Spaniard.'

'I mean her no harm,' Nicholas said, his eyes burning with a dark flame that chilled his friend. 'But think— even Miguel Cortes must come for his own bride. If she is snatched from beneath his very nose, his pride must suffer. He must respond to a demand for a ransom or lose all honour. Especially if it were a condition of the ransom that he comes himself to fetch her.'

'He would know it was a trap,' Henri argued. 'And if he were willing to pay, would you be satisfied—would you hand that child over to him, knowing how she would suffer at his hands?'

'No, of course not.' Nicholas raised his eyes to meet the disbelieving gaze of his companion. 'No, he shall not have her. I do not want his gold any more than I want my share of what we take from his ships. I shall kill him and return her to her father unharmed.'

Henri nodded. He knew that Nicholas used the Don's gold and silver for the good of others, having no need or use for it himself.

'I suppose your ruse might work if Cortes became angry enough to lose all caution,' Henri said doubtfully. 'But I cannot like your plan, Nico. Supposing something goes wrong? Besides, how are we to tempt Mistress Stirling to come with us? You said that she is determined to wed him, that she would not heed your warnings.'

'We must kidnap her.'

'*Mon Dieu!* Have you lost your senses?' Henri was shocked. He stared at Nicholas in dismay. 'You cannot steal a young woman of good family from her father. It is a hanging matter, Nico. Even your friendship with King James could not then save you from a terrible fate. No, you must forget this plan. We shall think of another way to tempt Miguel Cortes to sea.'

'If you want none of this you are free to walk away. I shall not blame you—now or ever.'

'You know I would never desert you. We are brothers in blood, to the death if need be.' Henri frowned as Nicholas continued to stare moodily into his tankard. Clearly his friend was determined to save the wench from herself. 'Supposing you manage to abduct the girl—where will you take her?'

'To my château in France. She will be safe with Marie to care for her. I mean her no ill, Henri.' Nicholas's eyes blazed suddenly. 'And if I do nothing—if I let her go unimpeded to her groom—what kind of a life will she find in that monster's bed? He is cruel in ways that a girl like that could never imagine. I would rather see her dead than wed to him.'

'It would indeed be a living death for a girl such as you describe,' Henri said thoughtfully. 'His touch would defile her, his cruelty break her spirit—but surely her father would listen to you? If he knew what Cortes was capable of he would in all decency refuse the match?'

'No, I think not,' Nicholas said. 'Apparently he knew Don Manola years ago. They were friends and he would not believe that the refined, honest gentleman he knew then could father such a son—or condone his evil ways.'

'Then we must find a way to save the wench from herself,' Henri said. 'We must be gentle and kind. She will be frightened at first. To be captured and taken away from her friends and family will be a terrible ordeal for her.'

'She will not be broken by it,' Nicholas replied. 'Mistress Stirling has spirit, Henri. She will fight us, especially when she realizes it is I who have stolen her—but she will not be afraid for long.' An odd smile played about his mouth, as if some pleasant memory had come to his mind. 'I warn you, my friend. She will not be an easy captive.'

Henri watched the changing emotions in his friend's eyes. This talk of abduction was unlike the character of the man he knew so well, this harshness foreign to his true nature. Once, before Isabella's murder, Nico had laughed more than he scowled, but now he was haunted by guilt—he believed that a trifling quarrel between himself and Miguel Cortes had led to Isabella's cruel death. Even so, this plan was wild and dangerous, and seemed at odds with the clever strategies Nico normally employed against his enemies. He was like a man driven by a force he could not control.

'Are you sure this is what you want to do?'

'I can see no other course but to take her with us, whether or no she wishes it…'

'But when shall you take her?'

'Her cousin is to be betrothed in the morning. The following day they leave for the north. I believe it would be better to strike now while they are still in London.

Our ship awaits us in Greenwich. We could be away on the tide before anyone is aware of what has happened.'

'How is this to be accomplished?' Henri asked. 'You can hardly steal her from her bedroom?'

'We shall keep a watch on the house and take our chances,' Nicholas said. 'I shall send a note asking her to meet me early in the morning. I shall say that I have something important to tell her—something she must hear.'

'Surely she will not come?' Henri was disbelieving.

'Oh, she will come,' Nicholas replied. 'If she does not, I must find another way. Yet, I believe she will not be able to resist…'

Chapter Four

It was no good! Try as she might, Deborah could not sleep. She had lain awake half the night, her thoughts going round and round in dizzy circles so that she became ever more confused. She could not believe that the young man whose portrait she had so admired could possibly be the monster the Marquis de Vere had described—and yet something deep inside her sensed that the marquis had been trying to warn her for her own good.

She had answered him proudly, dismissing his warnings—but that was because he had disturbed her, his kisses had enslaved her. She had needed to reassert her own will, to break his hold on her—but she had almost believed him.

She dressed in a simple gown, more suited to the country than the clothes she had worn of late, but which she was able to manage alone, then slipped on a dark cloak. She did not wish to call her maid. This restlessness must be subdued before she was prepared for the busy day ahead.

Going softly down the stairs, Deborah saw that no one was stirring as yet. The servants had retired late and were sluggards abed this morning. She pulled back the heavy bolts that secured the street door, glancing round as they screeched loudly. Surely someone would hear?

She peered into the street outside. It was still very early. A light mist was swirling across the river and into that part of the town that hugged its banks. No one was about, most of the houses still fast shuttered against the evils of the night air.

Pulling the hood of her cloak well up over her head, Deborah left the house where she and her family were lodged. She needed to clear her mind of the thoughts that so sorely troubled her, and she had missed the freedom she was used to at home in the country. There, she had been in the habit of walking often and alone.

Slipping from the house without having roused even the servants, Deborah forgot all the warnings she had been given about walking alone in London. It was very early. No one would trouble her, especially on such a morning. Anyone with any sense would not want to be abroad until the mist lifted. Even the beggars would not venture far until the sun broke through.

Her mind returned to the problem that haunted her as she walked, like a dog trapped on a spit wheel, endlessly turning its circle over the heat of the fire. Could it be true that Miguel Cortes was a cruel murderer? Surely not! The marquis must have lied to her. And yet there had been the ring of sincerity in his voice. He had seemed to care that Deborah might suffer some harm at the Spaniard's hands…

She shook her head as the memory of the marquis's dark eyes burning into hers forced its way into her conscious thoughts. He had looked so—so intense! So passionate! She could not help the little thrill of pleasure that invaded her when she remembered the way he had kissed her. But no, this must stop! It would be foolish to read too much into his kiss—or his words. She must not allow herself to think of a man who could never be anything to her.

Yet perhaps she ought to speak to her father of the marquis's warnings? Perhaps it might be better to ask if her prospective bridegroom would agree to a period of courtship before the betrothal? She must be certain she could both like and respect the man she married.

What was that? Something behind her, close by? Deborah was suddenly alert to the sounds of footsteps in the mist, echoing eerily in the half-light. She glanced over her shoulder, realizing that she must have wandered some way from her lodgings. Engrossed in her thoughts, she had not noticed where she was going.

A shiver of apprehension ran through her as she tried to take her bearings and failed. Everything was so unfamiliar in the mist. Where was she? Which way had she turned? It had all become strange and slightly sinister.

As she stood hesitating, three burly figures loomed out of the mist towards her. Some instinct warned her that she was in danger. She gasped in fright and turned to flee but there was someone in the way—a large, tall man. She was trapped between him and the others! She gave a cry of alarm as a blanket was suddenly thrown over her from behind, covering her in a shroud of darkness.

'No! Help! Help me...'

'Fear not, Mistress Stirling,' a man's voice said close to her ear. It was a French voice, and not one she had heard before. 'You will not be harmed. The Captain has ordered you be treated like a princess.'

Not harmed! Deborah tried to scream as she felt herself being lifted and hoisted on to a man's shoulder. Her indignation was equally as great as her fear. She was being carried as if she were a sack of straw!

'How dare you?' she muttered, her cries of anger lost in the wool of the blanket. 'Let me down at once. I demand that you put me down!'

She knew the covering over her head must muffle her protests. She could hear the sound of men's voices, laughter and jesting—and then a sharper tone, the voice of command. After that there was silence.

'What is happening?' she asked and attempted to struggle as she felt herself transferred to another captor, one who held her more comfortably. 'What are you doing to me?'

She was blinded and caught by the blanket, but somehow her senses seemed heightened. She was aware of being carried down steps and then felt a rocking motion beneath her. She was being taken into a boat! She screamed and struggled as violently as she was able, hampered by the confining weight of the blanket.

'Let me go! Let me go!'

'You are safe. There is no need to fear, *mademoiselle*.' That soft French voice again, though indistinct through the blanket. 'Do not struggle and hurt yourself. It is only for a little time. Soon you will be more comfortable.'

Now Deborah could feel a different sensation beneath her. The boat was moving. She was being rowed down the river. She had been kidnapped! She was being taken away from her father and friends. But who had abducted her—and why?

She felt her sense of balance returning. She was no longer in a man's arms, but sitting on a bench, his arm loosely about her, supporting her—she was no longer a prisoner. She knew that she must escape now, before she had been taken too far. She sprang up, trying to throw off the heavy blanket so that she could see, but somehow her foot caught against a rope or something similar and she fell forward, striking her head on a hard object. For a brief moment she felt pain and then she was falling into the darkness of a black hole.

Her head ached so! Deborah could hear voices and sense movement about her—or was the movement beneath her? She knew that she would have to open her eyes soon, but felt too ill to make the attempt. A moan escaped her lips; her dark lashes fluttered against pale cheeks, and then she was aware of something cool on her forehead. Gentle hands soothing her, stroking her hair and easing the pain.

'Forgive me,' a soft voice murmured. 'It was my fault you fell and hurt yourself, *mademoiselle*. I should have taken better care of you.'

Where had she heard that voice before? Deborah's eyelids flickered and then opened. She lay staring up at the man bending over her, feeling bewildered. Where was she? What had happened to her? The man had been applying a cool cloth to her forehead; now he removed it and smiled at her.

'Are you feeling better, *mademoiselle*?'

'Have I been ill?' she asked. Something was bothering her, but she could not seem to remember for the moment. 'Are you a doctor, sir?'

'No, *mademoiselle*, just the first lieutenant of the *Siren's Song*.'

'We are on a ship?' She realized that the odd motion she could feel must be the sea beneath them. She tried to sit up, then fell back as the dizziness hit her. 'Oh, my head hurts so much!'

'You hit it when you fell. Forgive me. It was not

intended that you should be harmed. The Captain was angry and very concerned that you might die. But I do not think that you will have more than a nasty bruise and a headache.'

Gradually, Deborah's eyes began to focus on the man's face. He was not handsome, but his smile was gentle, his eyes kind. His black hair was long and hung untidily about his rather thin face, and his nose was slightly crooked.

'Who are you?' she whispered, her throat hoarse. 'And why am I here?' She was struggling to remember...she had been walking in the mist and then something had happened to her.

'You are here because...' the man began, then broke off as someone moved forward into her line of vision.

'You were brought here because I ordered it,' a strong voice said—a voice that sent a thrill of recognition winging through her. 'Henri is not to blame, Mistress Stirling. It was I who had you abducted—though I much regret that you were hurt. That was never our intention, and I believe you brought it on yourself by your wilfulness.'

Deborah gasped as she looked into the dark eyes of the Marquis de Vere. She forced herself up against the pillows piled behind her, her eyes meeting his defiantly. She was angry despite the pain at her temple and the dizziness that once again swept over her.

'*You!*' she cried. 'How dare you make me your prisoner? How dare you treat me so ill?'

'You mistake the matter,' Nicholas said, smiling a little as he realized her ordeal had not damaged her spirit. When she had been knocked unconscious he had feared the worst, but it seemed that Henri was right. She had suffered no more than an unpleasant bump on her forehead. 'I would have you consider yourself my honoured guest rather than my prisoner.'

'Your guest?' Deborah's eyes glinted with temper. 'I was half-suffocated beneath a filthy blanket, terrified near to death, knocked unconscious and brought here against my will. How can you say I am your guest?'

'You have been treated extremely ill,' Nicholas admitted, his expression contrite but with a hint of humour about it. 'I do most humbly beg your pardon, Mistress Stirling—but it was necessary, believe me. Please do not imagine you stand in danger of any further…indignity. Henri will care you for until we reach the château, then my cousin will tend you. You shall have every attention, every comfort.'

'How can I be comfortable when I am your prisoner?' she cried furiously.

'My guest, lady.'

'I demand that you return me to my father at once!'

'Forgive me. For the moment that is impossible.' Nicholas frowned as he saw the distress in her eyes. 'Do not be concerned for your father. He has been informed that you are safe.'

'Safe! You dare to kidnap me, then assert I am safe? I find such behaviour unpardonable.' Her eyes snapped with temper. 'You shall pay for this, sir. I promise you shall be punished for your wickedness.'

'You have my word that you are as safe as if you were still in your father's care.'

'The word of a pirate!'

'A privateer, mistress.'

'As if there was a difference!'

'I assure you there is a vast difference between my ships and those of the Corsairs that roam certain parts of the Mediterranean,' he replied, a small smile about his mouth—a mouth she remembered too well from kissing it. 'But you should be resting, not quarreling with your host. I shall leave you for now. If the wind is fair we shall be in France within a few hours. I beg you to forgive any discomfort you have suffered and be assured I shall do all in my power to make you comfortable from now on.'

'Discomfort!' Deborah stared in disbelief as he bowed and left her. Her head felt as if it had a thousand hammers inside it—and he spoke of discomfort. 'You wretch! I wish you had my headache.'

'Is your head very bad?' Henri asked, coming forward again. He had withdrawn into the background while she was arguing with the marquis. 'Shall I prepare a tisane to ease your pain?'

She blinked. In her fury at discovering the culprit for all her ills, she had forgotten the Frenchman.

'I hate him,' she muttered fiercely as forbidden tears stung her eyes. 'How dare he do this to me? How could he?' She gazed at Henri. 'Why has he done this terrible thing?'

'Nico has his reasons.'

'You call him Nico?' She was curious, forgetting her anger for a moment.

'His name is Nicholas. It is a childhood thing.'

'You knew him then?' Deborah frowned as he nodded. 'You are his friend, are you not?'

'We are as brothers.'

'Yet you are a gentle man. I do not believe that there is any evil in you.'

'Nor is there evil in Nico, *mademoiselle*. There is a certain darkness, an anger that cannot be slaked but by blood, but he is not an evil man.' Henri hesitated, seeming unsure of whether to go on, then, 'You were taken hostage to prevent your marriage to Don Miguel Cortes. It was done in part for your own sake.'

'For my sake...' Deborah's words of furious denial died on her lips as she saw the expression in his eyes. 'Why do you look so? Please tell me—is Don Manola's son truly a monster?'

'He raped and then strangled a young woman of good family. The act was unprovoked and brutal beyond belief. No decent man could behave in such a manner, *mademoiselle*.'

Deborah's face turned pale and her heart jerked with fear. 'Then it is true...all the marquis told me. I did not believe it. Miguel Cortes...his likeness looked so pleasant...'

'Miguel Cortes has the face of an angel and the soul of the blackest demon this side of Hell,' Henri said. 'Isabella was not the only woman to have suffered at his hands—though perhaps the most vulnerable since she was innocent, little more than a child.'

'Isabella...' Deborah looked at him, an unconscious appeal in her eyes. 'Who was she? Please tell me about her?'

'Isabella Rodrigues was a young woman of good family but no fortune. She was betrothed to Nico for three months. Her parents were both dead, her grandfather too old to take proper care of her—or to exact revenge for what was done to her...'

Henri paused as if he found the tale too horrific to relate. 'Miguel Cortes saw her visiting the church a month before her wedding. She had refused his courtship some months earlier and the resentment must have festered inside him. He followed her as she walked home through her grandfather's orange groves and then...' His mouth twisted with disgust. 'Nico has sworn to take the life of the monster that subjected her to such a terrible ordeal that day.'

Deborah felt the sickness rise in her throat. The horror of the tale just unfolded to her was swirling inside her, and she seemed to see the young girl's struggle to fight off her attacker and hear her pitiful cries. She pressed a shaking hand to her lips, as she fought off the terrible images. Henri's story had been so harrowing that she could almost wish it untold.

'Is that why the marquis had me abducted?' she asked when at last she could speak again. 'Am I a part of his revenge on Miguel Cortes?'

Henri looked uncomfortable. 'Since the murder, Don Manola has forbidden his son to sail with his ships. He fears Nico's vengeance.'

'So I am the bait to lure Miguel Cortes from his home?' Her clear eyes accused him. 'I can see the truth in your face, sir. That *is* what the marquis intends, is it not?'

Henri nodded but could not answer.

'I see…thank you for telling me the truth. I was taken to serve the marquis's purpose because he believes Don Miguel must come to claim his own bride.'

'And for your own sake. Believe me—' Henri was silenced by her look of scorn.

'Not for my own sake, sir. Spare me such excuses, I pray you! I needed no help to make my own decision. Had I been given the time to consider, I might have decided against the marriage myself. I should in any case not have consented to the betrothal until I had had the opportunity to know Don Miguel—and if he is the monster you describe, I would have asked my father to take me home again.'

'Nico was certain you meant to wed him, that you would not listen to his warnings but go your own way.'

'The choice was mine. He had no right to interfere in my life.'

Henri inclined his head. She spoke only the truth, they had none of them the right to take her from her father and hold her hostage. What could he say in the face of her anger?

'Forgive me, *mademoiselle*. I shall fetch the tisane.'

Deborah lay back and closed her eyes as he left the cabin. Her head did ache so very badly. It was so very foolish of her to give way like this! She felt weak and wanted nothing so much as a good cry—but crying would not help her. She must be strong and conserve her composure. She had to think of a way to escape her captors.

Yet there was no possibility of escape while she was on board this ship. She could not swim back to England! She was helpless and it was her own fault. She should never have gone walking alone in the mist.

They must have been waiting for her to leave the house. She supposed that if the marquis was determined to capture her he would have found a way—but she need not have made it so easy for him!

Anger at her own carelessness banished her tears. She was not afraid of the marquis. Somehow she knew that he would not willingly harm her. The wound to her head had been caused by her violent attempt to escape.

Her real concern was for her father and how distressed he would be by her disappearance. Even if he had received word that she was safe for the moment, he would not be able to rest. She could imagine his agony of mind—and what of poor Sarah? Would her betrothal be postponed or would they decide that it must go ahead?

Would Deborah be returned to her father in time for her cousin's wedding? Her mind was in such turmoil! If the marquis intended to use her as bait to trap Miguel Cortes…and what was she to believe about the man she had thought to marry? Could he really be guilty of the crimes Henri Moreau had described?

Deborah shuddered at the pictures in her mind. What that poor girl must have suffered! It was too horrible to imagine. She was sickened by such cruelty and dare not think of what might have happened to her if she had been wed to such a man. It would indeed have been a living death.

The marquis had tried to warn her, but she had refused to listen. Perhaps if she had not so brusquely repudiated his arguments he would not have thought it necessary to kidnap her.

Moaning as she felt the throbbing begin at her temple once more, Deborah closed her eyes. It was all too difficult. She could not think any more. She needed to sleep.

'You are sure she said nothing to you?' Sir Edward looked sternly at his ward. 'If she has slipped away on some foolish errand—a surprise for one of us—then tell me. I shall not be angry, but I must know what has happened to my daughter.'

'She said nothing to me,' Sarah replied, frightened by the bleak expression in her uncle's eyes. He had always been so kind to her, so indulgent. She had never seen him like this before. 'I know you are anxious, sir…but I know nothing. Except…' She stopped, her cheeks flushing crimson. 'No, she assured me it was not a romantic tryst…'

Sir Edward's hand snaked out, grabbing at her wrist. 'What is this? Speak out at once!'

Sarah dropped her head. Deborah had been missing for hours. In another thirty minutes it would be the appointed time for her betrothal, but it could not go ahead without her cousin. Sir Edward was so angry, but if Deborah returned from a shopping errand she would be annoyed with Sarah for giving away her secrets.

'Tell me, girl! Or I vow I will cancel your betrothal.'

'No! That is not fair,' Sarah cried. Her head went up, eyes sparkling with indignation. 'Last night at the palace—she slipped away for several minutes alone with a man.'

'What man?' Sir Edward's eyes narrowed. 'If you are concealing something from me you shall be punished, girl.'

'That is unfair, sir,' Sarah protested. She did not know this suddenly old man who seemed almost driven mad by his fear for Deborah. 'She told me she had felt faint, that she needed air and—she left the hall with the Marquis de Vere.'

'That scoundrel!' Sir Edward turned pale. He staggered back as if from a blow and his hand dropped from Sarah's wrist. 'Why—why did she do such a thing? I did not press her to this marriage. If she has run away with this rogue rather than…'

Sir Edward turned as a servant approached hesitantly. 'Sir, a messenger has brought you this.'

'A messenger?' Sir Edward's heart caught. Had his daughter run away with that privateer? He snatched the small packet from the servant's hand and broke open the seal, staring at the words written there for some minutes before they penetrated his fevered brain. 'No! It is even worse than I feared… Oh, my poor child. My poor, innocent daughter. She has been snatched by that scoundrel and is to be held for a ransom.'

'A ransom?' Sarah stared at him in dismay. 'Oh, Uncle, I cannot believe that such a terrible thing could happen. What will you do?'

'I must speak to Señor Sanchez at once.' Sir Edward saw the crestfallen look in her face and frowned. Now that he knew the truth he was aware that he had a duty to his ward. Besides, it was best to see her safely betrothed before people began to gossip and speculate. 'But I am forgetting you, niece. Your betrothal must go ahead. It is even more important that you are protected from the shame and scandal this will bring on our family. Yes, I shall send for Señor Sanchez, but your betrothal must go ahead…'

Chapter Five

Deborah discovered she felt much better when she woke for the second time. She was able to sit up without the room going round and round like a mill wheel, and although her temple still felt sore and tender the pain no longer throbbed as it had.

She saw a tankard had been set on a little chest beside the bed. Henri Moreau had obviously left it there for her and allowed her to sleep on, thinking rest the best medicine as, indeed, it had proved. She reached for the cup and sipped at the dark liquid cautiously. Finding it tasted of cinnamon and honey, she drank several mouthfuls to ease her thirst.

Deborah noticed that the motion of the ship was different, a gentle swaying instead of the violent rolling motion that had contributed to her feeling of distress. Had they anchored? Had they arrived in France?

She rose from the bed and walked a little unsteadily to the small window, looking out curiously. The ship appeared to have anchored off what looked like a small sandy cove and a boat was already pulling for the shore. What was happening? Where was this place?

A knock at the cabin door startled her. 'Enter,' she

called and turned to see Henri Moreau hesitate in the doorway. 'Are we in France, sir?'

'We are anchored in the cove of Chalfont,' he replied. 'Nico has gone ashore to make sure that all is ready for your arrival and comfort at the château, *mademoiselle*. When the boat returns we shall follow.'

Deborah was silent for a moment. She still felt angry about the way she had been brought here without her permission, but of what use was it to protest? She must go with them. Her only alternative was to remain on the ship. Besides, she was well aware that she could be compelled to do whatever the marquis wished. She was his prisoner—his hostage!—whatever he might choose to call her.

'May I come up on deck?' she asked. 'It is airless and hot in this cabin.'

'Are you still feeling unwell?' Henri inquired, his tone one of genuine concern. 'You were sleeping when I brought the tisane. It was good, for the sea can sometimes be an unkind host.'

'You were considerate,' Deborah said and smiled. 'I tasted your tisane, sir. It was pleasant and eased my thirst. I thank you for your kindness.'

Was there a sheen of tears in her eyes? Henri's conscience smote him. He would follow Nico to the fiery pit itself, but he would never willingly hurt this woman. She was as brave as she was beautiful. And he was already a little in love with her.

'Please do not fear for the future,' he said gently. 'You are bewildered and distressed by what has happened, but I give you my word that in time all will be well.'

Deborah's eyes sparkled. Her head went up at once, pride banishing any desire to weep. 'You mistake the matter, sir. I am neither frightened nor distressed, merely angry. If your captain were a gentleman he would return me to my father immediately. He has behaved dishonourably.'

Henri was unable to answer her, for in his heart he had always believed Nicholas wrong to take a young woman from her family, no matter what the circumstances. He stood aside for Deborah to leave the cabin and then followed her on deck.

She stood for a moment to breathe in the salty air. The cry of seabirds echoing above her and the warmth of the sun on her head were comforting after her confinement below. She moved slowly to the side of the ship and looked across at the small, sandy cove.

A steep cliff lay behind it, but it was possible to see a series of deep steps cut into the rocks to make the ascent more accessible. Above the cliffs there seemed to be a plateau with a thickly wooded area, the haze of green giving the scene a softness it would otherwise have lacked. Despite herself, she admired the beauty of sparkling sea, golden sand and dark green trees, feeling a reluctant curiosity about the château and sheltered lands that must lie beyond.

'The climb is not as difficult as it looks from the sea,' Henri said, coming to stand beside her. 'By the time we reach the top, Nico will have returned with horses.'

'Is the château far?'

'A ride of some ten or twenty minutes, perhaps,' Henri answered vaguely. 'Less if one is familiar with the bridle paths through the woods.'

'And this cove belongs to the marquis as well as the land beyond?'

'Nico's father built the house within easy walking distance of the sea for his English bride. His vineyards lie some way further inland. The marquise loved the sea and she often came to the cove, for from the cliffs she could almost see her homeland.'

'Nico's mother?' Deborah echoed his use of the marquis's familiar name without realizing she had done so. 'She is dead?'

'Aye, and his father—she in childbed and he of grief. They died when Nico was but sixteen years.'

'Oh, how sad,' Deborah said. 'And then he lost his bride…'

'Life is sometimes hard, *mademoiselle*.'

'Yes, yes, I know.' Many women died in childbed, it was a fact of life. Most men married again within months for the sake of their children or their own comfort. The previous marquis must have loved his wife very deeply if he could not bear to live on without her. Such love was rare and, Deborah thought, very precious.

She lifted her head, her expression one of pride mixed with determination. She would not allow her heart to be softened towards the marquis. No matter that fate had delivered him some cruel blows, he still had no right to abduct a woman he scarcely knew and carry her off— even if he had wanted to save her from her own foolishness!

Would he still have kidnapped her if she had promised to reconsider her decision to marry Miguel Cortes? She felt a little surge of temper as she remembered that her captor planned to use her as bait to lure the evil Spaniard from his hiding place.

Now she was beginning to think of Don Miguel as a monster! She tossed her head defiantly. She would not allow the marquis to dictate even her thoughts!

Having heard and believed Henri's explanation, Deborah was not yet ready to forgive the marquis for his interference—or to admit that he might have been right in his actions.

She noticed that the rowing boat was returning to the ship and felt a tingle at the nape of her neck, a feeling that was part apprehension, part excitement.

'Are you ready, *mademoiselle*?'

She turned as the Frenchman spoke to her and smiled. From the beginning she had sensed that he was her friend, and she believed that he would do his best to keep her safe.

'Yes, I am ready, sir. You need not fear that I shall do something foolish and injure myself again.'

'I shall help you on the climb down to the boat.'

Deborah raised her head, giving him a confident look. 'When I was a child I often climbed to the hayloft, and my father built me a tree house outside my bedroom window. I have no fear of heights, sir.'

'You are brave,' Henri said. 'Will you not call me by my given name? I would be your friend if you will but permit me.'

'Would you help me return to England?'

'Forgive me, I cannot, *mademoiselle*—but while you are Nico's guest I shall not permit harm to come to you.'

'Very well.' She met the constancy of his liquid brown gaze. 'I accept your offer of friendship, sir— Henri.'

The sailors had brought the rowing boat alongside the *Siren's Song*. Deborah allowed Henri to help her over the ship's rail. He held her until she was secure, and a sailor went before her to make certain that her feet were tucked securely into each descending rung of the ladder. At times her gown wrapped about her legs and she cursed the awkward bulkiness of her clothing, but with some delay to free her limbs the descent was safely accomplished. It was as well that she was not wearing the elaborate gown she had planned for Sarah's betrothal!

'Next time I sail with you, I would prefer to dress in male apparel,' she told Henri when he joined her in the boat.

'I shall remember that,' he promised with a chuckle of appreciation.

Deborah sat facing the shore, watching as the sailors negotiated a narrow channel between ugly spears of sharp rocks, which could pierce the side of the boat and cause it to sink, dumping unwary oarsmen into the treacherous water. The water was particularly wild just here, swirling dangerously about the rocks, a current waiting to drag them down should they founder.

As the boat was successfully beached on the far side of the violent swell, her eyes sought the path leading up to the woods above. Even as the sailors beached and one of them leapt out to carry her to dry land, she could pick out the figure she sought. A tall, powerful man gazing down at them; behind him she thought she saw other men—servants, perhaps—and horses. The marquis began the steep descent moments after she had been deposited on the soft sand.

She made no attempt to move towards him, forcing him to come to her, her head held high, pride in every line of her body.

'Welcome to Chalfont,' Nicholas said, bowing to her as if they were at Court. 'Horses await you, Mistress Stirling, and my home is being prepared to receive you.'

'You do me too much honour, sir.' She tossed her head at him, her dark chestnut curls glinting with fire in the sunlight. 'Tell me, shall I find my prison comfortable? Will there be bars on the window—or am I to be cast into the oubliette?'

Nicholas laughed as he caught the mockery in her voice. 'I believe we can offer you something a little more comfortable, mistress.'

Deborah inclined her head but made no answer. They had been walking across the sand, which was difficult as her skirts dragged in the soft, clinging grains.

'Oh, I cannot put up with this a moment longer!' she cried, and pulled the ties which held her overskirt in place, letting it slip away so that she wore only her over-bodice and satin petticoat. The petticoat was slender and clung revealingly to her hips, but felt much less of a drag on her as she walked. 'That is better. I can move more easily without it.'

'I wonder that you were able to descend the ship's ladder with the skirt on,' Nicholas murmured. 'Had I been there I should have suggested you remove your gown.'

'Had you been more thoughtful of my comfort you might have provided me with a youth's hose and breeches to make my progress more comfortable, sir. Yet if you were a gentleman I should not be here at all!'

She ignored Nicholas's outstretched hand and began to climb the steep path to the top of the cliff, finding her way surely though slowly at first.

Nicholas bent to retrieve her discarded skirt, watching as she picked her way over the rocky incline. She was as surefooted and bold as any youth!

'You were right, *mon ami*,' Henri said softly at his side. 'She does have much spirit as well as beauty. Such a woman is rare. It would be a pity to let Cortes have her.'

'He shall never lay a finger on her,' Nicholas replied, a glint of anger in his eyes. 'But if we hope to succeed, we must pray his pride drives him to attempt to bargain for her.'

'And in the mean time?'

'Mistress Stirling is our guest. We should go after her—she has almost reached the top.'

Deborah had indeed gained the top of the cliff. She glanced down and saw that the two men had only just begun their climb. She smiled in triumph, pleased that she had managed it alone; then, observing the group of servants and horses waiting, she felt her spirits soar. Perhaps she would give the marquis a little scare. It would serve him right for the way he had treated her!

The servants bowed and welcomed her as she approached, and, at her request, one of them hastened to help her mount the mare, which had been prepared especially for her with an elaborate sidesaddle. With a wicked glance over her shoulder Deborah took the reins, urging her horse to a fast trot and then, as she gained confidence, to a canter and lastly a headlong gallop.

She heard a shout that was obviously meant as a warning behind her, but did not bother to glance back. The marquis had reached the top of the cliff in time to see her flight but not to prevent her making it. She laughed and raced on, following the narrow path that led through the thick woods. It was no more than a track but oft used and she found no difficulty in maintaining her pace, merely ducking her head to avoid overhanging branches.

She found the ride exhilarating, her blood singing wildly in her veins. She had stolen a march on the marquis and cocked a snook at him for his arrogance in assuming she would simply allow him to take her to his château. He would have to catch her first! It was amusing to have outwitted him and it gave her a feeling of exquisite pleasure.

She plunged on heedlessly, thrilled by the chase. For she knew beyond a doubt that the marquis was pursuing her. Perhaps she could do more than startle him! She might even find her way to the main highway and then a town where someone would direct her to the nearest port. There she could buy her passage home with the gold chain that lay hidden beneath her bodice and was valuable, having been her mother's gift to her. It was something she always wore every day of her life, though mostly tucked away for fear that the sight of it should bring back sad memories for her dear father. She would hate to lose it, but the sacrifice would be worth it if she could but find her way home.

Even as vague plans formed in her head, Deborah heard the crash of hooves thudding behind her and sensed that the marquis was catching her. She bent forward over the mare's head, urging the fine animal on ever faster. She would not give the marquis best! He was too arrogant, too sure of himself. Somehow she would escape him.

'Have a care, mistress,' Nicholas called as he drew nearer. 'There is a steep incline ahead. Your horse could stumble and send you tumbling to your death.'

She ignored him, plunging on regardless of his warning. He was lying, trying to frighten her into submitting—but he would not! She would show him that she was not a poor wretch to be taken easily.

He was beside her now, trying to catch at her reins. Deborah jerked away but he rode into her mare and succeeded in capturing the reins, bringing their wild flight to a certain and shuddering halt. She had to cling on to the hub of the saddle to prevent herself falling off. Then he had dismounted and was dragging her to the ground, shaking her roughly as if she were a straw doll.

'You foolish wench!' he cried. 'You do not know these woods. You could have killed both yourself and the mare.'

'If that is true I apologize to the horse,' Deborah said defiantly. She tossed her head, her hair, freed from its usual neat confines, falling about her shoulders in wild disarray. 'But you deserve no apology, sir. You had no right to make me your prisoner. I demand that you take me home at once!'

'You are my guest—and shall remain so until I choose to send you back to your father.' His face was harsh, his eyes cold and unyielding.

'I am your prisoner. I shall escape… You shall not keep me here against my will!'

She got no further, finding herself a prisoner indeed, crushed in his arms and held tight against his chest. Then his mouth sought hers, devouring it with a hungry desperation that thrilled while it shocked her. Her head felt as if it was spinning and she could no longer fight against the swooning sensations inside her. It was difficult enough to breathe. She knew only that her weakness made her want to cling to him with all her strength.

She gazed up at him as he let her go at last. 'You are no gentleman, sir. You have used me ill. I—I hate you.'

The emotion she was feeling at that moment was in truth far from hatred, but she was bewildered by the depth of passion he had aroused in her and needed to defend herself.

'Indeed, I had no right to kiss you,' Nicholas agreed, his dark eyes grave as they studied her. 'While you are my guest, honour demands that you should be treated as such and protected both by me—and from me. Forgive my lapse of manners. It was a momentary foolishness. Your recklessness made me forget myself. For a while

I feared that you might plunge to your death before I could catch up to you.'

What did he mean? Why should he be concerned for her—and why react in such a way? Unless, of course, the kiss was intended as a punishment. Yes, that must be it—he had been punishing her, humiliating her and forcing her to remember her own weakness.

Deborah lifted her head proudly. 'You shall not be so easily forgiven, sir. I have no power to prevent you doing as you will with me. I know that I am at your mercy, but my father is not without friends or influence. He will discover that you have taken me and then he will come in search of me. You will be punished for your insolence, I promise you.'

Nicholas inclined his head. 'I do not doubt that you would be glad to see me hang, mistress—but I have no intention of obliging you. As you have witnessed, it is not easy to enter the cove, and I have many who serve me faithfully. Should a raiding party come in search of you, they will be seen long before they reach the château and treated with scant respect by my people. If your father should come in peace, of course, he would become my guest.'

The glint in his eyes left Deborah in little doubt of his meaning. She glared at him. 'You are very sure of yourself, sir.'

'I protect my home and my people and they are loyal to me,' Nicholas replied. 'Miguel Cortes is my enemy. He would do murder here if I grew careless. Until that monster is in his grave anyone who calls himself my friend had best watch his back.'

'What have you done that Don Miguel should hate you so?'

'I once laughed at him and called him a fool,' Nicholas replied and his face was gaunt with grief and re-morse. 'For that he destroyed a vulnerable young woman—to punish *me* he murdered an innocent. It was my foolish temper that provoked him. I bear the guilt of Isabella's death on my soul.'

'Is that why you attack Don Manola's ships? Why you would use me as bait to lure his son to sea?' Her eyes searched his face for the truth but she found it impossible to read.

Nicholas inclined his head, his expression stony, in-decipherable. 'I see that you understand my purpose, Mistress Stirling. Even such a cowardly dog as Miguel Cortes cannot ignore this. I have stolen his intended bride—as he stole mine.'

'Do you imagine he will come?' Deborah's scorn hid her fear. 'Surely if he is the monster you think him he will ignore the challenge? What difference can it make whether he marries another or me? Why should he care for a woman he has never set eyes on?'

'Because the knowledge that I have snatched his bride will eat at his soul—because it makes him a fool,' Nich-olas replied, his eyes dark with anger. 'Don Manola has forced him to remain safe in their fortress home. The Don wants grandchildren, heirs to inherit his wealth and estates. He is well past his prime and believes himself too old to father more children, therefore he protects the miserable wretch he has the misfortune to call son. He needs an heir, but no Spanish lady of good birth will take Miguel Cortes for her husband. Don Manola sees you as his prize. Pride and desperation will force them to come looking for you.'

'And when they do?'

'I shall kill the son. I have no quarrel with the father. Indeed, I believe he was once a man of honour. Until his son shamed his name. He may go in peace if he chooses. I want only Isabella's murderer.'

Deborah was silent. She felt cold despite the heat of the sun, which filtered through the trees into the little glade they had reached, and could not prevent herself shuddering. A dark shadow seemed to hover at her shoulder, making her afraid—but of what? Was it the man who had made her his captive or another who would make her his wife for the sake of an heir?

Nicholas saw the fear and swore beneath his breath.

'Fear not, he shall never lay a finger on you,' he said hoarsely. 'I shall kill him before ever he comes near you. That monster shall never defile you as he did Isabella. I would kill you myself first!'

'I thank you for your care of me, sir,' Deborah said with a flash of spirit. 'But I prefer to live a little longer in the hope of returning to my father.'

Nicholas laughed. 'Believe me, lady. Miguel Cortes will be dead long before he even sees your face. I have sworn it.'

'You take too much on yourself,' she retorted. 'Who made you the arbiter of my fate?' Her head went up, eyes icy with pride. 'Why should I believe your tales? For aught I know, Don Miguel may be a fitting husband for any woman—and you no more than a pirate.'

His dark eyes bored into her, seeming to reach her very soul. His look sent tremors down her spine. She did not know what to think and could not bear his gaze upon her.

'Do you truly believe that I would lie to you in such a matter, Mistress Stirling?'

Deborah took a deep breath. A part of her wanted to defy him still, but she could not deny the sincerity in his tone. Why should he lie? He had her at his mercy. He had no reason to speak other than the truth.

'No, sir. No, I do not think you would lie over such a terrible thing—but that does not excuse what you have done. You should not have brought me here. You had given me your warning. You ought in all decency to have given me time to reach my own decision. Or at the very least to have set your case before my father.'

Nicholas frowned. 'Would you have married Cortes had I not acted as I did? Tell me the truth, mistress.'

'I had begun to reconsider,' Deborah admitted. 'Your words troubled me sorely, sir. It was because I could not sleep that I walked out alone in the mist. Had I not done so, you would not have found it so easy to snatch me from my father's care.'

'I had planned to send a note asking you to meet me. I was about to deliver it to your servants when I saw you leave the house. It was my intention to beg you to change your mind—but then…'

'So you and your men seized your chance?' She saw the answer in his eyes. 'So it was my own foolishness that led us to this situation. Had we talked without anger I might have been still with my family.'

She gazed into his dark eyes and it was as if something reached out from him, entering her mind, possessing her will so that she felt all resistance fading. He had not answered her and the silence stretched between them endlessly.

'Why did you bring me here?' she breathed, and for one wonderful, terrifying moment she thought she saw the answer in his soul.

Chapter Six

'I could not let you wed him, Mistress Stirling,' Nicholas said after what seemed an eternity of silence while her question lay unanswered between them. 'But had you given your word...I do not believe I would have taken you captive as I did. It was your obstinacy, your determination to go to that monster as a bride, that drove me to a desperate act.' He shuddered as if the thought filled him with horror and his next words were softly spoken, almost as if he spoke them to himself. 'No, I could never let him have you.'

She gazed up at him, trying desperately to understand his heart, to know his mind. 'And your plan to tempt Miguel Cortes from his hiding place?'

'Would have been forgotten. In time he must venture forth and when he does...' Nicholas shrugged.

'You almost persuade me that you acted for my sake, sir.'

Nicholas laughed softly as he saw the way her eyes challenged him. He sensed that she was still aggrieved by his treatment of her, but undecided, her manner softening despite her determination to resist him.

'Is that so difficult to believe? Can you not credit that a man might do much for your sake, lady?'

'Then will you not take me back to my father, sir? I will tell him that it was all a misunderstanding.'

'Why, Mistress Stirling,' Nicholas asked mockingly. 'Would you spurn my poor hospitality?' He held his hand out to her. There was charm in his manner, but also an imperious demand that would not be denied. 'Let me help you to mount. Come, trust me a little. I mean you no harm—but now that you are here I must hold to my plan. Your father has been told that you are my guest and he will inform Don Manola of your disappearance. In time you shall be returned to your home. I give you my word.'

His dark gaze narrowed, intensified, holding her own so that she trembled as she asked, 'You are determined on this madness? You will not change your mind?'

'I have no choice. Until Isabella is avenged I shall have no peace. I cannot forget the past until that monster has paid the price of his treachery.'

'Supposing he kills you?' Deborah asked. 'What will become of me then?'

'Henri will take care of you,' Nicholas replied gravely. 'You will be safe in my home, Mistress Stirling. When I go to meet Don Miguel I shall sail without Henri, who will remain here to guard you—and believe me, he will do so with his life. You have nothing to fear while you remain in my care. I would trust Henri as myself—he is an honourable man.'

'Yes, that I do believe,' Deborah said. 'He has sworn to be my friend and I have given him my trust.'

'Then shall there be a truce between us?'

'Why not?' She gazed up at him, her eyes searching

his face. 'I shall take your word that no harm will come
to me while I am in your care, sir.'

'I thank you, mistress.' Nicholas smiled; then, placing
his hands about her waist, he lifted her into the saddle.
'Let us have no more of these foolish attempts to escape.
Had I not caught you in time you might have fallen and
hurt yourself.'

Deborah's manner was more flirtatious than she knew
as she met his steady look. 'And would that have distressed you?'

'I believe you know the answer to that as well as I,
mistress.'

Deborah saw something in his eyes that made her
blush. She turned her face aside, telling herself she was
foolish to feel this way about a man who sought to use
her for his own purpose. It was Isabella he had loved,
Isabella he could not forget. Yet she believed him when
he said he would kill her rather than let Miguel Cortes
lay a finger on her.

If it was foolish to feel warmed by his words, then
she was foolish. She had begun by despising this man,
but somewhere along the line her feelings had undergone
a startling change. He was not a man to be treated lightly
in any respect. She had learned to trust him despite herself and—and to like him. She had no explanation for
the way in which his kisses turned her limbs to melting
bliss. At least none that a maiden might admit even in
the privacy of her own thoughts.

The marquis had her horse by the rein and was leading
it, firmly in command of the situation. When they passed
the steep incline he had spoken of, she realized that a
fall there might have left her badly injured or even dead
and a shiver ran through her.

No mention of the danger was made by either of them,

but once they were safely past it the marquis released the reins and allowed her to ride freely. She saw that the woods through which they had been riding had almost ended now and before her lay Chalfont, gleaming and golden in the sunshine—a house so beautiful and stirring to the soul that her eyes filled with tears.

It was not huge but larger than her father's house, the walls sturdily built of a thick buttery stone that looked warm and welcoming in the dying rays of the evening sun. The grey glass of small-paned windows had turned to rose in the sunset and gave the house an open, inviting appearance. She had seldom seen so many windows, for glass was fabulously expensive and very precious. It must have cost a king's ransom to build such a house as this.

'Oh…' she breathed as she reined in to stare in wonder. It seemed that everywhere was bright with colour: pink, white and purple flowers tumbling out of stone pots and over balconies. 'I do not think I have ever seen anything as lovely as your home, sir.'

'It was built for a beautiful woman who loved light and sunshine by a man who adored her,' Nicholas said, a faint smile of remembrance on his lips. 'I am glad you approve of my home, Mistress Stirling.'

'I had no idea it would be like this.'

'You imagined yourself on your way to a fortress, no doubt?' Mockery glinted in the dark eyes. 'It is but the residence of a country gentleman. My father loved his vineyards almost as much as he loved his wife. He was a man of peace, of solitude. I never heard him raise his voice in anger. When my mother died he could not bear to live without her.'

She was hearing from his own lips the tale Henri had

told her, and once again it touched her heart. 'He must have loved her very much.'

Nicholas bent his head in assent but made no further comment until he came to help her dismount. 'Come, my lady,' he said, holding out his hand. 'Let me show you my home. I believe you will find your apartments to your liking.'

Deborah was certain of it. Something about this place was already calling out to her, appealing to her senses on every level.

She allowed him to take her hand and lead her the last few paces to a short flight of stone steps to the veranda. The perfume of flowers wafted towards her and then she saw a woman standing at the open door—a tall, graceful, lovely woman with hair the colour of spun gold and hard blue eyes. She curtsied as they approached, bending her head submissively to the marquis.

'I am glad to see you safely returned, Nicholas,' she said in a soft, husky voice. 'I bid you welcome…and Mistress Stirling.'

As she spoke Deborah's name, her head came up and her eyes seemed to stab the younger woman with hatred. Yes, there was no other word that would accurately describe the expression in those icy eyes, thought Deborah. This woman was angry because the marquis had brought her here.

'Thank you, Marie,' Nicholas replied seeming unaware of her hostility towards his guest, and indeed the look was swiftly veiled so that he would see no trace of it. 'I am sorry to have given you so little notice of our arrival.'

'It matters not,' Marie replied, sweetly acquiescent. 'Your own rooms are always waiting for your return, of course—but it will be some minutes before the chambers you requested can be prepared. Perhaps some refreshment in the mean time?'

'Yes, that would be most welcome. Bring sweet wine and some of your almond comfits, Marie. I am sure Mistress Stirling would enjoy the biscuits as a temptation to her palate before we sup.'

'They await you in the small salon, cousin. Everything shall be as you requested.' Marie smiled and waved her hand in a gesture of invitation. 'You will forgive me, Mistress Stirling. I have much to do. Perhaps we shall have an opportunity to talk later?'

'Yes, most certainly,' Deborah replied. Had she imagined that hostile look earlier? There was no sign of it now. 'I thank you for your welcome. Forgive me, I do not know how to address you.'

'Mistress Trevern,' Nicholas said answering for his cousin. 'Marie is the daughter of my mother's brother. She came to visit me some eighteen months ago with her companion and liked the house so well that she decided to stay on.'

'The house lacked a woman's touch,' Marie said, giving him a teasing smile, which made her look startlingly beautiful. 'You neglected it and yourself, cousin. I have promised to leave you in peace when you take a wife. The remedy is in your own hands.'

'Nay, I would not have you leave,' he replied with a tolerant, amused smile. 'You know you are welcome in my home for as long as you wish to remain.'

Marie shook her head at him, excused herself and left the hall—but not before Deborah had read her secret in her eyes. She was in love with the marquis. She had stayed on at the château not because she liked the house, but because she loved its master.

It was little wonder that she resented the unexpected

arrival of a woman she had neither met nor heard of until that very day.

'Come,' Nicholas said, leading the way from the wide entrance hall into a moderate-sized square chamber with flooring made from a reddish pink, green and white material. The white was marble, of course, an expensive and beautiful substance used only in the halls of the great, but what was this wondrous stone set in pretty mosaic patterns here and there to delight the eye? Deborah was too awed to ask, but seeing her astonishment Nicholas smiled. 'Marble imported from Italy and agate dug from the heart of rocks beneath some swirling stream in far-off lands. My father spared no expense for his bride, and these were her favourite colours, especially pink.'

'As it is mine. I have never seen anything as lovely as this room,' Deborah confessed. Coming from a house that was considered extremely comfortable, its walls panelled with dark oak and hung with rich tapestry, she had believed herself privileged—but this was beyond her imagining. The airiness and lightness all about her gave her a feeling of freedom and space without seeming cold or dismal like parts of the English King's palace. The furniture was more elegantly wrought than she had previously seen, sometimes gilded and painted so that it added richness and colour to the whole, and at a window gauzy drapes moved in a soft breeze. 'This room is finer than the Queen's own withdrawing chamber at Whitehall.'

'Please do not tell His Majesty that,' Nicholas begged with wry humour. 'He would require yet more tributes from my coffers.'

Deborah's eyebrows rose. 'Is that why he pays no heed to Don Manola's demands that you should hang?

Because you give him gold and silver you have stolen from others?' Her tone was accusing, pricking at him despite their agreement to a truce.

'For that—and other reasons,' Nicholas replied, frowning as he saw the scorn she could not hide. 'Come, Mistress Stirling, we shall not quarrel. Take a cup of wine to slake your thirst.'

He poured wine from a silver flacon into goblets of gold chased with engravings and set with a band of tiny semi-precious stones about the foot, handing one to Deborah with a little smile before he tasted his own.

'Shall you be comfortable here? Or do you still fear my oubliette?'

She blushed, meeting his challenge with a toss of her head. 'That was foolish of me, sir. I confess I allowed my tongue to run away with me.'

'A noble apology,' he murmured. 'We shall forget 'twas ever said.'

His mockery stung her, though she had brought it on herself.

'Sir, you are the most…' Deborah's retort was lost as Marie Trevern returned, her sharp eyes noting their bantering mood and the rapport between them.

'Your chamber is ready now, Mistress Stirling.'

Deborah drained her cup and returned it to her host. As their fingers touched, she felt a shiver of pleasure run through her. Her eyes met the marquis's and her lips curved in a wicked smile that challenged while promising much.

'Your home is delightful, sir, as you know well. I am sure I shall enjoy my visit—of whatever duration it may prove.'

She turned then and went from the room with Marie Trevern, her back straight and her head angled high. The sound of Nicholas's laughter seemed to follow as she went into the hall and up a curving staircase, its wooden balustrades carved thickly with richly painted figures in classical dress, which spiralled to the gallery above.

'My cousin has given you the rooms formerly belonging to the Marquise de Vere,' said Marie. 'They have been kept aired since her death, but have not been used.'

'Then I am honoured to be allowed to use them,' Deborah replied, aware once more of the other woman's hostility.

'My cousin informed me that your maid and all your baggage was lost in a storm,' Marie went on, an angry glint in her eyes. She was clearly suspicious and resentful. 'He has requested that I lend you a gown until others can be provided—and any other articles you may require.'

Deborah was surprised and did not immediately reply. Why had the marquis lied to his cousin? Was it merely to save Deborah's blushes—or because he did not quite trust Marie?

'You are very kind. I dropped my overskirt on the beach so that I could climb more easily. Perhaps it could be rescued?'

'I believe you will find the garment in your chamber.' Marie's cold eyes swept over her with contempt. 'These are your temporary apartments, Mistress Stirling. A maidservant awaits you.' Had she meant to imply that Deborah's stay as an honoured guest would be of short duration? 'I have many tasks I must see to before we sup.'

She lifted a latch to open the door, then stood back, indicating that Deborah should go in alone. Clearly she considered her duty done.

'We dine shortly. Your maid will show you the way.'

'Thank you, Mistress Trevern.'

As the older woman turned aside, Deborah pushed the door open and went in, gasping in astonished delight as she saw what awaited her. The walls were panelled in wood that had been gilded and painted with pastoral scenes, then draped with pale cream silk, and the floors were once again of marble and that wondrous stone that had caught Deborah's eye before. Scattered on the floor—luxury upon luxury!—lay tiny, jewel-bright silk rugs. No one except perhaps royalty ever used carpets on the floors, they were far too precious, more fitted as hangings or table coverings! Yet here there was a profusion of them, giving warmth and more colour to the chamber. The bed itself was monstrous large and fashioned of four gilded posts with a canopy of swathed silk and draped about with hangings of rose damask.

Placed by an arched window was a large, flat-topped oaken coffer; it was banded and studded with iron, and a huge silver bowl filled with roses stood upon it. Close by was a gleaming, heavily waxed board supported by legs shaped like an inward-curving *X*. On its surface were strewn precious articles: scent bottles of Venetian glass banded with gilded silver, so rare and costly that Deborah had seen but one example in her life—a gift made to her mother on her wedding day. There was also a silver ewer and bowl and a hand mirror so fine that she hardly dared to touch it, besides combs of ivory and silver clips to fasten a lady's hair. An embroidery frame, a padded stool, and an oaken settle made this the most comfortable bedchamber Deborah had ever seen.

'Your pardon, *mademoiselle*,' a young woman said, coming in from an adjoining room. 'You would wish to bathe?'

Deborah stared at her in surprise. 'You have prepared a bath for me?'

'*Oui, mademoiselle*—pardon me. Mistress Trevern say I must speak always the English, but it is not good. You understand?'

Deborah laughed and nodded, feeling a wonderful sense of relief. A bath! What indulgence! She always took a bath once a month when at home, though it was not the custom to bathe so frequently. Often, she had to be content with washing herself all over. Too much washing was not thought to be healthy and was frowned on by many, but Deborah had noticed that it was good to feel clean and she went her own way in such things.

She followed the maid into the adjoining chamber. Here there was a private closet and several presses and armoires where clothes would be stored on shelves. In the centre of the floor stood a hipbath fashioned of painted wood lined with gleaming metal. The perfume emanating from the steaming water was enticing.

'You will disrobe, *mademoiselle*?'

Deborah assented to her over-bodice being unfastened at the back, and then she untied the strings of her heavy silk petticoat and stepped out of it. Another of a finer silk followed and then another of plain linen. She discarded her under-bodice and lifted her foot to dip a toe in the water.

'It is not too hot?' the maid asked.

'No, it is just right,' Deborah replied, settling into the bath with a sigh of content.

Her skin looked pink and pearly beneath the clear water, her legs smooth and well shaped. It was more usual for ladies to bathe wearing a loose gown to cover them, but none had been provided and Deborah let the soft water lap over her without feeling shame for her immodesty. What did it matter when there was none to see her? The maid was smiling, clearly uncritical of her new mistress as she handed her a jar of a soft and sweet-smelling soap.

Deborah began to rub the soap into her skin. She knew that many of those who did not bathe regularly needed an instrument to scrape the crust of dirt from their bodies, but Deborah's skin was soft and moist from the lotions she made herself and applied often.

'*Mademoiselle* has lovely skin,' the maid said. 'You like me to wash your back, yes?'

'Yes, please,' Deborah said and glanced at her. 'What is your name? I do not believe you told me.'

'It is Louise, *mademoiselle*—if it pleases you. Mistress Trevern calls me girl or wench, depending on her mood.'

'I shall call you by your given name, it is a pretty one,' Deborah said. She sighed with pleasure as the girl soaped her back. 'That feels so good. Thank you, Louise. I should like to stay here forever, but I was warned that my hosts dine soon. I must not keep them waiting. Will you hand me the bathing sheet, please?'

Louise wrapped her about with the large thick cloth that had been specially prepared and to Deborah's delight felt warm to her skin.

'You must tell me when you wish to bathe again,' Louise said. 'It is my pleasure to serve you, *mademoiselle*. I was a child when the marquise died but I remember how good she was, how generous to those about her. I have hoped a new mistress would come to bring the warmth and love back to this house—and to my master.'

Deborah looked at her curiously. 'Do you not like Mistress Trevern?'

The girl wrinkled her nose. 'It is not the same. She is not mistress of the marquis's 'eart. You understand?'

'Perhaps she would like to be.'

'For myself, I 'ope not,' Louise replied with a wicked grin. 'She is not a 'appy person to 'ave as mistress.'

'Ah, I see.' Deborah nodded. She smiled at the girl, feeling she had found a friend. 'Now I must dress quickly for I would not wish to keep the marquis waiting.'

'Sometimes it is good if a man wait,' Louise said. 'But we shall dress *rapidement, oui*?'

Deborah looked at the gown Louise had laid ready on the bed. The petticoat was of pink silk heavily encrusted with pearls; the overdress was a dark crimson, the hanging sleeves slashed through with silver.

'Is this the gown Mistress Trevern provided?' Deborah asked, amazed by the other woman's generosity in lending her such a lovely thing.

'Pah!' scoffed Louise. 'She bring that old brown thing I throw over there on the settle. This gown she belong to the marquise. It is much more becoming and it will fit you—no?'

'It looks as though it might almost have been made for me,' Deborah said, stroking the material with reverent fingers. 'But will the marquis not be angry if I wear his mother's gowns?'

'He will not know,' Louise replied with a little shrug. 'All 'er things are just left 'ere to waste. It does not matter. The marquise would 'ave given it with pleasure.'

Deborah stifled her misgivings and allowed herself to be dressed in the beautiful gown. Louise piled her long hair into an artless arrangement of curls and loops, fastening it with some of the combs and pins Deborah had seen earlier, and arranging a headdress of some fine material to perch at the back of her head. When she had finished, she stood back to admire her work with obvious satisfaction.

'There—it is done. You are *magnifique*, a mistress worthy to grace Chalfont this night, no?'

Deborah glanced at her reflection in the hand mirror. From what she could see of herself, her hair had never looked better and she needed no mirror to tell her the dress was becoming. It was of an era when the style of a woman's gown had been a little simpler and more elegant than the exaggerated court dress she had worn in London.

'You have made me look beautiful. Thank you, Louise.'

'*Mademoiselle* is beautiful,' the maid replied. 'I 'ave only dressed you, nothing more.'

'Shall we go down now?'

Deborah's heart was racing as she followed the maid from the room, along the gallery and down the imposing stairway. As she drew near the bottom, the two gentlemen standing below gazed up at her. This evening Henri Moreau was dressed in courtly clothes of blue and gold, which showed his wiry figure to advantage. The marquis was plain in black and grey, but his stature would always cast others in the shade. He bowed his head to Deborah, the gleam in his eyes as he saw her revealing his thoughts on the matter of her appearance.

'You look well this evening, Mistress Stirling. I believe...'

'How dare you? How dare you wear that gown!'

The angry, accusing tones of Marie Trevern cut across whatever Nicholas had been about to say. Deborah stood as if frozen to the spot, her cheeks crimson. She could only stare in dismay as the other woman came forward to challenge her.

'Your gown would not have fitted me…' She offered the excuse lamely, knowing that she could not explain what had truly happened for that would have exposed Louise to her anger.

'Then you should have worn your own,' Marie said. 'That gown belonged to my aunt—Madeleine, Marquise de Vere. No one but me has touched her things in years, and that only to preserve and air them. You had no right to take her gown.'

'Forgive me…' Deborah glanced at the marquis awkwardly. 'I did not mean to offend you, sir.'

'Nor have you,' said Nicholas. 'My mother would have begged you to make free with her hospitality had she lived. I believe that gown was hers when I was but a lad. I remember she wore it once for my birthday. It becomes you well, as it did *Maman*.'

'It is very beautiful. I consider it an honour to be allowed to borrow it.'

'Nonsense! You may use and enjoy anything you find in your apartments, Mistress Stirling. An old gown is but poor recompense for the situation in which you find yourself. I shall put the seamstresses to work to make new gowns—but until then I beg you to use what you will.'

Nicholas's words had brought a dark crimson colour to his cousin's cheeks. She was angry, jealous and humiliated. Clearly she had coveted the marquise's possessions for herself but had not dared to take them for her own. She was hardly able to contain her fury at seeing them given carelessly to another. Yet after a few moments she hid her chagrin behind a smile.

'Forgive my outburst, Nicholas. It seemed sacrilege to

see another woman wearing your mother's things. I imagined it must cause you pain.'

'Forget the incident, Marie.' Nicholas frowned at her. 'If you desired the gown you should have taken it for yourself, cousin.'

'It would not suit me,' she replied, averting her eyes so that he should not read the truth. 'I merely kept my aunt's things in good order for the sake of her memory.'

'I thought them discarded long ago. But it is as well that you were so assiduous in your care, for now they serve a worthwhile purpose. I thank you, cousin—and now we shall sup together. Henri will escort you, Marie, if you please?' He smiled at Deborah. 'Come, take my arm, lady, and tell me whether your apartments please you?'

'How could I not be pleased?' She looked at him shyly. 'You were considerate to give me your mother's apartments. I have never before stayed in such beautiful apartments.'

'My father would never give my mother less than the best he could provide. I would think myself shamed if I did less for you. You did not ask for my hospitality, Mistress Stirling, but now that you are here I would have you offered every comfort.'

'I thank you, sir. I am very comfortable.'

'A little better than the cage you imagined?' Nicholas could not resist the taunt, his wicked eyes mocking her.

Deborah blushed. He would never allow her to forget the foolish things her temper had caused her to say. Yet how could she have guessed at the outset how generous he would be?

'I was…disconcerted to find myself on your ship, sir. Pray forgive me for my unruly tongue.'

Nicholas's eyes gleamed with his appreciation of the

apology politeness had forced from her. 'Only disconcerted, lady? I vow I should have been vastly put out
had I been treated as you were. You were quite right—
that blanket was filthy.'

Deborah caught the wicked teasing note in his voice
and laughed. She had a high, clear laugh that sounded
joyous and caused the others to turn and look at them
curiously.

She realized they would be a larger gathering than she
had imagined. Besides Marie and Henri there was an
older woman, who, she was later to learn, was Mistress
Roth, companion to the marquis's cousin. Two other
gentlemen, clearly close friends of Nicholas, had come
to sup with them. Both were French and young, attractive men. Later that evening Henri told her that both
were captains of their own ships as part of the marquis's
fleet.

The atmosphere was merry at table, the gentlemen
laughing and jesting with each other in the manner of
old friends. Often they spoke in English out of deference
to the ladies, but sometimes they lapsed into their native
tongue.

Her father, who spoke French well and had spent
some time in the country during his youth, had taught
Deborah himself. Sir Edward had had his daughter educated as he would have his longed-for son. She was
able to understand the gist of what they said, though
sometimes they spoke too fast for her to follow all of it
and in a dialect that was strange to her. However, they
were such kind, thoughtful hosts that Deborah found the
evening sped away. She had seldom enjoyed being in
company so much and began to feel that she was truly
an honoured guest rather than a hostage.

After they had dined Nicholas played on a lute and

sang in the manner of a troubadour, songs of love and courtly pleasure. His voice was melodious and had an attractive quality that made it a pleasure to listen to his songs. One of the other gentlemen, whose name was Pierre, told them a story about the brave deeds of Charlemagne, the founder of the Holy Roman Empire and ruler of all Frankland in his age. And so the evening passed away happily in a haze of laughter, music, talk and wine.

When it was time for Deborah to retire she was aware of a feeling of reluctance to leave these charming people, but since the other ladies had made it plain they wished to go to their chambers she could not stay on.

She wished the company goodnight and left the gentlemen to their wine and talk. However, Nicholas insisted on accompanying her to the foot of the stairs. He kissed her hand, smiling at her in a way that set her heart racing wildly and made her even more reluctant to part from him.

'Will you ride with me tomorrow, Mistress Stirling? I would like to show you my estate—and to warn you of the dangers of leaving it without an escort.'

'Do you still suspect me of meaning to escape?'

'I believe you might try if the opportunity arose. Am I not right?'

'Perhaps,' Deborah replied, though at that moment she had no desire to leave this man or his home.

'As I thought, you are high-spirited,' he said. 'There is no harm in that—but I beg you to consider carefully. You are safe here. Don Manola will not attack me on my own land, for he knows I am too strong, too well guarded—but once he knows you are my guest he might attempt to snatch you by stealth. If you were foolish enough to leave my protection, he might grab his chance to steal you back.'

'Then I shall not behave in a reckless manner again,' Deborah gave her word easily. 'You have given your promise that I shall be returned safely to my father one day and I am content to trust your honour in this.'

'So we progress,' Nicholas said and looked as if her words had pleased him. 'You have the freedom of my home and lands, mistress. And for your entertainment there shall be guests who will be your friends, music and dancing.'

'Is it always as it has been this evening when you are at home, sir?'

'I like to gather friends about me,' he replied. 'For some long months I confess I have not found solace in music or dancing—but this evening pleased me well.'

'I also,' said Deborah, a high colour in her cheeks. 'If the time always passes so—so pleasantly in your home, I see little wonder that Mistress Trevern chose to stay on.'

'Marie came to visit with her brother and companion. While they were here Master Trevern died suddenly of a fever. He was but eighteen and had no wife or child, and perforce his estate passed to a distant cousin. Marie believed she would not be welcome in her cousin's house. I offered her a home here for as long as she wishes and she was pleased to accept.'

Nicholas's statement was accompanied by a careless shrug. He clearly had no idea of Marie's feelings for him.

'You were generous, sir. Mistress Trevern would no doubt have been found a husband had she returned to her home, but not necessarily of her choosing. A woman is at the mercy of her relatives, and they are not always as kind as I think you might be to those you care for.'

'Your compliment is accepted, mistress. I thank you.' Nicholas smiled. 'But you must leave us now. Sleep well—and do not have bad dreams. I promise that you are safe here.'

'Yes, I know. Good night, sir.'

He inclined his head but said no more. Deborah sensed that he had not moved, was still there watching her with those dark, intense eyes. There was such power in his eyes—the power to make her melt and lose herself in him. But such thoughts were dangerous, especially when she was his hostage, at the mercy of his whims.

The nape of her neck tingled with a strange sensation, and it was all that she could do not to turn around, but somehow she kept her head high and walked along the upper gallery to her own apartments.

Chapter Seven

Louise was waiting to undress her. She greeted her mistress with smiles and chattered on as she helped Deborah to disrobe, bringing out a night chemise of the softest lawn to slip over her head and finally brushing her hair until it shone. Deborah was content to listen to her, smiling but saying little.

After she had dismissed the girl she went over to the window, which had not been shuttered, as it would have been at home, though it was securely fastened from the inside. Gazing out at the moonlight, Deborah thought she would like to walk in what was clearly a beautiful garden, for she could see a profusion of climbing roses and other scented flowers. She wished she dare go down and explore some of the secret walks; she was not afraid of the night air, even though it was said to be evil, nor of the dark itself.

At home she had sometimes walked in her own walled garden late on a summer's night, and here she knew it would be warm and still, the air perfumed with the scent of flowers that seemed only to give out their true sweetness at night.

But she could not go down. It was not her house. She

was a guest here and she must behave with proper respect.

Sighing, she turned back to her bed. Louise had taken off the heavy covers of silk damask, leaving only a light covering. More would not be needed on such a warm night.

Deborah slipped into the bed, settling back against the pile of downy soft pillows. She felt a little sleepy now, but as she closed her eyes she saw again the marquis's dark eyes gazing into hers. What was it about him that affected her so, making her insides melt in unfamiliar heat?

Was the feeling he aroused in her desire? The feeling that she had heard drove both men and women to the edge of madness, and led young girls to their destruction and shame?

She had never felt anything like it until the marquis kissed her, but now just to look at him, to feel his gaze upon her or the touch of his hand against hers, caused her heart to beat wildly. In her father's village, Deborah knew, country lads and lasses were sometimes forced to wed because they had come together in unholy lust. The Reverend Howarth had condemned them for their wicked sins from his pulpit. Was she wicked to feel as she did when Nicholas touched her?

Surely such pleasures could not be evil if the couple were blessed in wedlock—but if they were strangers? Deborah was aware that her father would frown on a marriage between her and the marquis, even if Nicholas had asked for her—which he had not! Nor was it likely, she told herself severely. And yet those eyes promised so much…or perhaps that was her imagination?

Oh, why must she be plagued with such wanton thoughts? Deborah groaned as she realized that it could

not be other than sinful to allow her mind to dwell on a
man's kisses—a man who was not her husband nor yet
her betrothed. He should never have kissed her! That
alone was enough to ruin her if it were known.

Perhaps she was already ruined in the eyes of the
world. By taking her from her own secure world, the
marquis had committed an unforgivable sin in the eyes
of her peers—and one that by implication also damned
her.

She closed her eyes as her thoughts became too mud-
dled, willing herself to sleep and forget the marquis.
Drifting into a state of slumber, she allowed a smile to
curve her mouth. For in her dreams there was no right
or wrong, no conscience to chide her, merely a sweet
content that held her until the dawn crept in at her windows.

'My master sent word that you were to break your
fast in bed,' Louise said, setting a platter of soft rolls,
butter and honey on a stand by the bed. 'I 'ave brought
for you a cordial of fruit, *mademoiselle*—but there is ale
or wine if you should care for it, and water cool from
the spring.'

'I shall try a little of your cordial,' Deborah said,
stretching luxuriously. She felt so good after her sleep,
which had been deep in the end. 'But it is my habit to
drink nothing but water to break my fast.'

'I think you will like the cordial,' Louise said. 'But I
shall remember the water in future.' She smiled. 'My
master says you are to ride with him after you eat. He
say I should bring to you the marquise's riding gown.
You would like this, *oui*?'

'Yes, thank you, Louise.'

Deborah bit into the soft roll she had spread with

honey; it was light and crispy outside and tasted delicious.

'Oh, this is so good. I feel wonderful this morning.
So alive!'

'*Mademoiselle* slept well?'

'Yes, thank you.' Deborah stretched once more, wrig-
gling her toes in blissful pleasure. 'The bed was very
comfortable.'

'Me, I warmed it with the pan to make sure it was
not damp,' Louise told her. 'You do not want to catch
the agues, no?'

'No, certainly not,' Deborah replied laughing.

She was aware of feeling happy as she finished her
meal, then hopped out of bed to wash herself in the
warm water Louise had provided in a pewter ewer.

Spread out on the bed waiting for her was a riding
gown of black and silver. The skirt was cut on simple
lines, so much easier to wear than the voluminous gowns
that were so fashionable at the English Court; the marquise had obviously been a lady who knew her own
mind and dressed as she pleased!

When Deborah was dressed and Louise had finished
fastening the bodice, she looked as elegant as she had
the previous night. A small hat with a huge curling
feather perched on the back of her head, and soft leather
gauntlets completed her toilette.

'The marquise was slender like you, *mademoiselle*,'
Louise said with a look of satisfaction when she had
finished. 'And her feet were as tiny as yours. Mistress
Tavern, she 'as the big feet. She could never wear the
marquise's things; they would look foolish on 'er.'

'You should not say such things, Louise. No, really
you should not. It is unkind.'

The maid shrugged. 'I say only the truth, *mademoiselle*.'

Deborah smiled but shook her head at her. Indeed, their conversation was brought to an abrupt end when, after a perfunctory knock, Marie Trevern swept into the room. She frowned and set her mouth in a prim line as she saw how Deborah was gowned, but made no reference to the fact that she was using the marquise's things.

'I trust you slept well, Mistress Stirling?'

'Very well, thank you, Mistress Trevern.'

Marie's eyes were cold and disapproving: her hostility seemed to be growing rather than dissipating. 'My cousin has invited you to ride with him this morning, I believe. He is not in the habit of being kept waiting and asked me to inquire if you were ready?'

'I am quite ready.' Deborah nodded to the serving girl. 'Thank you, Louise. I am very pleased. You may go now.'

'*Oui, mademoiselle*.' She curtsied and left.

For a moment Marie deliberately blocked Deborah's way, preventing her from following. 'Who are you?' she asked, her eyes narrowed and suspicious. 'My cousin says you were caught in a storm and he brought you here to safety until your family could be reached—but I think he is lying. Are you his latest whore?'

'How dare you!' Deborah cried, outraged by both the question and the manner of its asking. 'You have no right to say such a wicked thing to me. I am no such thing.'

'Then why are you here? Why have you no clothes or possessions of your own?'

'You should address your questions to the marquis.' Deborah lifted her head proudly.

'He will not tell me.' Marie glared at her. 'But I shall

discover your secret, Mistress Stirling. Believe me, I have my ways.'

'There is no secret—or none that could cause me shame,' Deborah said and swept past her.

She raised her head, determined to give no sign of her deep unease. The other woman clearly meant to be as unpleasant as she could, but Deborah was not about to let her attitude upset her. She was smiling as she went down the impressive staircase to discover the marquis waiting for her.

'You look delightful, Mistress Stirling,' Nicholas said. 'I hope you rested well?'

'Yes, thank you. Very well.' She felt the heat rise in her as she met his smiling gaze.

'Are you ready to go riding?'

'Quite ready, sir.'

'Then let us waste no more time. The air is fresh this morning. Later it will be too warm for riding.'

Deborah smiled her agreement but said no more, merely following the marquis outside to where the horses were waiting. A pretty chestnut mare had been saddled for her; it tossed its silken mane and danced skittishly as she approached but was soon gentled by the marquis's touch and soothing voice. He placed his hands about Deborah's waist, lifting her effortlessly to place her on her horse's back.

She took the reins, controlling the mare's slightly nervous prancing as she waited for the marquis to mount his own fine horse, which was a huge black creature with wicked eyes. Then she followed Nicholas's lead and trotted behind him out of the courtyard, which had just begun to warm in the early morning sunshine. As they came to a pretty park their pace increased to a gentle canter but not yet a gallop. It was too fine a morning to race, and the leisurely pace allowed Deborah to glance about her.

The park had wonderful ancient trees, the branches dipping almost to the ground in majestic grace, but there were plenty of open spaces and areas where it might be pleasant to walk. She saw a group of fountains playing into a deep pool where lilies grew in profusion; there was a Grecian-style temple for taking one's ease away from the fierce heat of the afternoon and occasionally she caught sight of deer grazing in the distance. It was an idyllic place, perhaps as close to Paradise as she was ever like to see.

After they had been riding for some twenty minutes or more the park gave way to pasture where sheep and cattle grazed, and once they had gained the crest of a small rise she saw vast vineyards spread out beneath her as far as the eye could see.

'Is all this your land?' Deborah asked as the marquis reined in beside her so that their horses stood side by side at the top of the rise. 'It seems to go on forever.'

'There is a village beyond,' Nicholas said, 'and a stream to the north. We have the cliffs to our backs...so you see we should be warned if an enemy thought to strike at us.'

'Could we visit the cove?' Deborah asked. 'Is there another way in other than from the sea or those steep cliffs?'

'Not to the cove where we landed,' he replied a frown in his eyes. 'But there is another beach to the south of the vineyards. Would you like to see it?'

'Yes, please.' Her eyes were aglow as she looked at him. 'I love to walk by the sea. Our home is but an hour's ride from a sandy shore and in the summer my father and I often went there...' The glow faded suddenly and she gave a little choke. 'My poor father. How anxious he must be for my sake.'

'If you wish to write a letter to Sir Edward I will have it delivered to him.'

'Would you?' Her eyes lit up once more. 'It would ease my mind if I thought Father was not worrying too much over me.'

'Then it shall be done.' Nicholas smiled at her. 'Come, I shall show you the beach—though I must ask for your promise that you will not go there alone. It is our one vulnerable spot. It would be possible for men to land there from the sea. We should have warning long before they reached the château, of course, but if you were there alone...'

'Yes, I understand,' Deborah said. 'You have my word, sir. Since I believe that your motive in kidnapping me was in part for my own sake, I shall take care. I have no wish to wed with the man who so cruelly treated your betrothed.'

'I thank you for your promise, lady. I shall feel easier in my mind when I am away if I know you are safe.' Nicholas inclined his head, then turned his horse away for her to follow, but not before she had seen that dark brooding expression in his eyes.

Deborah understood that her mention of Isabella must have caused him pain. Obviously, he had loved her very much. It was clear that her death haunted him. And when he spoke of going away, it was because of his appointment with Isabella's murderer—an appointment with destiny. For some reason that made her feel cold inside despite the warmth of the sun.

For some time they rode in silence. The beach when they came upon it was a surprise. Here there were no rocks or cliffs, but merely a stretch of coarse salty grasses that sloped sharply to the sea. Beyond the grass-land the blue water lapped gently against a beach of soft golden sand, curving into a wide bay between two high ridges of rocks that became solid cliffs again a little farther on.

'Oh, this is wonderful!' Deborah cried. 'I shall race you to the sea.'

She spurred her mare forward to a gallop and was soon in headlong flight towards the shallow edge. Nicholas swiftly caught up with her, their horses keeping pace as they pounded the wet sand, salty water flying up in a cooling spray about them.

Deborah laughed for sheer delight. And when at last they brought their horses to a stand and Nicholas lifted her down, it seemed only right and natural that he should kiss her. It was not a demanding, challenging kiss as the others he had given her had been, but softer, sweeter and somehow tender.

Deborah's heart and mind were swept into tumult, and she clung to him breathlessly. Her eyes, did she but know it, were like to rival the night's stars as she gazed up at him.

Nicholas reached out to trace the curve of her cheek with his fingertips. 'So soft,' he murmured, 'so lovely. You tempt me sorely, Mistress Stirling. I am minded to keep my prize now I have it.'

What could he mean? Deborah's heart raced, her throat catching with emotion as she wondered at the way he looked at her. The burning heat in his eyes thrilled and yet terrified her. He could be so intense at times! She felt as if she were drowning in the flood of sensations he aroused in her, being drawn into him, possessed.

She moved away, fearing what might happen if she did not. She was his captive, his hostage. He could do

as he willed with her and there was no defence for her;
even that of her own pride was denied her for she had
been acquiescent in his embrace. His hand touched her
shoulder as she continued to look away, a gentle touch
and yet compelling. She swung round to face him, lips
parted, eyes wide and anxious.

'Do not fear me,' Nicholas said. 'I would never harm
you, Deborah—never dishonour you.'

He had used her given name. His tone made her weak
with the longing to be back in his arms. She knew that
she must fight against the desires that had made her his
willing conquest.

'Some would say you already have, sir.' Her eyes met
his, steady and a little reproachful. 'Some would say my
reputation was besmirched the moment you snatched
me...or even when you kissed me first.'

Nicholas nodded, his mouth thinning to a grim line.
'You do well to reproach me, mistress. I was like to
forget myself. My honour is also hazarded here. I have
given you my word you will not suffer for what was
done—and I must keep it. I beg your pardon for my
lapse of manners. Come, let me help you mount. We
should return to the house.'

Deborah gave him her hand but said nothing. She
avoided his eyes as he swept her up into the saddle once
more. She had fought his passion and won but she felt
no triumph, only a sense of loss. His charming, flirtatious
manner had stolen her heart and she would miss his
smile if he became silent and withdrawn.

He rode a little ahead of her all the way back to the
château. Her eyes centered on his back, noting the stiff-
ness of his shoulders. She had angered him by her ac-
cusations and he had withdrawn from her. When he
helped her down once more he was polite, courteous,

but she was aware of coldness—that darkness she had sensed before.

Then she had wondered at it, but now she understood that he was remembering his lost love. Her heart ached as he led the horses away, leaving her to go into the house alone.

Deborah spent the afternoon walking in the rose gardens. The flowers were large and brilliant of hue; they spilled out their powerful scent into the fierce heat of the afternoon. She gathered a few blooms to scent her bedchamber, sighing as she thought of how pleasant it must be to be mistress of such a house.

There was a profusion of roses in this garden and their petals could be used in so many ways, for perfumes and lotions, cordials and even in sweetmeats. She had also noticed an herb garden where many things she used in her simples grew in neat borders. There were some that were very costly to buy in London, and others that she did not recognize.

She might ask Louise to tell her their names and what they were used for one day. She had bent to touch a sweet-smelling leaf that felt a little furry and was strange to her when she heard a man's heavy footsteps and swung round, her heart racing as she saw the marquis.

'I came to tell you the seamstresses are ready to take patterns for your new gowns,' he said. She saw to her relief that his eyes were not cold, as she had feared, though his manner was more reserved than it had been of late. 'You will find various bales of silks and damasks in your chamber, Mistress Stirling. You may choose whatever you will.'

'Thank you,' Deborah replied. 'But I have been quite happy to wear your mother's things, sir. There was no need for such expense. After all, I may not be here for long.' There was a touch of unconscious pride about her as she looked up.

'No matter how long or short your visit, you deserve the best I can offer,' Nicholas said. 'No woman should have to wear another's old clothes.'

He frowned as he spoke, and Deborah thought that perhaps he did not like to see her using his mother's things after all. She nodded to indicate that she had accepted his right to order these things as he would, but said no more. She was a guest here—or perhaps a prisoner. He had allayed her fears with kindness and honeyed words, but she was no less his captive for all that.

'I shall go at once, sir.' She curtsied to him, then turned to leave. He laid a restraining hand on her arm. 'Nay, stay but a moment, mistress. I would have us friends. I was too free with you this morning, but the thrill of the chase heated my blood and your beauty would tempt any man to madness. I shall not overstep the bounds again while you are my guest.'

'Then there is no need for constraint between us, sir. For my part I would willingly be your friend.'

His smile was her reward. 'You are always generous, Deborah, even when pushed beyond what is normal and right. I believe that must be why I enjoy your company so much.'

His compliment almost took her breath away. She glanced down shyly, her heart racing like a mad March hare.

'And I yours, sir.'

Deborah moved away and this time he let her go. Her thoughts were in turmoil, her pulses beating as a thousand drums. She walked swiftly into the house, leaving him alone in the herb garden. What had he meant—

while you are my guest? Was it a mere pleasantry—or would he consider himself free to kiss her again when all this was over and she was once again under her father's protection?

The only way he would be able to kiss her then would be to court her with Sir Edward's blessing, and she doubted that could ever be won. A little shiver ran through Deborah as she imagined her father's anger with the man who had stolen her away. He would never accept a proposal of marriage from such a man, even if it were to be made.

It would be foolish to hope for anything in the future. She was merely a hostage of fortune, a woman at the mercy of men.

Her spirits lifted a little as she entered her chamber a few minutes later and saw the profusion of materials spread out on the bed. There were glorious silks and damasks, velvets and lace in wonderful hues: cloth of gold, pinks of every shade, deep crimson, yellow, dark and light green, deepest blue and silver.

'Are they not lovely?' Louise asked as she approached the bed. 'The marquis had them all stored away in coffers.'

'Beautiful…' Deborah murmured, and touched the materials with the tips of her fingers. 'I have never seen such exquisite silks. I believe they must have been very costly.'

'And meant for his bride,' a sharp voice said from the doorway.

Both Louise and Deborah swung round in surprise. They saw Marie standing in the doorway, watching with jealous eyes.

'Yes, I suppose they must have been,' Deborah agreed.

'Now he has given them to you.' Marie stared at her angrily. 'The seamstress awaits your orders. Shall I send her up to you?'

'Yes, if you will,' Deborah replied, then, as the other woman was about to turn away, said, 'Mistress Trevern. Will you not choose some of this silk for yourself? There is such a profusion here I cannot need it all.'

'Wear what Nicholas intended for his beloved bride?' Marie's tone was like a whiplash, sharp and stinging. 'No, I thank you, Mistress Stirling. You but exchange the clothes of one dead woman for another. I prefer my own.'

Deborah went white. She felt as if she had been slapped in the face. Seeing that her thrust had gone home, Marie smiled coldly.

'He adored Isabella. You may replace her in his home. He may give you her things as he gave you his mother's—but you will never have his heart. That was buried in Isabella's grave.'

Deborah could find no answer for Marie's spite. It was obvious that the older woman hated her. She met her angry gaze with a look of pride, and in the end it was Marie who turned away and left without another word.

'She is bitter and jealous,' Louise said after she had gone. 'Since she come to this house she try to make the marquis look at 'er with the eyes of a lover, but 'e does not go to 'er bed as she desires. If 'e want a mistress, 'e take one of 'is own choosing.'

'Louise! You should not speak of your master so,' Deborah said, but she did not look displeased.

'My master—'e likes you very much, *mademoiselle*.'

'How can you know that?'

Louise shrugged carelessly and smiled. 'If one is aware, one can see in many ways, *mademoiselle*. The marquis looks at you with the 'unger—you understand? And there is tenderness, no?'

Deborah blushed. 'Louise, you really should not,' she said, but the girl's observations eased the sting of Marie's spite. If it were true that he liked her very much, then perhaps Nicholas might come to love her in time. She had known that he desired her. How could she not when his kisses were so sweet? And yes, as Louise had averred, hungry. But desire was not necessarily love. Only a foolish woman gave herself to a man without love—or a wedding ring. For herself, Deborah wanted both.

Deborah's thoughts were distracted by the arrival of a seamstress and her apprentice. They measured her body with a tape they had marked out to certain proportions and the apprentice made strokes on a slate she carried on a little girdle at her waist.

'*Mademoiselle* desires all the silk made into gowns?' the seamstress asked. 'There is much of beauty 'ere, *oui*?'

'I need only four gowns at most,' Deborah asserted. 'Two for evening, one for riding and one for afternoons.'

'Zees is not 'ow the marquis say,' the woman protested, looking disappointed. 'For evening zere must be at the minimum six gowns, for riding two, for walking also two and four for afternoons. Also a lined cloak and the night-chemise—no less than seven.'

'I shall not need the half of those,' Deborah began, but Louise was agreeing with the seamstress.

'Zees is the least you need, *mademoiselle*,' Deborah was assured. 'And it would be a pity to return all this beautiful silk to the marquis's chests, would it not? In time it will only go to waste and rot.'

'Oh, very well.'

Deborah gave in. If Nicholas wished her to be dressed as befitted a woman of his own rank, what objection could she make? None that would not sound ridiculous. As for Mistress Trevern's spiteful words, they might not have been spoken. Deborah had not objected to wearing the marquise's clothes, and though she had realized that the lovely materials had very likely been purchased as a gift for Nicholas's intended bride, she did not think that a sufficient reason to refuse them. Poor, unfortunate Isabella had not lived to enjoy the gift.

The knowledge that Nicholas had adored his betrothed had not come as a shock. Deborah already knew that Isabella's death and his need to avenge her murder haunted him.

That did not mean he could never love again—did it? Many men took several wives, for women often died in childbed, but some remained faithful to their memories. Deborah's own father was one such man. She suspected the marquis might be another. Yet something deep inside her would not let her despair.

If passion were all that Nicholas had to offer her it might be enough. And that was sufficient to bring a flush to her cheeks. Such unmaidenly thoughts! Had she no shame? It seemed not, for the prospect of lying in her captor's arms gave her only pleasure.

When had he become Nicholas in her thoughts? Was it when he had kissed her on the beach—or when he came to her in the herb garden?

She could not be certain. She knew only that something deep inside her had irrevocably changed. A part of her belonged to the man who had stolen her away and she had, indeed, become his captive whether he had intended it or not.

Chapter Eight

That evening was spent much as the first, except that Deborah was asked to sing for the company, which she did shyly but sweetly. The hours passed pleasantly and all too swiftly. Once again the night was warm and enticing, but Deborah resisted the urge to go down after she had officially retired, even though the moonlit garden called to her.

She did not see much of Nicholas the next day, but rode instead with Henri and Nicholas's friends. She knew them now as Pierre and Jean. Both were free and easy in their manners, but they treated her with the utmost respect, addressing her always as *mademoiselle*.

When Deborah requested that they should ride to the beach, they agreed at once. She noticed that all three were heavily armed and thought it sad that such precautions should be necessary in this beautiful place. The feud with Don Manola and his son had intruded even here into this paradise.

It was a merry party who set out that morning. Everyone laughed and sang as they rode at a gentle canter. There was no need for haste. All three gentlemen were plainly there to amuse and guard—or protect—her while Nicholas was away.

He was away all that day and night, and Deborah missed him. His friends tried to amuse and entertain her as before, but somehow their jests fell flat without the man who was the very centre of this world.

When he returned the next afternoon he brought a small cavalcade of three ladies and four gentlemen with him. Deborah was introduced to all the guests in turn and greeted warmly by them. She was a little disconcerted to discover that they seemed to take her presence at the château for granted, showing no surprise that she should be there without companions or relatives to attend her.

Deborah had taken a long, leisurely bath after her ride that morning, and her hair was freshly washed with scented soap. That evening, Louise brushed it back and secured it with a rolled bandeau of green velvet and cloth of gold, leaving a few tendrils to escape and curl enticingly about the perfect features of her face.

The seamstress had somehow managed to finish an evening gown. The underskirt was of a pale primrose yellow, lightly traced with pearls where the dark green overskirt fell back in a deep frill. The sleeves were puffed at the shoulders and split to show silk ribbons of a deep yellow colour.

Louise had just finished dressing her when they heard the knock at the door.

'Come in,' Deborah called. She was expecting it to be Mistress Trevern and did not rise from her stool. She was startled when the marquis entered. 'Oh…my lord. I did not think it was you.'

'I hope I do not disturb you, mistress?'

'No, not at all. Louise had finished her work. I was about to come down.'

'I have brought you a gift,' Nicholas said. 'If your maid will remove the ribbon about your neck…' He took a string of large creamy pearls from inside his doublet. 'I believe these will compliment your gown.'

'But…' Deborah stared at the beautiful pearls. 'Are you sure you wish to lend me something as valuable as these, sir?'

'They are not a loan,' he replied. 'Nor were they my mother's. I bought them yesterday for you from a goldsmith. They are a gift of friendship, and I hope you will accept them as such.'

'They—they are lovely,' Deborah said. She knew she ought to refuse. Such a gift was too costly to accept and yet she did not want to see the warmth fade from Nicholas's eyes. 'You are too generous, sir. I can only offer you my thanks. I shall always treasure your gift.'

'Then I am well rewarded,' he said, smiling at her. 'Will you allow me to escort you downstairs?'

Deborah stood up, slipping her arm through his. He was so tall, such a powerful, strong man—and being close to him set her whole body trembling with delight. Yet this feeling between them was not just a physical thing; she was truly happy and proud to be escorted by this man, for she was coming to like him more and more as she came to know him. How could she ever have thought him harsh or cold? Now that she knew what caused the bleak look that shadowed his eyes at times, she understood it. There was darkness in him, but she was not afraid of him.

'You look beautiful,' Nicholas told her as they walked down the gallery together. 'Is that a new gown?'

'Yes, my lord. The seamstress must have worked all night to finish it.'

'I told her she must complete the first by this evening. I hope you are pleased with it, Deborah?'

'Yes, my lord. It is elegant and fine and fits me very well. I am grateful for your thoughtfulness.'

'I do not ask for gratitude,' he replied with a little frown. 'Only that you should find your visit pleasant.'

'I am…strangely, I am happy,' Deborah admitted truthfully. 'Perhaps I ought not to be, but I confess I believe any woman would be privileged to live in such a place.'

Nicholas's eyes seemed to caress her, making her heart sing for pure joy. She felt her cheeks grow warm and her pulses went wild. Was he about to kiss her? He had promised it would not happen again while she was his guest—but oh, she wanted him to kiss her! She wanted to feel his lips on hers, to know again that wondrous sensation that only his touch could arouse in her.

'I am honoured by your presence in my home,' was all Nicholas said, and then he was drawing her down the stairs to join the assembled company.

Their moment of intimacy had passed. For the remainder of the evening, Nicholas was the perfect host, giving his attention equally to each of his guests in turn.

He had engaged a small troupe of musicians and tumblers for their entertainment that evening. After a sumptuous meal of many rich courses, which far outshone anything Deborah had ever tasted, the guests watched as the tumblers performed their amazing somersaults and juggled with flaming torches. The minstrel sang his song of courtly love and after he had finished the musicians set up a merry tune and the company began to dance.

Nicholas took Deborah's hand for the first, which was

not as wild as the one they had danced together at the English Court, but a lively country romp in which everyone joined hands in circles. After their dance Deborah was claimed by each of the gentlemen in turn, and Nicholas danced with various ladies, including his cousin.

Deborah could not help noticing how intensely Marie gazed up at him. Surely Nicholas must be aware of her passion for him? Deborah wondered that he did not appear to notice the expression of longing in Marie's eyes.

He had allowed her to remain at the château—but might it not have been kinder to give her a dowry and see her wed to another? She was young and lovely, and it would be a shame if she were to wither away into a sour old maid because her passion was not returned.

Deborah noticed that Jean looked at Marie often. Was it possible that he felt a *tendre* for her? It would not be surprising, for she was a beautiful woman and when she smiled and laughed she could be charming. It was only to Deborah that she showed her scowling face.

'So—you are enjoying your stay at Chalfont, Mademoiselle Stirling?'

Deborah turned to look at the pretty young woman who had come to stand beside her.

'Yes, very much, thank you, Madame Dubois.'

'This is good,' the Frenchwoman said with a smile. 'We who care for Nico have long wanted to see him happy in a woman's arms. I think you will make this happen, *mademoiselle*.' She gave Deborah a swift kiss on the cheek, then laughed and walked away to join her husband.

Deborah's face felt as if it were on fire. She could not fail to mistake the other woman's meaning: she thought there was an understanding between her and Nicholas. And since she was unmarried and here without family or companions to protect her, she must obviously be his mistress!

She had denied it angrily when Marie accused her of it, but had thought it merely spite on Marie's part. However, the well-meaning Madame Dubois's remarks had made her aware of how others must see her.

Her reputation had been lost from the moment she came here. How could she have been so stupid as not to realize it? When she was sent back to her father, she would never be able to raise her head again amongst her own kind. She would be a fallen woman, besmirched by what had happened to her through no fault of her own. No matter that she was still innocent, no one would believe her. The old tabbies would whisper behind her back and the men would look at her with knowing eyes.

She had allowed her pleasant surroundings—and her captor's charm—to lull her into a feeling of false security. Shame washed over her and she suddenly longed to be alone. She had thought the marquis's friends kind and understanding, but now she saw that they had accepted her as his mistress.

The mistress of a powerful and wealthy man was often accepted in society—but what happened when she was discarded, passed over for another? She would not necessarily be welcomed then. Deborah had always been above gossip, her rank as Sir Edward's daughter giving her respectability and position, but she had heard the spiteful tongues directed at others and knew that a disgraced woman had no choice but to retire from the world.

Deborah felt the tears sting her eyes. By appearing to acquiesce to her situation, she had completed her own ruin. When the marquis brought her here by force, she ought to have stayed in her chamber and refused to come down. She had been enjoying her visit, acting as if she were indeed an honoured guest. It was no wonder that Nicholas's friends believed she was his mistress.

Suddenly, she felt as if she could not bear to be a part of this merry company a moment longer. She turned and would have left the room at once, but Nicholas came to claim her for the next dance.

'You look pale,' he said, and when she tried to move away he detained her by resting his hand on her sleeve. 'Are you unwell, Deborah?'

She clutched gratefully at the lie. 'I—I have a headache,' she said in a voice so low that he could hardly hear it. 'I think... I beg you will excuse me, sir. I would seek the quiet of my chamber.'

'Of course, if it is your wish.' His gaze narrowed as if he were suspicious and wished to read her thoughts. 'Come, I shall escort you.'

'I would prefer that you stay and attend your guests. Pray excuse me.' Deborah walked away, leaving him to stare after her in exasperation.

The tears she was too proud to shed stung her eyes. She would not weep! It mattered not what these people thought of her. She had only to wait and she would be returned to her father. He would take her home and she would live quietly away from the world and never see the marquis or his friends again.

'Deborah!' Nicholas caught her at the bottom of the stairs. She had thought he would let her go, but at the last moment he had come after her. 'Mistress Stirling, I pray you stop a moment. I must speak with you.'

She turned reluctantly, knowing he must read her distress in her eyes. 'Yes, my lord? What must you say that will not wait on the morrow?'

'You are angry.' His gaze narrowed, intensified. 'What has been said to make you look at me thus?'

'Have you no eyes or ears?' she asked scornfully. 'You give me fine clothes to wear and costly jewels, and treat me as your honoured guest—what must your friends think of me? I have no companions about me, no guardian to protect my honour.' Her fine eyes accused him. 'You had done better to cast me into a cage, sir. Then at least I might have kept my reputation.'

'So that is it,' he said softly. 'I knew that Jeanne had said something to you. Whatever it was, she meant no offence—she likes and approves of you and told me so at once.'

'Madame Dubois, Mistress Trevern—all of them!— believe I am your mistress.' Deborah tossed her head at him, eyes flashing like emeralds in sunlight. 'Can you deny it?'

'They have not heard it from me,' Nicholas said. 'But the world being what it is, they may suspect it. However, they would not think less of you if it were true. Men and kings must have their mistresses and many love where they cannot marry. Is that so very terrible?'

'I have lost my reputation, sir—and with it my right to be a wife.'

'Are the men you know so foolish, then?' Nicholas asked, eyes watchful, voice soft. 'Would they discard a priceless ruby because it had been worn on another's hand?'

'You are pleased to jest,' Deborah said, her cheeks pink. 'I do not think so lightly of my honour. And it is unfair since I am not nor have I been your mistress.'

'Perhaps you would not mind so much if it were true? Shall I make you mine, Deborah? Would that content you?' The caressing tone of his voice almost overset her, setting up forbidden longings. How dare he look at her so? How could he be so careless of her feelings?

'I shall never, never be your mistress,' she vowed in a low, passionate tone. 'You have ruined any chance I might have had for happiness—no decent man would have me now—but I would rather die a maiden than be yours!'

With that, she turned and ran up the remainder of the stairs. At first she feared he would follow, but he did not and she gained the safety of her chamber without hindrance. Louise was surprised to see her back so early, but one look at Deborah's face held her silent as she attended to her gown and brushed the flowing tresses that reached almost to the small of her mistress's back.

Left to herself at last, Deborah sat on a seat by her window, looking out on the moonlit gardens. She felt desperately unhappy and humiliated. She had been so naïve, so foolish! Her anger at the way she had been snatched had melted too swiftly in the warmth of the marquis's charm. She had been enchanted by his home and by him—only too willing to surrender her heart... and her body if he had pressed his advantage when they kissed so sweetly.

Shameless! Shameless! She deserved that Nicholas's friends should take it for granted that she was his mistress, for her eyes must have been as revealing to them as Mistress Trevern's were to her.

She felt so wretched...so lost and alone. If she could but turn back time, be as she had been before they met. But that was impossible. The damage was done. She had lost both her heart and her reputation.

How could she face the marquis or his friends in the morning? Oh, she wished she might die! Might be free of this ache in her heart...if only she was free. This situation was impossible! Anger was beginning to replace her feelings of humiliation. Perhaps she would carry the scars of her encounter with the marquis for the rest of her life, but that did not mean she had to remain tamely in this gilded cage. For it was a prison and she a prisoner for all its comforts.

The marquis would have returned to his guests. Now was the time to escape. She had gained enough knowledge of the château and its grounds to be able to find the stables and steal a horse, and she knew in which direction she should ride. Beyond the vineyards lay the village of Chalfont and a highway—leading where? She did not know, but it could not matter. Once she was away from the château she would find someone to help her.

She had given the marquis her promise that she would not try to leave his protection. She had been foolish to do so, and it must be broken. He'd had no right to demand such a promise of her. It had been given under duress and was therefore not binding, she told herself, though her conscience told her otherwise. No matter! She had a duty to escape and she would. Somehow!

Deborah shivered with excitement as she began to dress. She chose her own gown, the one she had been wearing on the fateful morning she was kidnapped. It was simple to fasten, and besides, she wanted nothing that belonged to Nicholas. No, no, the marquis! She must not think of him with her heart, only her head. He was a wicked rogue who had carelessly brought her to ruin, and the fact that his kisses made her melt with pleasure meant nothing.

The sound of music and laughter floated up to her as she walked softly down the stairs, hesitating now and then to listen and watch. If any of the servants saw her she would tell them she was taking a walk to clear her head. However, there was no sign of anyone. It seemed that all the servants were in the banqueting hall attending to the guests. Perhaps because of her promise the marquis had relaxed his guard a little and there was no one to hinder her leaving the house.

The air outside was sweet and cool, the gardens heady with the scents of roses, honeysuckle and oleanders. Deborah paused for a moment, breathing in the heavenly perfume. For a moment her determination weakened. She could be so happy here if only the circumstances were different—but they were not and she would be foolish to give in to the little voice in her head that was prompting her to stay.

She straightened her shoulders and turned in the direction of the stables, which were to the side of the house and beyond a courtyard that was used for exercising the horses. Once or twice she glanced back, thinking she heard something, but it was too dark to see and the shadows might hide many things.

Tales of the evil that walked abroad after nightfall came to mind, making her nerves jangle. A shiver ran down her spine but she scolded herself. She was not afraid of shadows!

It was just nerves! Why should anyone follow her? If she had been seen there would have been noise and shouting as the alarm was given. No, it was simply her guilty conscience pricking at her, because she was breaking the promise she had freely given.

She could smell the strong earthy tang of the stables now. Some of the horses were housed in buildings of grey stone, which formed a semi-circle about a courtyard, others ran free in paddocks behind the buildings. Deborah had no idea where the mare she had ridden previously was housed. She would just have to open the top half of each door in turn until she found a horse that looked gentle enough for her to manage alone.

She attempted to draw back the bolt on the first door. It was stiff and resisted stubbornly. After a few moments of wasted effort, she went on to the next and tugged as hard as she could. This bolt moved more easily and she was able to swing open the top of the split door.

The warm smell of horse came out to meet her nostrils, and she made an encouraging noise with her tongue as a dark shape loomed out of the interior.

'Oh, it's you, old fellow,' Deborah said as a nodding head poked out at her. She had chosen the stable of the great black brute Nicholas always rode. It tossed its head and snorted at her, wicked eyes gleaming in the darkness. 'Good boy…would you like to come for a ride?' She stroked the stallion's nose and wondered if she dared to take the marquis's own favourite horse. It would surely be too strong for her. Besides, she could not take an animal that Nicholas was clearly fond of. 'No, perhaps not…perhaps I should look further—'

'A wise decision.' The sound of the marquis's voice close behind her made Deborah jump. She swung round to see him standing a few paces away, half-hidden in the shadows as he went on. 'Had you entered his stable he might have trampled you to death. Nero is an unpredictable creature and responds to authority, not kindness.' Nicholas glared at her as he stepped forward. 'Perhaps some women might respect the bridle more than the soothing glove.'

Deborah blushed as she heard the suppressed fury in his voice. She could not see his face clearly in the shadows of the stable yard, but she knew that he was very angry with her.

'You were following me!' she accused. 'I heard something earlier but thought it imagination. Why did you not make yourself known sooner?'

'I thought to see what you intended, Mistress Stirling,' he said coldly. 'I had believed your word fairly given, but it seems that I may not trust it.'

'It was given under duress,' Deborah replied, her cheeks hot for shame as she lied. 'You had no right to ask for my promise. I am your prisoner in this place and it is my right to escape if I can.'

'Shall I make you my prisoner, mistress?' Nicholas moved even closer, making her jump with fright as she sensed the menace in him. He was angry and she knew she had deserved his anger. 'Shall I show you what it is like to truly be at the mercy of your captor?'

'You wouldn't dare!' she cried. 'Oh, I know I meant to break my promise—but my situation is intolerable. I feel so…ashamed.'

'You have no need to feel shame.' Nicholas stared down at her, his expression softening a little. 'I have not shamed you, Deborah, nor shall I. Let others think as they will. We know the truth and in time it will be made plain to all. I give you my word that I shall restore to you all that you have lost. Give me a little time and you shall have no need to repine over what has happened to you.'

'What do you mean?' she demanded. 'How can you restore my reputation? It is not in your giving.'

'I can give you position and rank,' he replied. 'In my home you would have the respect and deference shown to my lady—believe me, many would accord the Marquise de Vere as much homage as the Queen of France.'

'The Marquise…' Deborah felt as though she could scarcely breathe. Her heart was beating so fast, setting her senses spinning in such a whirl that she hardly knew what she was asking. 'Are you saying that you would take me for your wife?'

'It is the only resolution to the situation in which I have placed you, Mistress Stirling. I brought you here and I accept that any damage to your honour is of my making. What I did was wrong and careless, and I beg your pardon for it.' Nicholas inclined his head. 'I have sworn never to marry until Isabella is avenged, therefore I cannot wed you until I return from my appointment with Don Miguel. However, I shall have my notary draw up the papers so that you will be provided for should my plans go awry.'

'I do not wish to wed you,' Deborah said, knowing that she lied. 'Let me go home to my father now and I shall forget you.'

'I think not,' he replied. 'You are a stubborn wench, Deborah, and contrary, but in time I shall make you more reasonable. You were right when you said my actions had ruined your chances of a good marriage, therefore, I shall behave honourably and put right the wrong I have done you.'

'I do not wish to be married so that you feel your honour has been vindicated,' Deborah said, tears starting to her eyes. She blinked them away angrily. 'I am not your possession to do with as you will.'

'Are you not?' he asked softly and his voice sent tremors down her spine. 'I have you captive, Deborah. I can do exactly as I will with you.' He moved towards her, sweeping her into his arms, holding her crushed against him so that she could feel the warmth of his breath on her face. 'Shall I show you the delights of that seduction you fear, sweet wench? Shall I show you that to be mine in every way can give nothing but pleasure to us both?'

'Oh, you wretched man! I hate you.'

'I think you lie,' he said and chuckled softly. Then he bent his head and kissed her, his mouth possessing hers so that she was indeed his captive, swept away on the tide of passion that was set loose between them. One leg went round her, freeing a hand to move down her body, pulling at the gown that hid her from his eyes. He bent his head lower, his tongue flicking delicately at the hollow between her breasts, then lower still until his mouth found the rose-pink tips and took them in, each in turn, sucking and teasing at her until she moaned with pleasure. 'Shall I take you to my bed, sweet Deborah?' he murmured throatily. 'Shall I take all the rights of a sovereign lord? For I am your lord whether you would have it so or not.'

'Oh, you wicked, wicked rogue. I do not want to lie in your bed,' she lied desperately.

'Then shall I take you here against the stable wall? Shall I put my mark on you so that you can never leave me?' His voice was murmuring against her ear, soft but husky with passion so that she felt her whole resistance leave her and longed for him to do all he promised.

'I hate you, I hate you,' she whispered, but she was melting into him, her mouth opening to receive his tongue as it explored the sweetness of her and sent her senses on a dizzy spiral once more.

'I think you want me, my fiery wench,' Nicholas breathed against her throat as his lips ventured further. 'You may not love me yet, but you will one day. I vow I shall have you begging for my loving, sweet temptress. We shall explore the realms of heavenly delights together and sup at the wells of the goddess of love herself.'

'No…no…' She denied him with her words even as

her body welcomed and invited him. 'You are a devil and I shall never love you. You may take my body, but you cannot compel my heart.'

'Then I shall make do with passion,' Nicholas said. 'And since I mean to have you, I may as well begin this night...'

Deborah pushed at his shoulders with her hands. 'Please, I beg you, no,' she cried desperately. 'Do not make me your whore. If it is your true wish that we should marry I—I shall accept, but let me come to you as a virgin on our wedding night. I beg you, my lord. Do not shame me. I cannot say you nay, for you know well that I am weak and you are strong—but in all honour, that honour which you hold so dear, let there be nothing between us until I am your wife before God and man.'

Nicholas swore. He was far gone in his need and denial now was agony to him, but she had somehow reached through the mist of desire that had almost carried him beyond the point of no return. Yet her words halted him, making him aware that if he continued with this he would break his promise to her, and even though she had been about to break her word to him that did not release him from his own vow.

'Your pardon, lady,' he muttered as he released her from the hold which had her fast bound to him. 'Indeed, I would be the devil you named me if I pleasured you here like a tavern wench. You deserve more than that, and so do I. Give me your solemn word that you will not try to leave me again, and I shall wait until we are wed.'

'I swear it.' Deborah gazed up at him, her face pale but determined. 'I was wrong to try and leave in the dark of night like a thief. I give you my word I shall not leave without your permission. Will that content you?'

'If I could believe it.'

'I swear it on my mother's memory. I shall not run away from you—but we shall talk of whether we should marry another time, when we are both in control of our senses.'

'You shall marry me, lady,' Nicholas said. 'But until then you shall remain as chaste as you were when I took you.'

'I thank you for your restraint, sir. What happened here shall be forgot.'

'As you wish, my lady.' Nicholas's eyes gleamed like black coals. 'But I shall have the papers drawn up for our wedding—and you shall sign them before I leave.'

'Leave?' She stared at him, her heart jerking with sudden fright. 'When do you leave?'

'My rendezvous with Don Miguel is in six days from now,' Nicholas said. 'I must leave in three days to meet him at the appointed place and time. Until then, we shall feast and make merry—and you shall wear my betrothal ring and all my friends will say that they always knew I meant to wed you.'

Deborah could not answer him. He had countered all her complaints. By wedding her, he restored reputation and respect, for few would wish to spurn the hospitality of the Marquis de Vere. Her father might be angry at first, but he would see the advantages in time and come to accept what was done, though he might never forgive.

So she merely took the arm Nicholas offered and allowed him to lead her back to the house. After all, what else could she do?

Chapter Nine

Deborah spent a restless night, sleeping only fitfully and waking late as tired and listless as if she had never slept at all. She groaned as Louise came into the room bearing a dish of ripe fruit, soft rolls and honey.

'It is such a lovely morning,' the girl announced, her excitement so obviously bursting out of her that Deborah eyed her warily. 'The seamstress has sent a new gown, *mademoiselle*, and my master 'as said 'e as something important to announce today.'

'Something important?' Deborah pushed herself up against the pillows. 'What do you mean, Louise?'

'It is to be a special day. The marquis 'as asked for a feast to be prepared and served outside in the gardens. Everyone is to share in the 'appiness. It is good, no?'

Deborah nodded but made no answer, nibbling cautiously at a slice of fresh, juicy melon. She was remembering what had happened in the stable courtyard the previous night, the way Nicholas had come close to ravishing her against the wall. Only her appeal to his sense of honour had saved her. It was that same sense of honour that had made him decide they should marry.

As she ate a few mouthfuls of the delicious food Louise had prepared for her, Deborah considered whether or not she wished to be wed for the sake of honour—hers or Nicholas's. It would not be the marriage she had dreamed of, for she had hoped to be loved in the same way her mother had been by Sir Edward, but it would not be so very different from the match her father had meant to make for her when he took her to Court.

The marquis was both handsome and charming. She knew him to be generous and imagined he would be kind to those under his protection—but what of her own feelings and desires? She had come to feel so much more than respect or liking for this man. Would she be able to conceal her own needs and longings from his penetrating gaze? She thought it might be painful to love too well if that love could never be returned.

Nicholas was still in love with Isabella. He might marry for the sake of honour—and yes, he was a man and needed the comfort of a woman in his bed. She had felt the throb of his passion as he held her clamped against him in the stable yard, and the memory of the heat that entered her from him set her flushing all over now. Deborah knew that he desired her, and also that it would give her pleasure to lie with him—but would it also cause her pain?

What a foolish child she was to cling to romantic dreams of love! The marquis had offered her a way of restoring all she had lost and it was the only solution. She must accept his betrothal ring, and she must sign the papers that would bind them almost as surely as the vows they would later take in church.

Deborah settled the matter in her mind. She would behave as though the previous night had never happened, and pretend that there had been no abduction, no broken promises. Her manner must seem to indicate that the betrothal had always been planned, that she had always been Nicholas's intended bride and never his hostage. After all, she was a gentlewoman and her years of discipline and proper behaviour must stand her in good stead now.

Nicholas came to her chamber just as Louise had finished dressing her in a gown of sea-green silk, her glorious hair left to spill over her shoulders in a riot of wild chestnut brown curls.

'You may go, Louise,' he said. 'I would speak with my lady in private.'

Louise giggled, shot a glance at Deborah and ran away, but not before Deborah had seen the satisfaction in her eyes.

She stood facing Nicholas in silence as he reached for her left hand. He slid a heavy gold ring set with a large blood-red ruby on to her third finger. It fitted loosely and felt heavy.

Nicholas frowned. 'The ring is not right for you but will serve to show my intention. I have already let it be known that I shall announce something important at our feast, and the papers will be ready this evening. Although not blessed in church, our union will be legal—and therefore you need feel no shame for what has happened between us.'

Deborah could not meet his gaze. Something deep within her was urging her to throw off his ring and tell him that she would never marry without love, but her mind would not form the right words or her tongue speak them. She seemed to have lost the will to defy him. It was easier to smile coolly and lay her hand on the arm he offered, allowing him to lead her down to join his friends. Pride and breeding must carry her through.

From the moment the day of feasting and merriment

began, it was clear that everyone was aware of the marquis's intentions. Deborah could see pleasure in Madame Dubois's eyes, a faint anxiety in Henri's—and a burning hatred in Marie Trevern's. She said nothing to Deborah and slipped away just before Nicholas made his announcement. Perhaps she could not bear to stay and hear that another woman had been given all that she had coveted.

Everyone else pressed forward to congratulate Nicholas and shower gifts and compliments on Deborah. She was overwhelmed by their kindness, brought close to tears by their expressions of good will.

Deborah wondered where all the gifts had come from. How had Nicholas's guests known there was to be a betrothal? It had not been decided until the previous night in the stable yard. Only Henri seemed a little doubtful as he presented her with a cross of silver set with garnets and pearls.

'You are content, mistress?' he asked. 'Nico must always have his way, but I would not have you forced to something against your will.'

'No, I have not been forced,' Deborah replied. 'Or only by circumstance and honour. I was brought here against my will—but I stay because…because I wish it.'

Henri nodded, smiled and kissed her hand. 'I am content,' he said. 'It is sometimes strange how good may come from evil. I was uneasy when we took you from your father, even though I could not stand by and see you given to a monster—but now I see much that was hidden before.'

'You speak in riddles, sir. Pray tell me what you mean.'

Henri laughed and shook his head, turning away as the tumblers began to entertain the company. Music and laughter filled the air as Deborah strolled apart from the company to a scented rose arbour. She was glad of a few moments alone to calm her thoughts. Was any of this real? Sometimes she almost believed herself dreaming, expecting to wake up at any moment in her own bed at home.

'So—you think yourself very clever,' the sharp voice said behind her. 'You wear his ring and have his promise to wed you—but you will live to regret it.'

Deborah swung round to face the bitter, angry words. Marie was staring at her with such all-consuming hatred that it made her shiver, an icy chill running down her spine.

'What do you mean? Why should I regret being married to the marquis?'

'I know how you came here,' Marie went on heedless of the question. 'You were meant to be the bride of that Spanish devil. That is why Nicholas snatched you and brought you here as a hostage. He is paying the Don in kind for what he did to Isabella. Do not imagine he cares for you—this is all a part of his revenge. He does not love you. He will use you, humiliate you and then discard you.'

'How can you know that?' Deborah looked at her scornfully. 'You are jealous because he did not ask you to be his wife—because you want him for yourself.'

'Yes, I want him,' Marie said, her eyes glittering with malice. 'I love Nicholas and he wants me. When he has finished with you, he will come back to me.'

'You deceive yourself. If he loved you, he would not have asked me to marry him.'

'You think not?' Marie's smile was chilling. 'Unwanted wives are easily disposed of, Mistress Stirling.

When he has taken his revenge, you will simply not exist for him.'

'You lie! Nicholas would never stoop to such a thing. He is too fine, too honourable.'

'What he might not care to do may be done by others,' Marie said. Again her smile was so chilling that it made Deborah shiver. 'Make the most of your time in the sun, Mistress Stirling—it will not last long.'

Deborah watched her walk away. For the moment the viciousness of her hatred seemed to linger after her, casting a shadow over the day. Surely she could not have meant to sound so threatening?

'Why have you hidden yourself away?' Nicholas spoke from behind her, making Deborah turn with a guilty start. 'I hope you are not already regretting our bargain?'

He was frowning, his eyes narrowed and intense. Deborah could not answer him for a moment. To have complained of his cousin's spite would seem petty on such a day, and besides, she did not believe one word Marie had said to her.

'No, I am not regretting it, sir—though I regret the manner of its making.' She meant that she wished they had been betrothed with the blessing of her father but she saw his frown deepen and realized he had mistaken her words. 'I wish my father were here, that is all. I fear that he will be angry when he learns that I have given my promise without first asking his consent.'

'Your father will forgive you,' Nicholas said, his expression softening. 'Write him a letter this evening and I shall see that it is sent to him.'

'You are very good, my lord.'

'Am I, Deborah?' The shadows were in his face once more. 'I believe I have treated you ill, but I shall do my

best to make up for our unfortunate start in the future.'
He held out his hand to her. 'Come, my lady. We must
return to our guests before they begin to wonder where
we have gone and draw their own conclusions. We
French are hot-blooded and our thoughts dwell over-
much on making love—but today you shall have the
respect due to my lady.'

Deborah blushed, giving him her hand but making no
reply to his teasing words, though she knew well enough
what he meant. She went with him to join his friends,
who were now also hers, and after a while she found
that she had begun to feel happy again. The shadows
had lifted and there was no more need for shame or
anxiety. She was acknowledged as the marquis's intended bride and was content. Even Marie's brooding
hatred could not destroy her pleasure as she danced and
played foolish games, and knew that Nicholas smiled at
her.

The marriage contract was signed that evening with
three of their guests as witnesses. When she left Nicholas
to retire later that evening, Deborah knew that she was
now legally bound to him, though the marriage ceremony would not take place until his return from his
meeting with Don Miguel.

She dreamed that night, a dream so vivid and so terrible that she woke trembling to find her body bathed in
a fine sweat. She had seen Nicholas lying dead at her
feet—and herself wed to a Spaniard with the face of an
angel and the soul of a devil.

It was a long time before sleep claimed her again, but
at last she drifted away.

Deborah woke only when Louise came to rouse her.
The frightening dream had faded by then and she put it

from her mind determinedly as she dressed to go riding with the marquis.

Later that afternoon she wrote a long and loving letter to her father, asking for his forgiveness and explaining that she had come to admire the Marquis de Vere. She would have his blessing if she could and hoped that he would come to visit her often once she was the marquise. Sealing her paper with wax from the writing desk Nicholas had provided, she gave it into his care that evening.

'It shall be sent immediately,' he told her. 'We must hope that once Sir Edward's just anger has cooled he will give us his blessing on our union.'

'Yes.' Deborah smiled bravely. It would hurt her deeply if she were to be forever estranged from her beloved father.

She knew it would take some days for the letter to reach him. Even when Nicholas's messenger reached the shores of England he would have a long journey before him, and it would be several more days until a reply could come to her. She must pray that the marquis's messenger found her father at home. Surely he would have returned there to await news of her?

And yet she knew he would have been anxious for her safety. It was possible that he might have decided to search for his lost daughter. Would he come here? Would he know where to begin his search? And how would she feel if he believed her lost?

'Why do you look so sad?' Nicholas asked. 'You are not unhappy with our bargain? You do not fear your future here?'

'No...' She gazed up at him. 'I am neither afraid nor unhappy, my lord. Only a little uneasy because you must leave tomorrow.'

Nicholas laughed softly. 'Fear not, my lady. Within a week my business will be done and I shall return to claim you. Our wedding day shall be no more than two days later.'

A little thrill of excitement mixed with apprehension went through her. Those dark eyes held a wicked promise, and one that brought a faint blush to her cheeks as she recalled how close she had come to surrendering that night in the stable yard.

'I shall pray for your safe return, my lord.'

'Never doubt it, Deborah. I am impatient for my wedding night.'

She was breathless of a sudden and could not answer him, though she knew that she too was eager for their marriage to be a true one.

Nicholas escorted her to the door of her chamber that night. He gazed down into her eyes for several moments.

'Do not forget me, Deborah. Nor that you are mine— for I shall never let you go.' And then he kissed her softly on the lips. 'Sleep well. God keep you safe until I return.'

'And you, my lord,' she whispered as he turned and walked away. 'I pray God brings you back to me swiftly.'

She turned cold suddenly and crossed herself. Nicholas was so confident of vanquishing his enemy—but supposing he was killed or badly wounded? She wished then that she had confessed her love, but Nicholas had gone and her pride would not let her go after him.

'My daughter—have you heard anything more of her?' Sir Edward demanded of the Spaniard. 'Tell me at once, I beg you, *señor*.'

He was standing on the deck of Don Manola's ship,

the *Santa Maria*, and the Don himself had that moment come on board, as it lay anchored off the shores of Cadiz.

'Quiet your fears, my friend,' replied the Don. 'Mistress Stirling is in a fair way to being recovered. As soon as we received the ransom demand our plans were made...'

'That rogue has demanded gold from you?' Sir Edward's face turned red with fury. He had lived in constant fear during the voyage to this Spanish port and his impatience tumbled out in an angry spate. 'By God! He shall hang for this.'

'I hope to have that pleasure myself,' the Don replied. 'Our ships sail to the appointed meeting in the morning.'

'You will accede to his demands?'

'He has demanded that my son hand over the gold in person. De Vere hopes to settle a quarrel between them and take Miguel's life.'

'A quarrel?' Sir Edward's eyes narrowed. 'Between your son and the marquis? I have heard naught of this—why do they quarrel?'

Don Manola's eyes did not meet those of his old friend as he replied, 'It was nothing—a mere spat between two hot-blooded young men, but de Vere has turned it into a vendetta.'

'So my daughter was snatched because of a quarrel between your son and de Vere?' Sir Edward's eyes narrowed in suspicion. There was more here than he had yet realized. He had left England with Señor Sanchez only hours after hearing of his daughter's abduction, giving Sarah into the care of her betrothed, his one thought to find his daughter and see her safe.

'You shall have your revenge for any disrespect shown her, my friend. Within a few days *Le Diable* will be dead and your daughter restored to you. Then we shall have a wedding.'

'If that rogue has harmed her…'

'He would not dishonour her,' Don Manola replied. He did not add that if he had doubted it the girl would have been left to her fate, worth neither the ransom demanded nor the trouble of rescuing her. 'Rest easy in your mind, Sir Edward. De Vere may be ruthless and I have good cause to wish him dead—but he would not dishonour a maiden. He thinks too highly of his honour.'

'I must pray that you are right, *señor*.' Sir Edward's eyes were bleak. 'I shall have no peace until I have her back—and as for the wedding, Deborah's consent must be won. She may be too distressed to think of marrying just yet.'

'We shall give her time, of course,' the Don assured him smoothly.

The lie trickled silkily from his tongue even though the giving of it shamed the man he had once been. There had been a time when his honour had been as spotless as de Vere's, but no longer. There was a stain on it that would not be washed away by a thousand Hail Marys or a lifetime of penance.

He knew that what he did would burn him like the fires of Hell, and that he would not escape eternal damnation, for his sins were heavy and he was about to compound them. God forgive him! He was in torment now and had been since he had discovered the truth about his son.

Yet he had no alternative. His plans were set and must be followed to their end. He had the father in his power and soon he would have the girl. She would be wed to the son he despised and loathed because there was no choice.

He had done much that had sat ill with his conscience for one purpose. A purpose that rode him like the devil, never giving him a moment's peace.

Miguel must provide an heir and the mother must be well-born, worthy of his name and lineage. After that... Don Manola's thoughts shut off abruptly. Once he had his heir, he would do what must be done.

Chapter Ten

Nicholas had been gone two days and to Deborah it seemed much longer. Although Henri remained at the château, all the other guests had departed that morning. Deborah felt bereft, lonelier than she had been in all her life with only Marie and the servants for company.

'I feel as if I am deserting you,' Jeanne Dubois had said as she kissed her goodbye that morning. 'It will not be for long, I promise you. We shall return for your wedding, if not sooner, but my husband has business that will no longer be ignored.'

They had become friends, and Deborah had been sorry to part from her and the others, but in her heart she knew it was Nicholas she was truly missing. It was his voice she longed to hear, his touch she hungered for with every fibre of her being.

Marie's open hostility had driven her from the house soon after the guests had left. She wandered about the garden disconsolately, unable to forget that very soon now Nicholas's ships would reach the appointed meeting with those of Don Manola. What would be the outcome? She feared a bloody battle with much loss of life on both sides.

Supposing Nicholas was amongst the wounded? It was no use! She needed something to drive these foolish thoughts from her mind. A good hard ride would help. She entered the house and ran upstairs, asking for her mare saddled while she changed into a suitable gown. As she did so, her betrothal ring came off and, not wishing to lose it, she laid it aside.

When she came down again, she found Henri waiting for her. 'You wished to ride, Mistress Stirling?' he said. 'With your permission I shall accompany you.'

'There is no need if you have other duties,' Deborah replied. 'I know you are busy and I meant only to go as far as the park.'

'Nico would not forgive me if you went unprotected.'

'You must think me a troublesome wench,' she said and laughed. 'It is overwarm for riding, I know, and it is foolish of me to be so anxious—but I cannot rest.'

Henri smiled in return. 'You must know that it pleases me to please you, lady. I understand your unease. This is the first time Nico has sailed without me, and I cannot rid myself of the feeling that he is in trouble—though I know such thoughts are foolish. He has no need of my protection.'

'Oh, poor Henri,' Deborah said. 'You must be fretting as much as I—it was unfair to leave you behind.'

'I am honoured by the trust Nico has placed in me,' Henri assured her. 'Someone must remain to protect you. We have men who would fight to the death for you, but someone must command.'

Deborah nodded, understanding that he was torn between his desire to protect both her and Nicholas. The two men were as close as brothers and Henri could not be easy in his mind until his comrade returned.

He helped Deborah to mount her mare, then swung

into the saddle of his own horse. Deborah flicked her reins, and the two horses trotted out of the courtyard side by side. Soon they were cantering in the park; it was very warm even there and after a while Deborah suggested they ride as far as the beach.

'It will be cooler there,' she said. 'We can easily be there and back before darkness falls.'

Henri seemed to hesitate for a moment before agreeing. He had his sword as always, but why should he have need of it? Deborah saw no need of caution. Nicholas was on his way to an appointment with his enemy. There was surely no fear of an attack while the Don and his son were waiting elsewhere?

'If it is your wish,' Henri said. 'I confess I am too restless to do nothing. A hard ride will help to ease this feeling I have inside.'

Deborah did not need to ask what he was feeling. She had a growing sense of foreboding. Supposing Nicholas had sailed into a trap—supposing the Don's ships fired without warning? They were meant to meet under a flag of truce, but she could not help the tormenting thoughts that came to her mind.

Riding helped a little. Deborah knew her way to the beach now and she urged her mare to a gallop as they neared the rise, which then sloped gently to the beach beyond. As she crested the rise, she halted at the sight that met her eyes. A ship had anchored off shore and two boats had beached. The beach itself seemed crowded with armed men. Had Nicholas returned sooner than expected?

As Deborah hesitated, uncertain of what was happening, one of the men on the beach saw and pointed at her, shouting to the others. In that moment she realized that they were not Nicholas's men but Spanish. Don

Manola, seizing the chance to attack while Nicholas was away and his home vulnerable, must have sent them here.

Henri had seen them too. He was shouting at her, gesturing for her to ride away. There were so many men—perhaps thirty or more. What would happen if Deborah rode back to the château? She could reach safety for the men on the beach had no horses as yet— but what of Chalfont's people? She knew instinctively that these men had come for her and would if need be storm their way into the château to take their prize.

Because of his own strict code of honour, Nicholas had believed they would meet him to bargain for her return under a flag of truce, but he had been tricked into leaving his home vulnerable to attack from the sea.

'Come, mistress,' Henri was urging her. 'They cannot follow if we ride fast. It was fortunate we came this way. They meant to attack us while we slept—but now we shall be ready for them.'

'But our people may die…'

'They will die bravely for Nico and for you.'

She stared at him in an agony of uncertainty. If she saved herself she would be the cause of so much bloodshed. She hesitated a moment longer and then all at once it was too late. Several shots rang out and Henri's horse went down beneath him. Deborah screamed as he fell and was rolled on by the agonized beast in its dying throes. She threw herself down beside him, kneeling on the coarse grass.

'Henri,' she cried. 'Henri—speak to me. Forgive me.'

He lay white and still, eyes closed. She knew the fall had killed him and gave a wild cry of distress, as the Spaniards were suddenly all around her, grasping at her, hauling her to her feet.

'He is dead,' she accused them bitterly. 'You have killed him, murdered him. My friend. He is dead… dead!'

They had laid hands on her, were dragging her away from Henri and her mare, which had skittishly kicked up its heels and was eyeing them nervously from a safe distance.

Deborah looked back desperately, her heart aching with pity for the man who had given his life so needlessly for her stupidity. Had she obeyed Henri at once he would still be alive; she would never forgive herself for the hesitation that had cost his life.

The Spaniards were excited. They called out to one another in a language she could not understand, gesturing at her in triumph as if they could not believe how fortunate they had been. She was being dragged towards one of the boats amid shouts and laughter—and then all at once her captors fell silent, glancing at one another uncertainly.

A man came towards her. He was more richly dressed than the others, his armour black with a gold eagle emblazoned on the breastplate. As they met, he removed his pointed helmet and she saw the colour of his hair— it glinted like spun silver in the sunlight.

Deborah knew him at once. She raised her head, her manner proud and dignified as she looked straight at him.

'Pray tell your men to take their hands from me, *señor*. I am a lady and not to be treated so roughly by common soldiers.'

Don Miguel's eyes narrowed as he saw her. He had seen her likeness but she was more beautiful in the living flesh, her hair blown by the wind into a tangle of red-brown curls, and her eyes gleaming like precious emeralds in the sunlight. Her pride was obvious, her bearing regal. She was clearly the wellborn lady his father had demanded he marry as the price of his silence. She must be treated with respect by the dogs that served him. He spoke sharply in Spanish and the clutching hands fell away instantly.

'You know me, Donna?' he asked, a glint of ice in the blue eyes. 'You are the daughter of Sir Edward Stirling?'

'Yes, I am she,' Deborah replied. She saw the way his mouth had formed a thin cruel smile and knew instinctively that everything she had been told about this man was true. He would delight in tearing the wings from a butterfly or watching a wounded bird flutter as it died. There was something in him that provoked an instant revulsion in her, making her shudder inwardly. She must be careful. One man was already dead because of her. She would have no more deaths on her conscience. 'You are Don Miguel Cortes?' she asked and then as he inclined his head, 'I thank you for coming to my rescue, *señor.*' She was a queen demanding homage from her subject, showing no fear even though it consumed her inwardly.

The Spaniard inclined his head once more, but his smile did not reach his eyes—those curiously empty, repelling eyes. The artist had not painted his eyes faithfully, Deborah thought, but perhaps it had been beyond him—or simply that he dared not.

'How came it that you happened to be riding here with that man?'

Deborah felt the sickness in her throat as she gazed into the Spaniard's face. He was evil. She could sense it, feel it, almost touch it and her fear all but choked her, but still she would not allow it to show.

'He was my servant,' she lied, outwardly calm, inwardly in turmoil. 'He had helped me to escape from my guards at the château and had arranged for a boat to meet us here. The fishermen must have been frightened away by your galleon, *señor*.'

She saw his hesitation. He was suspicious, unsure whether or not to believe her. Deborah took a step towards him, her hand stretching out as if in supplication. She sighed and then pressed trembling fingers to her eyes as if faint, swaying towards him. He caught her. He was wearing a heavy perfume, which masked another peculiar odour that made her feel nauseated, and now, in truth, she was close to fainting.

'You are unwell, Madonna?' The term of endearment on his lips chilled her but Deborah did not flinch.

'It is merely shock—and the relief of seeing you, *señor*. I thought I should never be released from the marquis's stronghold.'

'There are many guards?' He looked at her intently. 'This fortress has stout walls and is well defended?'

'Oh, yes,' Deborah lied. 'It would take many more men than you have with you to breach its walls.' She clutched at his sleeve in real distress as she thought of that sunlit house so open to destruction without the protection of its master. 'Oh, do not risk your lives in useless fighting, I beg you. Pray take me away from here before it is realized that I have escaped.'

Again the Spaniard's eyes narrowed as though he would doubt her word. He studied her thoughtfully, and then one of his men spoke to him urgently. Deborah glanced behind her. She saw someone standing at the crest of the grass bank—a peasant from the village. He became aware that he had been seen and, seizing Deborah's mare that, left unchecked, had wandered away, swung himself into the saddle and raced off in the direction she knew would take him to the village.

'He will rouse the alarm...'

'We shall go,' Don Miguel said, reaching his decision. 'Come, Madonna. I shall help you into the boat.' His grip on her arm was painful to Deborah, but she allowed it to go unremarked. For now all she wanted was that these men should leave the beach and return to their ship. She dared not think beyond that. His next words were addressed to one of the soldiers, 'We have what we came for. There is no point in wasting time. We have more important work ahead.'

Deborah was half thrust into the boat. She could scarcely breathe for the frantic pounding of her heart. How could she bear what was happening to her? Yet she must. She would rather die herself than see the marquis's people slaughtered for her sake.

Glancing back towards the place where Henri lay, she stifled a sob of despair. She had been reckless to come here while Nicholas was away. Henri could never have protected her against so many. Had she stayed within the confines of the château she might have been safe— and yet that would have brought pain and death to so many.

Perhaps it was better that fate had brought her here to this place at this moment, even if it had caused Henri's death, for the sake of the innocent men, women and children who might have been killed, if not for her own.

Her heart was breaking. She was being taken from people she liked and doubted that she would ever return. Nicholas would not be able to snatch her from the Don as easily as he had taken her from her father. She would truly be a prisoner from now on.

'Nicholas...oh, Nicholas.' Her heart wept while she

stared resolutely ahead of her as she was rowed out to the ship. She would never see him again, never feel his lips on hers—never be able to tell him of her true feelings. 'I love you so. I love you so.'

Deborah felt numb as she was forced to climb the rope ladder that was taking her on board Don Miguel's ship. She stood on the deck waiting, seeing nothing but the face of the man she loved, her mind closed to what was happening to her.

'Now, Madonna. You will go to the cabin and wait until I have time for you.' She hardly heard Don Miguel's words, conscious only that she must not let this man see her weakness. Some inner intuition told her that only pride would keep her safe from him. If she once faltered…it did not bear thinking of!

Deborah's arm was taken by one of the soldiers who had helped capture her on the beach. His grip was less cruel than Don Miguel's had been, but Deborah was oblivious to physical pain. There was nothing left for her—her heart was dead and she wished that she too could die from the mental agony that was beginning to torture her.

Where was Nicholas? If there were no need for a truce between them, the Spaniards would not respect the flag of their enemy. They would fire on Nicholas's ships first in the hope of killing him and destroying his fleet.

Oh, God, let him not die! Let him live. Only let him live and her own life would be forfeit. Henri was dead because of her and she truly mourned him, but she could not bear that Nicholas should be killed, too.

It was a moment or two before her mind cleared sufficiently to realize that she had been left alone in a cabin. It was richly appointed, clearly the property of a wealthy man—Don Miguel's own, of course. She recalled that he had ordered her to wait for him. And what would happen then? Supposing he treated her as he had Isabella Rodriguez?

She felt the sickness in her throat and the fear was almost overwhelming. She could never give herself to such a man. It would be better if she were to die—better to plunge into the sea now than let him take her to his bed. Her feeling of apathy fell away and she went to the cabin door, only to find it securely locked from the other side.

Of course! What else had she expected? Don Miguel had no reason to trust her. Finding her riding freely on the beach had aroused his suspicions. He might wonder if she had gone willingly with Nicholas. If he believed that—believed she had been Nicholas's mistress…as she so nearly had…there was no telling what he might do to her.

Returning to the bed, Deborah sank down on the edge. She had no means of escape. From the moment she had dismounted to kneel by Henri this had been inevitable. There was no way out for her—unless she could somehow send word to her father. Perhaps he could influence his old friend, and yet she did not believe it possible. Sir Edward had been deliberately lied to, deceived into consenting to her marriage to the Spaniard. It was unlikely, then, that he could save her now.

There was only one man who might help her—and he was about to sail into a trap that would surely mean his death.

Deborah lifted her head as pride came to her rescue. She would not live as Don Miguel's bride. She would sooner take her own life, even though it was a terrible sin and meant that she would be eternally damned.

* * *

'You plan to fire on de Vere's ship under a flag of truce?' Sir Edward stared at the Spaniard in disbelief. 'But to do so would break every code of honour. I cannot stand by and see this happen. I protest, *señor*. De Vere must have his chance to explain why he has acted so badly towards my daughter.' Sir Edward looked at the man he had thought of as a friend and did not care for what he saw. There was a ruthlessness in this man, something he had not seen or suspected when they had known each other years before. 'Besides— you do not know whether Deborah is on board his flagship. If you sink it, she could be killed.'

'Do not concern yourself, my friend,' the Don said. 'I know the way de Vere's mind works. He did not come for gold. He hath no need of it. This is his way of getting to my son. It was a condition of the ransom that Miguel handed over the gold in person. He hopes to force him to a fight—a duel of honour between them, which would end in Miguel's death.'

'If de Vere is such a man, why does he quarrel with your son?' Sir Edward's eyes narrowed in suspicion. He had begun to think there was more to this as he watched the Don's ships prepare for a fierce battle. 'What has Miguel done that another man—a man of honour by your own account—should hate him this much?'

'It was nonsense.' Don Manola dismissed the rape and murder of a young woman with a wave of his hand, though it would not so easily be dismissed from his dreams. 'We shall kill de Vere and put an end to this for good.'

'And my daughter?'

'My son will soon have rescued her. He has taken a band of fighting men to attack de Vere's château while he is away. Never fear, *señor*, they will bring her back to you safely.'

'At what cost?' Sir Edward demanded.

He wanted Deborah restored to him, and he would see de Vere arrested and tried for his crime if he could, but this treachery disgusted him. A gentleman's honour was all that separated him from the flotsam of debased humanity that flourished in the gutters, and was beyond price.

'I cannot allow you to do this,' he said again. 'What has been done at de Vere's château cannot be helped, though I would not have agreed to this plan had I known of it—but a flag of truce must be honoured. I demand that you allow de Vere to board this ship without firing at his. He must be given a hearing. He should in all decency be brought to stand his trial before God and his peers in an English court of justice.'

Don Manola stared at him in silence for a moment. 'Then I am afraid I must ask you to go below, *señor*. I cannot have my orders countermanded.' He nodded to one of his officers and the next moment two soldiers were taking hold of Sir Edward's arms.

'What is this?' Sir Edward struggled to throw them off but found himself a prisoner. 'More treachery?'

'I regret that it is necessary,' the Don replied. 'I would not have shown you disrespect, *señor*, but I repeat that I cannot allow you to interfere with my plans.'

What a fool he had been to put himself in this position! He had no servants at his command, no power to defend himself. It was useless to argue. As he allowed the Don's men to take him to his cabin, Sir Edward cursed himself for not taking more thought before he embarked on his desperate journey. He had trusted Don Manola, believed the Don's son a worthy bridegroom for his daughter.

He would not consent to a hasty marriage! Yet he was effectively a prisoner, caught in a trap of his own making, his daughter a pawn in this evil game between ruthless enemies.

'My poor Deborah…my poor child.' His fears were all for his daughter. She might even now be in the clutches of the Don's son and, for some reason he did not understand, that made him very much afraid.

For some while he was sunk in thought, and it was the sudden booming of guns that roused him. What was happening above? Had he imagined it—or had it been another ship that fired first? He had believed it was the marquis who would be taken by surprise, but if his guns had spoken first…

His thoughts went reeling in confusion as he felt the *Santa Maria* shudder violently. They had been struck and by more than a single blast. The other ship must have sailed in with all guns blazing and there was a furious battle going on above his head.

Sir Edward was suddenly spurred into action. If the ship went down while he was locked in this cabin, he would be caught like a rat in a trap. He must get out! At least then he would have a chance of survival. He owed it to Deborah to escape from this tomb.

He looked about him for a weapon with which to break the lock on the cabin door, choosing first a heavy candlestick and battering at the stout wood furiously but without much success. Such a damned fool, to let himself be brought here without a struggle! But he would not stay to be condemned to a watery grave. He glanced round for something more substantial and then wrenched an iron spike from the wall, driving it deep into the stubborn lock and jabbing at it until he heard the wood splinter and part company with the door.

The ship was shuddering from stern to prow, taking water fast, and listing to one side as if it had been badly holed. As everything went sliding across the floor, he increased his attempts and saw that the lock was hanging out. He wrenched the door open, staggering as the ship heaved drunkenly to one side and then back again as it struggled in its death throes, blasted by yet another deadly round of cannon fire. Whoever was in charge of the other ship knew what he was about!

He was out of the cabin now, scrambling towards the hatch above. It was closed but not battened down and he thrust at it with all his strength, pushing it back and hauling himself out on deck. As he crawled on his belly, unable to stand because of the list, he gagged on the stench of burning wood and flesh; the air was acrid with gunpowder and blood. Confusion was all around him. Masts had been brought crashing down, bodies lay everywhere and the screaming of the wounded was horrific.

He looked for the Don but could not see him. Men were abandoning the ship, which was clearly lost. Sir Edward caught a rope, clinging to it, pulling himself hand over hand towards the rails, knowing his only hope was the sea. There at least he might have a chance of being picked up by another ship, for they were all around him, seemingly engaged in what looked to be a fight to the death.

Reaching the rail at last, soft hands torn and bleeding from the rope, Sir Edward stood and prepared to jump into the sea, pausing momentarily to seek a clear patch, away from the swirling mass of debris churning in the waves below. It was in that moment of hesitation that a shattered mast broke free from its last rope and came crashing down on him, rendering him unconscious and sending him headlong into the mass of debris below.

Chapter Eleven

She had been here a long time alone. Dusk had fallen hours ago and she had lit a lanthorn, which hung from an iron hook embedded into the cabin wall. Deborah was calmer now, her determination hardened. To show fear would make her vulnerable—and somehow she knew that the Spaniard would enjoy seeing her humbled. It would avail her nothing to beg and so she would not— no matter what was done to her.

Although desperately tired, she refused to sleep. She would be ready when Don Miguel came to her. She sat in the heavily carved chair that was set before a table strewn with maps and charts of the seas. They were beautifully drawn with pictures of strange fishes and creatures of the sea. Did such beasts truly exist? she wondered as she amused herself by trying to discover the meaning of various notes written in the margins.

'What are you doing?'

Don Miguel's voice startled her. She had not heard him enter. He must have moved softly, perhaps hoping to find her sleeping. She would have been vulnerable then, and helpless if he had decided to force his attentions on her.

'I did not hear you knock,' Deborah said, surprised at her own calmness as she faced him. The fear she had felt earlier had faded for the moment. 'I am not accustomed to gentlemen entering my chamber without first asking my permission.'

The Spaniard's eyes narrowed. 'I vow you hath a sharp tongue, lady. You are not in your own bedchamber. This is my cabin and you are...'

'Your intended bride, sir.' Deborah looked him in the eyes. Something deep within her was prompting her, telling her how to behave. 'And as such I demand to be treated with respect. You will in future request entry. No gentleman would do less.'

'And the Marquis de Vere?' Don Miguel's voice was soft but somehow menacing. 'You were accorded this respect while his prisoner?'

'Indeed, yes,' Deborah replied. 'How could it be otherwise? The marquis was demanding a ransom for my return. It would hardly be paid had I been dishonoured. Besides, the marquis was seldom in my presence.'

Deborah's heart contracted with fear as she lied. It was so important that he believed her. If he suspected that she had promised to wed Nicholas...that he had kissed and made passionate love to her...she would have no hold on this man and her fate would be sealed. She silently thanked God that her betrothal ring was lying on the table in her bedchamber at the château. Had she been wearing it when she was taken, the Don would have had good reason to doubt her.

'De Vere is a fool,' Miguel said suddenly, his mouth twisting in an ugly sneer. 'He had his chance for revenge within his grasp and let it slip. Only a fool would leave himself at risk. He should have known I would not accept his demands and kept you fast.'

He was gloating because he had outwitted Nicholas!

Deborah itched to wipe that hateful sneer from his mouth but knew she dared not. She must not let him guess how she felt—about Nicholas or the fact that she was now his prisoner. Here on this ship she was completely at this man's mercy. He could do whatever he wished with her. She knew that he possessed a cruel and vicious nature. Only her own courage would protect her from him.

'When are we to be married?' she asked with an imperious toss of her head. 'My father—you must send word to my father as soon as we reach Spain.'

'Sir Edward will be awaiting your arrival, Madonna.' Don Miguel blinked as though he had been in some kind of a trance and her demand had brought him back to himself. 'He sailed immediately for Spain with Sanchez. My father will arrange the wedding when our work is done.'

'What work is that, *señor*?'

'De Vere has been a thorn in my father's side too long. He will be dealt with and forgotten.' An unpleasant smile touched the Spaniard's lips. 'We shall be wed soon enough, Madonna. I promise you.'

Some quality in his voice made the sickness rise in Deborah's throat as she saw his gloating look. If she were once his wife and bound to him by the laws of God and man, with no redress, he would delight in hurting her. She wondered why he did not begin now. She had seen the temptation in his eyes and there was no reason for him to restrain himself. Had he been determined to rape or punish her she could not have stopped him.

'My father will like you,' Don Miguel said, seeming to speak to himself rather than her. His hand reached out, touching her hair. She fought the revulsion that whipped through her, praying it was not reflected in her face. 'He would not be pleased if you had been damaged. His son's wife must be beyond reproach. She must be chaste on her wedding night…untouched until then. The mother of his heir must be worthy…'

A chill of horror went through Deborah as she realized that he was hardly aware of her. He was repeating the words as a kind of litany—or a charm to ward off evil! A glazed look had come into his eyes and it chilled her.

He was not quite sane! Not mad like the poor lunatics who must be chained for their own good and the safety of others—but strange and unpredictable, his mood changing in an instant.

'Why are you staring at me? I hate women who stare!'

It was the unpredictable nature of his mind that was dangerous. He was clever, cruel and ruthless—but there was an unbalanced side of him that she suspected, once let loose, even he might not be able to control.

'I have no wish to stare,' Deborah replied proudly. Her only defence was to remind him always of who and what she was. 'I wish to retire, *señor*—and I shall have the key to my door, if you please. It is not fitting that any man should be able to enter at will.'

'They would not dare. They know me too well.' His eyes glittered.

Deborah's instincts were all she had to guide her now. The words came to her mind as if they had been sent from a guardian angel.

'Should one of them dare and my maidenhead be lost, Don Manola would not be pleased. He has entrusted me to your care, *señor*. You must be sure that when I bear a child it is of your own blood.'

He stared at her. She saw that whatever had ailed him had passed. His mind was his own once more.

'You will lock the door after me,' he said. 'I pray for your sake that you have not lied to me, Madonna. You will suffer for it if I find you not a maiden on our wedding night.'

Deborah inclined her head, giving him a haughty stare. It seemed to satisfy and then please him, as if his thoughts were amusing. He smiled in a cold, calculating way, bowed his head and laid a key on the table, then he turned and walked to the door.

'It will be a pleasure to teach you how to be a wife, Madonna.'

Deborah could not move as the door closed behind him. She felt ill and was trembling from head to toe. He was evil! She could never have imagined how evil. His mind was warped and distorted by some sickness that had made him the monster he undoubtedly was.

Poor, poor Isabella! How she must have suffered before she died.

Gathering her courage, Deborah picked up the key and went to lock the cabin door. At least she could sleep without fear of being disturbed. If she could keep Don Miguel from ravishing her while she was on board his ship, she might yet find a way of escape.

Whatever happened, she would die before she went to his bed as his wife—and if he raped her before that, she would not long survive the ordeal.

Returning to the bed, Deborah lay down fully clothed.

'Nicholas,' she whispered to the pillow. 'Nicholas, my love. Where are you? God keep you safe. Please come for me. I beg you—do not desert me if you live. And if you are dead, let me know it so that I may die also.'

'What of our patient?' Nicholas asked Pierre as he came to him on the poop of the *Siren's Song*. 'Has he recovered his senses?'

'No—not yet. He has a fever. The blow to his head

was severe. Men die of such wounds.'

'We must pray for my lady's sake that he recovers,' Nicholas said and frowned. 'Had your sharp eyes not picked him out amongst the debris he would have un-doubtedly drowned.'

'I saw at once that he was not a Spaniard. He wore no armour and I was curious how he came to be aboard the *Santa Maria*.'

'No doubt he sailed from England with Sanchez in search of his daughter—and joined forces with Don Manola to destroy me.' Nicholas's frown deepened. 'Speaking of our prisoner—has he asked for me?'

'He refuses to answer when questioned about the whereabouts of his son. Not one word has passed his lips since you forced the surrender of his ships.'

'Don Manola is a proud man,' Nicholas acknowl-edged. 'You have told him that he will be returned to Spain unharmed when I have what I want?'

'He has been told your terms.'

'We have the captains and officers of his ships secured below, and one of his ships is forfeit as our prize, but the others have been allowed to go their way with what remains of their crews on board. The Don knows all this—and yet he refuses to speak?'

'He has been told that his officers will be released when Don Miguel meets you face to face.'

'He has lost his flagship and two others—what more will he sacrifice for that unworthy dog of a son?' Nich-olas asked. 'I do not wish to threaten him with death. My quarrel is with Miguel Cortes, not his father.'

'Even though he was prepared to fire on you under a flag of truce?'

'I never expected the truce to be respected—nor in my heart did I believe Don Miguel would be here at the appointed time.' Nicholas smiled oddly. 'Why do you imagine I left behind more than a third of my fighting men and your own ship, Pierre?'

'I thought you asked me to sail with you because Henri stayed behind.'

'To guard my lady and the château, of course. The men under his command were warned to stay out of sight. I did not want Deborah or the other women to be afraid for their lives. I knew there was a chance of treachery but if Cortes has attempted a surprise attack, he will meet with more resistance than he imagined. The cliffs are watched constantly as is our most vulnerable spot. It will be at the beach that an enemy lands.

'A simple mistake that any might make. Easy enough to beach their boats, but too far to the château to have any possibility of surprise. My men will be warned and ready for them before they could hope to reach the house. They will be surrounded and overpowered long before they are within sight of the château.'

'I should have known you would not be fool enough to sail into a trap,' Pierre said and laughed. 'Henri never spoke a word of this to me.'

'I warned him to be silent,' Nicholas said grimly. 'I knew there were men watching over the safety of our women. I left him in command, though I knew he would rather be with us.'

'He will be like a hen without its chick,' Pierre jested. 'And so—now we sail for home?'

'We shall be eagerly awaited—and we have a wedding to celebrate,' Nicholas replied. He was smiling, but then, as he recalled that Deborah's father lay at death's door in his cabin, the smile faded. 'I pray God that Sir Edward lives. My lady may never forgive me if I have killed him.'

'You were not to know he was on board that ship.'

'No—but my lady will not exonerate me so easily. She loves her father dearly. And, in truth, I am to blame. Had I not snatched her that day he would likely be at home even now preparing for Mistress Palmer's wedding.'

Nicholas's eyes brooded as he stared into the distance. With Don Manola his prisoner he was in a position of strength, but the victory gave him little pleasure. He could think only of the woman he had left behind and what she would feel when she learned his news.

It might be that his wedding must be delayed until Sir Edward's health improved. And what if he died? Would Deborah hate him for the part he had played?

He remembered the sweetness of her surrender to him in the stable yard. Yet later she had denied that her heart was his. She was a fiery wench and her tongue was sharp when she chose. He had thought that she lied because she was angry and he had wounded her pride somehow, but perhaps he had allowed himself to be deceived. There were women for whom passion was not always a matter of the heart. He had not believed Deborah one of them.

She had acted oddly on the morning of their celebration. He had asked her more than once if she had regretted her promise and she had denied it. She had told him her sadness came from the breach with her father...

Once again he felt the cold hand of fear about his heart. Why could he not be at ease in his mind where Deborah was concerned? He knew the château was well protected. He would not have left it or his people vulnerable to attack. This strange feeling must be because he was uncertain of ever being able to win her love.

He hoped and almost believed that she would learn to love him when they were wed—but supposing her father's death lay between them? An insurmountable barrier that he could never breach.

No, it must not happen! He must be able to return to her with a clear conscience.

'Take command,' he said to Pierre. 'I am going below. Deborah's father must live. He shall live—if I have to drag him back from the devil's clutches myself!'

A grim smile hovered about his mouth as he made his way to the cabin where Sir Edward hovered between this life and the next. He knew that this might be his hardest battle yet, but somehow he would win—for Deborah's sake and for the love he bore her.

Deborah stood on the deck of the Spanish galleon and watched the activity ashore. It was a busy port and there were many ships either anchored some way out or moored at the quayside for unloading. Most of the vessels were clearly merchant ships. Spain was a wealthy and powerful country and traded with far flung lands as well as those of the Mediterranean basin, bringing back spices and rare goods bought with silver from the New World.

'Are you ready, Madonna?'

Don Miguel's voice spoke softly from behind her. She was not startled. She had known he was there, though he had come upon her quietly, hoping to shock her. She turned to face him, cold and proud, every inch the great lady. Her manner had served her well thus far. She had seen a reluctant respect grow in both him and his men because of it.

'Thank you, *señor*. I am quite ready.'

The ship had been brought in close to the harbour. She was able to walk down a solid plank to reach dry land. The sun was very hot, for it was midday and the sky free of cloud. She could smell the tang of rotting filth from the water swirling about the ships in harbour, where rubbish had been swept out of their holds and into the sea.

'Horses have been provided,' Don Miguel said. 'It is no more than an hour's ride to my father's *casa*. Once we are there you will be able to rest and change your gown, Madonna.'

His caressing tone made her shiver inwardly; he was like a cat toying with the bird it meant to kill, savouring the pleasure to come. She hated the way he looked at her, measuring her, stripping her naked in his mind: his unclean, strange, evil mind. Who could tell what such a man might think or do?

'That will be most welcome.' She inclined her head. 'I thank you for your consideration, *señor*.'

Don Miguel nodded. He glanced about him, seeming preoccupied, clearly expecting to see something—or someone.

'My father said he would be here to meet us. I see none of his ships…' A flicker of uncertainty showed in the ice-blue eyes.

Deborah made no reply. She sensed the Spaniard's unease, but ignored it. Whatever was keeping Don Manola from returning to port was good news as far as she was concerned. The wedding could not take place until he returned—and in the meantime she might discover some means of escape.

Six horses were brought. One of the soldiers helped Deborah to mount hers, then swung into the saddle of his own horse. Don Miguel continued to look about him, seeming almost to have forgotten she was there. He spoke sharply to his men as he mounted himself, jabbing at his horse's mouth cruelly with the bit as he pulled hard on the reins. It was obvious that his father's tardiness had unsettled him.

With an escort of five heavily armed men, any escape attempt was doomed to failure. Deborah did not even think of it—but she did take note of the road they travelled as far as she was able.

After the busy port and city were left behind, they seemed to be heading for the hills that lay beyond the rocky coastline, following roads that were often no more than sheep trails. The hills themselves were browned by the fierce sun, in places bare rock burned dry of any but the hardiest vegetation. At other times they came upon woods of cypress and clusters of mimosa with a few blossoms from a late flowering. Here, tiny birds fluttered amongst the trees, twittering in the otherwise silent landscape. Occasionally, crude hovels could be seen clinging to the sides of the hills, and there were signs that peasant farmers eked out a precarious living on these slopes.

It was almost an hour before they came to the village—just an inn and a few poor houses clustered about a church. Some of the inhabitants sat outside the inn, drinking wine in the sunshine. Two old women dressed in black gossiped in the street, but disappeared hastily inside their houses as the small cavalcade approached. A man leading a donkey turned his head aside and spat in the dust as they passed.

Deborah sensed fear and hatred all about her. These people must look to the Cortes family for their living, but they did not do so willingly. She remembered Henri telling her that Isabella was not the only woman to have suffered at Don Miguel's hands. How many of these men's wives and daughters had been raped or abused?

She felt a sense of hope. Perhaps she might find help amongst these people? If they hated Don Miguel...and yet they must also fear him and his power. Would any of them be brave enough to defy him for her sake? And why should they?

Her hope faded as they began the ascent to the fortress at the summit of a hill. It looked a forbidding sight, built of grey stone and enclosed by thick walls and an iron portcullis. An army would be needed to break down these defenses. If she had hoped that Nicholas would come for her the hope died stillborn.

The heavy iron gate was raised as they approached and lowered as soon as they were inside the courtyard. Deborah looked at the house itself and her heart sank as she saw the bars over what windows there were. Most of the air and light came from narrow arrow slits, at least on this side of the castle. She felt that this was indeed a prison.

Her only escape from here would be to die by her own hand.

'Welcome to your home, Madonna.'

Deborah saw the gleam of triumph in Don Miguel's eyes. He had her now. She should have tried to escape during their ride or jumped into the sea!

Her head went up proudly. She would never show fear. Somehow she would hold him off until the wedding, and if no help came before then... She was not afraid to die. She would find some means of taking her own life within the fortress: perhaps a knife or a sword. She prayed only that she would have the courage when the time came.

Entering the dark, gloomy house, Deborah held her head proudly, her back straight as servants came run-

ning. One was a man dressed plainly in black. He bowed
to her. From his manner of dress she judged him a steward or secretary. He smiled gravely and gestured to an
old woman to come forward.

'This is Señora Anna Martinez,' he said in perfect
English. 'She will serve you, Mistress Stirling. And if
you need anything more I am at your service.'

'And your name, *señor*?'

'Carlos Montana. I am Don Manola's steward. In his
absence and by his authority I welcome you to this
house.'

'Enough!' Don Miguel said sharply. He barked something at the old woman, who looked at him sullenly.
'The woman will take you to your apartments, Madonna.
And *you* come with me!' He glared at the steward as if
enraged that he had dared to speak to Deborah in such
a manner.

Anna was pulling at Deborah's arm, gesturing urgently that they should leave. It was clear she spoke no
English and equally clear that she did not like her master's son. Her expression seemed to warn Deborah, and,
as they left the small dark hall behind and began to
mount a twisting stair, she placed a finger to her lips and
shook her head.

Deborah glanced back once at Señor Montana. He and
Don Miguel seemed to be arguing. She had noticed that
the steward did not appear to be afraid of his master's
son and that intrigued her. Why was he not afraid when
Don Miguel's own men went in fear of him?

Montana had appeared very confident, very much in
control. Was that because he had the authority of his
master? Deborah had gained the impression that Don
Miguel was a little afraid of his father. Could that be

why the steward was so confident?

She suspected that the only reason Don Miguel had not subjected her to rape during the voyage was because his father would not approve—had, perhaps, forbidden it. Obviously, Don Manola had a strong hold over his son. Was it only the father's influence that had protected him from hanging for the murder of Isabella Rodriguez—or was there more to it?

Deborah could not know the truth, but the steward's presence in the house gave her hope once more. He might protect her if she needed it—and perhaps, when her father and Don Manola returned she might persuade them to allow her to return home.

It was, she knew, a forlorn hope, but at least her father would be here. Surely he would not stand by and see her forced to marry a man such as Don Miguel?

'You are certain?' Don Miguel's eyes narrowed to thin slits, veiling his feelings from the steward. 'My father's flagship was sunk—and he is *Le Diable*'s hostage? You are sure he was not killed?'

Carlos Montana saw the gleam of triumph the younger man had tried to hide, and the sickness turned in his stomach. His master should have had this monster shut away long ago when the strange moods began to come on him—but at first he had not believed it was happening, even though the evidence that Miguel had inherited his mother's madness had been strong.

'De Vere would not be foolish enough to kill such a valuable hostage,' he said. 'He will bargain for your father's life. We have only to wait and the demand will arrive. Perhaps he will accept gold for Don Manola's release.'

'He wants me dead,' Miguel replied and his lips

curved in a sneer. 'He wants revenge for that wench—
though why he should bother is beyond me. She was a
snivelling child and not worth the effort. I never thought
she would cause me so much trouble.'

Montana's disgust showed in his eyes. Only his respect for the father kept him from showing it openly as
he stared in silence at the son. Miguel was a monster
and should have been strangled at birth, but Don Manola
could not bring himself to do it.

Montana knew that his master had desperately loved
his wife, even when he realized she was not as other
women, and he had given her a child. The steward knew
that his master had suffered agonies for what he had
done, punishing himself by doing penance for years, but
he had gone on loving his lovely young wife until the
day that she died of a fever. And he had tried to love
the son she had given him, but from the early years it
had been apparent to most that Miguel's mind was
flawed.

As a child he had contented himself with torturing any
creature that came within his grasp, and it was only as
he grew to manhood that the true depth of his depravity
had begun to show through.

'Why should I pay gold for my father's return?' Miguel asked, but Montana knew that he was speaking to
himself and did not realize he had said the words aloud.
'If he does not come back, I am master here.'

'You know that I have command in Don Manola's
absence,' the steward said. 'The deed is lodged with the
notary and the Don's men will obey me. I shall pay
whatever is demanded for my master's return.'

Don Miguel looked at him calculatingly. It was true
that such a deed existed. His father had told him that
during an interview he would prefer to forget. He shud-

dered as he remembered the place he had been taken to that day, his father's warning still as terrifying to him now as it had been then. Once as a child he had been shut in a dark place that smelt of death and decaying flesh; he was afraid of the dark. Demons shrieked at him in the dark and their claws tore at his flesh.

His father had threatened him with the demons of hell if he did not mend his ways, but Miguel did not believe in heaven or hell—only in the horror of that dark place.

'Not the woman,' he said. 'Gold, if you will—but not the woman. She is mine. Father wants her for my bride. You know that, don't you? He would not be pleased if you gave her back.'

God forgive him, Montana thought as the sickness churned in his guts. He knew it well and had argued against it from the start. He had served his master well and faithfully, but this wickedness was beyond all that had gone before. He thought of the young woman he had just welcomed to this house and the fate that awaited her as this monster's bride.

'Nothing can be done until Don Manola returns,' he replied coldly. 'There will be no wedding until my master is here to see it done properly.'

'Get him back,' Miguel muttered. 'Don't bother me. I have other things to do—more important business.'

The steward watched as Don Miguel walked away. Who knew where he went to when the sickness was about to come upon him—or what he did? It was better simply to look the other way.

But could he look the other way when it came to the matter of the wedding?

Chapter Twelve

'Why did you save me?' Sir Edward asked in a voice that was little more than a whisper. He gulped greedily at the water in a cup being held to his cracked lips. 'Why have you shown me such kindness, such devotion? You must know I am your enemy—that I would see you hang if I could?'

'I hope we shall not always be enemies, sir,' Nicholas replied gravely. 'Indeed, I would have us friends—for Deborah's sake, if no other.'

'My child—how dare you speak to me of her?' Weak though he was after two days lost in a fever, Sir Edward struggled to sit up and to glare at the rogue who had snatched her. 'What have you done to her? Where is my daughter? I swear I will kill you if you have harmed her!'

'Rest easy, good sir. She is safe at my home,' Nicholas said. 'She has promised to wed me and we hope for your blessing.'

'Over my dead body!' Sir Edward fell back against the pillows, his strength spent. 'Never, never shall I consent.'

'Neither Deborah nor I would welcome your death, sir. Indeed, I know it would sorely grieve my lady to be estranged from you. It has caused her much distress to know you must be anxious for her sake.'

'*Your* lady? By God, sir! You take too much for granted.'

'The marriage contract is already signed. The wedding was to take place two days after my return, but may wait easily until you are well enough to give the bride away. I know Deborah would be happy if you were to stand by her side in church.'

Sir Edward's eyes narrowed. 'Are you telling me she consents to this of her own will?'

'She does—and will tell you so herself.'

'I thought you took her for a ransom—or was there more to this?' Sir Edward frowned. 'This quarrel between you and Don Miguel is of long standing, I believe. My daughter was but a pawn in some plan of revenge.'

'Not a pawn, sir,' Nicholas said swiftly. 'I never meant to give her to the Spaniard. Heaven forfend! I took her away to save her from a fate worse than death. I know it to have been a reckless act and I do sincerely beg your pardon for any pain I caused you. I ought in all conscience to have come to you and told you the truth...'

'Indeed you did, sir! It was a wicked, cruel thing you did to snatch a daughter from her father. I thought her lost to me forever—mayhap dead.'

'She was never in danger—I beg you to believe that I would protect her with my life. I was afraid you would not listen—and I could not bear that Miguel Cortes should defile Deborah as he has others.'

Sir Edward closed his eyes. His head was aching and he felt ill, both in body and mind.

'You are not well, sir. We shall continue this discussion another time, when you are feeling better.'

'No, no, I am listening. Pray tell me everything.'

He listened in silence as Nicholas told him of Isabella's murder and of other things he had learned since, which he had told to no one else because they were too horrible to speak of except when it was needful.

'The man you have described is the devil incarnate.' Sir Edward crossed himself and shuddered as he struggled to come to terms with what he knew must be the truth.

'Miguel Cortes is not a lunatic, though I suspect he may lose control at times. When himself, he is clever, cruel and evil—with the cunning of a serpent that creeps up unseen on its victim. I once called him a fool to his face and he killed the woman I would have wed. Knowing this—could I let a woman I admired above all others go to him as a bride?'

'You should have told me, that was your duty.' Sir Edward looked hard at him and something in Nicholas's eyes suddenly made everything clear. 'You could not risk my being too stubborn to listen. You loved her— Deborah. You took her because you *loved* her.'

'I did not like to admit it even to myself,' Nicholas acknowledged with a rueful smile. 'But it is true. I love her with all my heart and did so from the moment I first saw her. I had vowed never to marry until Isabella was avenged but, though Miguel Cortes has escaped me yet again, I shall wed your daughter, sir. Revenge is nothing but bitterness and in sweet Deborah Ann I truly believe I have found my salvation. So I shall wed her as soon as it can be arranged.'

'With or without my blessing?' Sir Edward demanded.

'I would have it for her sake,' Nicholas replied. 'But

she is mine and I cannot let her go.'

Sir Edward nodded. He too had known such a love. A reluctant smile touched his mouth. The man was undoubtedly a rogue, but perhaps… He was about to speak when the cabin door was thrust open and Pierre entered.

'We have just sighted the *Antoinette*,' he said, his expression anxious. 'There is an urgent message. Henri wishes to come aboard…'

'Henri?' Nicholas stared at him, an icy coldness trickling down his spine. 'Henri has brought the *Antoinette* to meet us? I ordered him to guard the château and my lady with his life. How dare he disobey me?'

'My God!' Sir Edward gave an anguished cry. 'I had forgot. While you were absent, Don Miguel went to your home to seize my daughter. If your trusted lieutenant is here…'

Nicholas was reeling from the shock. How could it be that Henri was sailing to meet them—had signalled that he had an urgent message?

'If that monster has my daughter…God help my child…' Sir Edward put a hand to his eyes and gasped. 'God forgive us all…'

'We shall get her back, I swear it.'

'If Don Miguel is as evil as you told me, it might be too late. Better perhaps that she should die than live with such shame…better for us to forget she ever lived.'

'Never!' Nicholas cried, face white, eyes dark with horror. 'I shall find her and do what must be done.'

If he killed her and then himself, at least she would not be trapped in a living hell.

Sir Edward had fallen back against the pillows and was moaning, severely distressed. Nicholas pitied him but could not stop to comfort him.

His thoughts were grim as he went on deck. He had

never felt so angry or so desperate in his life. How could his plans have gone so awry? It was not possible for the Spaniards to have sprung a surprise attack—even if they had crept up in the dead of night they would have been seen. Surely his own men had not run like craven cowards? He could not believe that—and yet something must be wrong or Henri would not at this moment be sitting in a boat being rowed towards the *Siren's Song*.

'What do you mean—she went of her own free will?' Nicholas stared at the man he had until this moment considered his best friend. 'Damn you! I do not believe it. She would never have gone with that monster willingly.'

'I urged her to ride away, but she would not be swayed—and then my horse was shot from under me and I was knocked unconscious as it rolled on me. I did not witness what happened next, though...' Henri hesitated as he saw the fury in Nicholas's eyes. 'I was told that she went with them willingly. She did not fight them, Nico—and I have been told that they treated her with respect rather than as a hostage.'

Nicholas swung away as the pain ripped through him. She had broken her word to him, persuading Henri to ride to the beach in the hope of escape... Yet she could not have known the Spaniards would be waiting. Unless he had been betrayed by others... No, no, it could not be! He would not believe that she had left him willingly.

He was tortured by his thoughts, which would turn him against even those he loved and trusted most. Damn that green-eyed wench for deceiving him! She had bewitched him with her smiles and the taste of her lips... she deserved her fate!

'He has but one day's start on us,' Henri began. 'I

was not able to follow immediately, for my wits were
wandering some hours. Our ships are faster. If we make
good time we may be able to overtake him while he is
still at sea.'

'No! She chose her bed—let her lie on it,' Nicholas
said and swore furiously. 'Why should I risk good men's
lives for a lying witch?'

Henri stared at him, shocked into silence momentarily.
What had happened to this man he loved as a brother?
Then, all at once, his own anger erupted. 'May God
strike you down if you let this happen. Damn you, Nico!
I shall go alone if you will not come with me. Whatever
your private quarrel with Mistress Stirling, you cannot
condemn her to a living hell with that brute—or you are
not the man I thought you.'

Nicholas stared at him, wanting to strike him, but then
the truth of his words began to penetrate the mist of pain
and disappointment in his head, and he knew that Henri
was right. If Deborah had gone of her own will, it was
because she did not believe Nicholas when he told her
Don Miguel was a monster—and he had only himself to
blame. He had snatched her from her father and forced
her into a situation where her only choice was to marry
the man who had besmirched her reputation.

He recalled the way she had melted in his arms, the
sweetness of her lips, and knew that he could not stand
by and see such softness and beauty destroyed. His love
wrenched at him, twisting like a knife in his belly as he
asked, 'Why did she leave me, Henri? How could she
prefer that evil creature to the life I offered her?'

Henri saw the pain in his eyes and pitied him. 'I do
not know,' he said softly. 'My memories of those last
moments before I went down beneath the horse are hazy.
I know she hesitated—but I cannot recall what she said

to me just before the shot that felled me. Yet in my heart I do not believe she wanted to leave you.'

Nicholas smiled at him regretfully. 'I have not asked if you were badly hurt—forgive me?'

'Bruised—and dazed for some hours,' Henri said ruefully. 'But, in truth, I believe I deserved more for my carelessness.'

'Why did you take her to the beach? You knew the risk.'

'She was restless—as was I,' Henri confessed. 'I thought the ride would settle us both. Forgive me. I believed it safe enough. You had done all that was needed to protect the château. We had ample time to escape if...' He faltered and Nicholas frowned.

'If she had not stubbornly refused to go with you?' He was suddenly tortured by pictures of Deborah subjected to the vile attentions of the Spaniard. 'No matter! Whatever the reason, she must not be left to her fate. You were right, Henri. We must go after them.'

Deborah glanced at her reflection in the small hand mirror Anna had brought for her use. She saw that her hair had been dressed in the Spanish way, the crown pulled flat with clusters of ringlets at each side of her head. Her gown had wide panniers, which felt heavy and cumbersome, and was not as elegant as the gowns the French seamstress had made for her.

'Thank you,' Deborah said and smiled at the old woman, who had been kind to her. 'You have done your work well.'

Anna was apparently satisfied, for she gave Deborah a toothless smile and chattered away in her own language. As a knock came at the door, she put a finger to her lips and shook her head as if to warn Deborah to be careful. It seemed even the servants here disliked and distrusted their master's son.

However, when the door was opened, Deborah saw that it was Don Manola's steward. He too had changed his clothes for the evening, but was as plainly garbed as before, though the stiff ruff around his neck was edged with silver lace.

'I came to escort you to dinner, Mistress Stirling. I believe we shall be alone this evening. Don Miguel hath business that detains him elsewhere.'

'What kind of business?' Deborah detected something in his manner. 'Pray tell me, *señor*—what kind of a man would they see me wed?'

Carlos Montana hesitated, then offered his arm to her. 'Walls have ears, Mistress Stirling. We shall talk in a little while. I have taken the liberty of having our meal served in my master's apartments. It is not as large as the banqueting hall and more comfortable. My master often dines there when he wishes to be private.'

'You are considerate, *señor*.'

He smiled at her but said nothing until they were inside a small room, which was panelled with dark wood and had shelves for books and rolled parchments; there were, besides, a heavy table, two carved chairs and several coffers banded with iron. The table had been set with plates of silver, goblets and an engraved wine ewer, also a water jug.

'We shall not be disturbed until I order our meal to be served,' Montana said. 'Will you take wine, my lady?'

'I thank you, no. Water will serve.'

'You may trust me—the wine is not drugged.'

'I have thought from the first that I might trust you. I seldom drink wine, *señor*.'

'As you wish.' He poured water into a goblet and handed it to her, helping himself to red wine. 'You wished to know what I can tell you about my master's son?'

'Yes, please.' She raised her clear gaze to meet his steady grey eyes, studying him for a moment. He was a man in his mid years, neither particularly attractive nor ugly, but with an air of decency about him that marked him out as an honest man. 'I have thought…at times…' She took a deep breath. 'Tell me, *señor*—is Don Manola's son insane?'

His expression was unreadable, giving nothing away. 'Has he harmed or frightened you?'

'No—though I saw something in his eyes that made me fear he would ere long.'

'Don Manola is a good man,' his steward said. 'But he was wrong to seek this marriage. He wants an heir—it is an obsession with him, you understand—but it is not fitting. The sickness may be passed on to yet another generation if he allows this abomination to take place.'

So she had been right! The Don was ill in his mind, even though at most times he seemed in command of his wits.

'The Don knows of his son's…sickness?'

Carlos Montana sighed and looked grave. 'In all my years of service we have never disagreed save over this one thing. I cannot understand why he is so determined to have his own way. He must know that this merely compounds the original sin.'

'What sin?' Deborah asked, but the steward shook his head, unwilling to elaborate.

'Of that I may never speak,' he replied sorrowfully. 'I have served my master well and faithfully and hope to do so until one or both of us are dead but…I cannot stand by and see this wickedness go on.'

'You mean—you will help me?' Deborah's voice rose as she stared at him in sudden hope. 'You will help me to escape from this place?'

'Hush, lady. Even here we cannot be certain no one is listening. Don Manola's flagship has been sunk in a battle with the Marquis de Vere. I expect to receive a demand for my master's ransom at any moment...'

Deborah's heart jerked wildly and she felt a surge of excitement. The Don's ship sunk! Then Nicholas had won his battle. He would come for her. Surely he would try to get her back? Oh, please God, let him want her back! He must, he must!

'What do you plan, *señor*?'

'If, as I believe, Miguel hath the sickness on him, we may not see him for several days. As soon as news comes of my master, I shall offer your return for his.' He saw her frown and gave an apologetic shrug. 'My life is here, lady. I must have good reason to let you go or risk Don Manola's displeasure.'

'Supposing Don Miguel recovers before you receive the ransom demand? I beg you, *señor*. Help me to leave now, tonight, before it is too late.'

'Forgive me, I may not—but I can control Miguel. He fears his father's anger and in Don Manola's absence I rule here. I could, if need be, have him chained, shut away from the world and no danger to himself or others—that is within my power.'

Deborah nodded. 'I sensed that you had some authority. His men fear him, but you do not.'

'His men have cause enough, but Miguel does not dare to raise his hand against me. He knows that would be an end to his father's patience. The Don would have him shut away.' The steward smiled. 'Do not be afraid, sweet lady. I shall protect you until the time comes for you to leave. I pledge my life that that monster shall not lay his bloodstained hands on you.'

Deborah accepted his word. He was prepared to do so much and no more. There was nothing she could do or say that would persuade him. His first loyalty was to the master he served.

She looked at him anxiously. 'Have you heard anything of my father, *señor*?'

'Nothing as yet, lady. I believe he was expected to join my master at Cadiz, but I do not know what happened after that.'

'I cannot bear to know nothing of him. I am uneasy, *señor*. I do not think I can eat anything.'

'You must eat,' Montana said. 'You will need your strength to sustain you through the hours of waiting.'

'Yes, I thank you, *señor*. I have eaten little since I was taken from France.' She had almost feared to eat or drink lest some foul poison contaminated the food. She sighed, realizing that she must do as this man said for she had no other friend here. 'I shall be patient since I must.'

'You should pray,' he said. 'Put your faith in God, lady. For no solace can come but from him.'

Deborah inclined her head in assent. Yes, she would pray, had done so constantly since finding herself in Don Miguel's power—but she would put her faith in Nicholas. Only if he came for her could she hope to leave this place alive.

She had a sudden fearful thought. 'What if Don Manola was killed in the battle?'

The steward was silent for a moment, considering. 'I believe he was taken hostage; but if he has since perished... Then I should have no choice—Don Miguel can never be master here. He is hated and feared by all who know and serve his father. I should have to shut him away in a secure prison, where he would be cared for and treated according to his rank but never allowed freedom. You would be returned to your father. I am a good Catholic, and you have done me no harm. I would not have the sin of murder on my soul.'

'Then I shall eat with you and rest easy in my mind, *señor*, for I believe you are an honest man—and I hope your master lives since you wish for it so sincerely.'

He smiled at her, then went to the door and shouted for the servant to bring food. Deborah moved about the room, glancing at precious items that stood here and there displaying the wealth of the castle's owner.

Servants were carrying dishes and platters into the room. After a few moments she was aware of something that made her feel uncomfortable and she had a prickling sensation at the nape of her neck…as though she were being watched. When she turned around to look, she saw that only Anna and the steward were present and neither of them was looking at her.

A shiver ran through her. Montana had spoken of walls having ears. Was it possible that someone had been watching and listening to their conversation all the time?

No, of course not. How could it be possible? The walls were built of solid stone and covered by thick layers of solid hardwood. No one could possibly spy on them. She was letting her imagination run away with her.

She turned as the steward spoke her name and smiled at him. There was nothing to concern her. Don Miguel was ill, and by the time he recovered she might already be on her way home to France.

Lying in the narrow aperture above the ceiling of his father's apartments, Miguel Cortes fought the swirling mist in his head. It was threatening to cast him into that dark place from which he feared there would one day be no return. Especially if that traitorous dog Montana had his way!

Oh, he would delight in that one's death! He had waited, biding his time, knowing that the moment would come. Now at last he saw a way to be free. His father was a prisoner. If no ransom was paid de Vere would no doubt hang him, and Miguel would be free at last of all restraints. For, if his father were dead, the steward would follow soon enough and no one would have the power to defy him. He would take his rightful place as master here—a place that had been too long denied him.

Miguel remembered his father's threats to have him locked away if he ever harmed another woman as he had that stupid wench. That had been a stupid mistake. Village wenches were beneath his father's notice—but she had been of good family. He could not remember why he had wanted her…his head ached too much to think now…but it was something to do with his enemy. He would kill de Vere too when the chance came! Oh, how he hated that French devil!

He was slipping away. No, it must not happen! He tried to hold on. He wanted to punish that proud witch who had treated him as if he were as the dirt beneath her feet. Pretending she was eager for the wedding and planning all the while to escape. Oh, she despised him, thought him mad—but he was the only one who understood. They were all fools, for they did not know he had them at his mercy, that he knew everything that was said and done against him—this was not his only spyhole. He had learned years ago that it was safer to know more than others.

That proud bitch had thought to cheat him with her lies. She had been de Vere's whore! Oh, but she would suffer for it. Before he was finished with her she would wish she had never been born. He giggled as he recalled how the other one had begged on her knees and called out to God to help her.

How could God help her? There was no God. Miguel had heard the voices and he knew that only the Devil had the power of life and death—and he was the true flesh of the Devil. Had his father not told him so that day?

Now they would all pay for daring to despise him. First Montana, and then the woman. He wanted to laugh as he thought of what he meant to do but he was losing control, slipping into the darkness where the demons waited. She would suffer. After Montana was dead… when he was himself again.

Chapter Thirteen

The two ships lay side by side in the bay off the coast of southern Spain. Henri had gone ashore more than an hour ago, his purpose to buy horses for their journey. Pierre had volunteered to take the ransom demand to Don Manola's fortress.

'I would go myself, for I know you risk your life in dealing with Miguel Cortes,' Nicholas had told him when they discussed who should go on this dangerous mission. 'Yet it is a risk I am forbidden to take by common sense. Miguel would rather see me dead than have his father back.'

'I shall go,' Pierre insisted. 'You say I must speak with this Montana, the Don's steward—and no one else?'

Nicholas nodded. 'Don Manola broke his silence when I told him we would ransom him for Deborah. He stressed that we have no chance of reasoning with his son, and I believe him.'

'You would trust the Spaniard—when he meant to sink you under a flag of truce if he could?'

Nicholas gave a wry smile. 'They say all is fair in love or war. When I saw that Miguel's own ship was not with the Don's fleet, I had no intention of sticking to the truce I had offered. It was evident they meant to fight for their cannons were being loaded even as we struck. We defeated them in battle, yet Don Manola knows I am not his enemy. I have told him that with Deborah's return the feud between us ends. He has my word that I shall no longer prey on his ships, and he has given his promise that she shall be returned to me.'

'I would have a care of him, Nico. He may turn on you and stab you in the back.'

'Don Manola needs an heir,' Nicholas said and frowned. 'Now that I have promised to forgo my revenge, he may be able to find another bride for his son. It is a little odd…but I cannot doubt his sincerity or his desire for an heir.'

Nicholas recalled the look in the Don's eyes as he had spoken of his need for an heir.

'I cannot entrust my name and fortune to Miguel,' he had said stiffly. 'But his wife may bear a legitimate son…who may be more fitting.'

'Why do you not marry again yourself, *señor*? You are not too old to have the hope of another, more worthy son.'

Something had flickered in the Spaniard's eyes, some secret sorrow he kept hidden from the world.

'That is between my God and me, sir.'

Nicholas had respected his silence, yet he sensed that the Don had only hatred and disgust for his son who had brought shame on his name. Why had he not punished Miguel for his wickedness and taken another wife so that she could give him the heir he craved?

It was a mystery, but it did not exercise Nicholas for long. His anger had cooled and now he had but one thought—to recover Deborah.

Supposing she had been subjected to the kind of brutality that Isabella had endured before her death? No, he would not let his thoughts dwell on such horror or he would run mad indeed. Don Manola had assured him that Miguel would not touch her until his wedding night. Nicholas could only pray he was right.

Somehow he must get her back before she became that monster's wife.

Would Miguel wait for Don Manola's return as he had been bidden? Or would he seize the chance to disobey his father?

Deborah sighed over the needlework she had been given by Anna. It was a tapestry begun by someone else and looked dusty, as if it had been lying untouched for years. The colours had faded here and there, and she had begun to unpick the stitching, but she had no heart for the task. Indeed, she felt a kind of depression hanging over her, as if this place and its secrets had already begun to crush her spirit.

She would rather die than live here!

It was the morning of the third day since she had been brought to this gloomy castle and it seemed a lifetime. She was restless, tired of being forced to spend so many hours alone. Even when she walked in the small walled garden, which was pleasant enough and had a pretty lily pond with fish swimming beneath its clear water and a little fountain, she felt as if she were suffocating.

Where was Nicholas? Why had he not come for her? Was she too impatient? But it seemed so long since she had seen him…so long!

Hearing the sound of Anna's footsteps, she looked round and saw the old woman beckoning to her.

'You want me to come with you?' Deborah stood as

the old woman smiled and nodded, beckoning urgently. 'Where are we going?'

Anna said something in Spanish, but she spoke so fast that Deborah had no hope of understanding, though she thought the word garden was mentioned. Anna's manner was that of a conspirator and she looked pleased, nodding and smiling encouragingly, which somehow caused hope to spring anew in Deborah because she knew Anna liked her.

As she had thought, she was taken directly to the garden where she saw Carlos Montana waiting for her. He was clearly dressed for riding with a short cloak strung over his shoulder, and as he came towards her she sensed that he had news. He was smiling, anxious for her to reach him.

'I have heard from my master,' he told her. 'He bids me bring you to the church in the village. We are to go alone, and the exchange will be made in secret. The Don fears his son may try to stop us so we must hurry.'

'I am ready to leave,' Deborah said. 'Where is Don Miguel? I have not seen him since the day he brought me here.'

'He sometimes disappears for days on end,' replied the steward with a frown. 'No one knows where he goes or what he does.' He shivered and crossed himself. 'Perhaps not even Miguel himself.'

'Then let us go before he returns.'

Deborah also made the sign of the cross over her heart. These past days and nights she had feared Don Miguel might come to her chamber at any moment, had prayed that he would not. It seemed that God had answered her prayers.

The steward looked anxiously over his shoulder. 'Yes, even though the appointed hour is not quite yet, better that we leave the castle before Miguel learns what we intend.'

Montana led her to a small gate in the wall, which he unlocked with a key from inside his doublet. Outside, a man waited with two horses. Deborah hesitated only a moment before discarding her heavy overdress. She would find it difficult to ride in such a gown and the underdress was perfectly adequate, even though it was now mid-September and the wind could be cool at times despite the heat of the sun.

The groom came forward to help Deborah mount her horse and then stood back. Montana had sprung quickly into the saddle, looking anxiously over his shoulder as if to reassure himself that no one was watching. And then they were riding down the narrow hill road that led to the village and the church.

A sense of relief flooded through Deborah as she felt the wind in her face and saw the open spaces about her. She had never thought to leave that terrible place alive when she entered it with Don Miguel. Now she was on her way to meet Nicholas. Soon she would be with him again and everything would be as it had been before the Spaniards took her prisoner.

Perhaps her father would be with the Don? She had heard nothing of him from Carlos Montana, and she did not know whether he had been with Don Manola on his flagship when it was sunk. Don Miguel said that her father would be waiting for her in Spain, but the steward seemed to know nothing of him. She could only pray he was safely in England.

Montana paused as they approached the village, which seemed completely deserted: no women gossiping in the street, nor even a stray cur sniffing at the roadside. The steward waited for Deborah to bring her horse to a stand beside his. He appeared to be waiting for something and she sensed his unease before he spoke.

'What is wrong?' she asked, looking at him anxiously. 'Why are you worried?'

'I am not sure. It is so quiet. No one is in the street. It is usually this way when…'

Before he could finish there was a shout and the sound of running feet and then several men came pouring out of the houses to surround them. Deborah knew at once that these were not Nicholas's men.

'Get away!' the steward cried. 'It is a trap.'

His warning came too late. Neither of them could break away. The soldiers—Miguel's men—had heavy guns pointed at them. And a man was leaving the church, another soldier dragging a black-robed priest behind him.

'So you have come to my wedding, Montana. I am honoured.' Don Miguel's eyes glittered. 'You promised you would see me shut away before I wed her, but I am always one step ahead of you. You are a fool and a traitor—and traitors deserve to die like the dogs they are.' He raised his arm and, without further warning, pointed the pistol he was carrying and shot his father's trusted steward in the heart.

Montana's body jerked, then he slumped forward and fell to the ground, his blood seeping into the dust.

'Murderer!' Deborah cried as her horse reared in fright and she struggled desperately to hold her seat. 'Devil! Devil!'

The soldiers nearest caught at the reins, wrestling with and subduing the terrified beast, and then they were pulling her none too gently from its back. She struggled and railed at them furiously, but they were too many and too strong. Her head went up defiantly as they dragged her to stand in front of Miguel.

'You are insane,' she told him coldly, knowing that the time for pretense was over. 'You have killed a good man. You may as well shoot me too, for I shall never marry you.'

'Oh, but you will,' he said softly, a cruel smile on his lips. 'You have no idea what pain is, Madonna—but you shall learn. I promise you shall learn very soon now.'

'Do as you will, you shall never have me—merely my broken body. And I shall not wed you. You cannot force me to be your wife. I despise you, Miguel Cortes. You are nothing to me.'

'Stupid witch,' he muttered, furious at her defiance even now. She should have been begging for mercy, as all the other women had. There must be a way to break her. His gaze fell on the priest and he smiled. 'Bring the priest.' The soldiers hastened to obey and the poor man was dragged in front of Deborah. 'You see this craven creature? He fears to die. Even though he preaches of heaven to those foolish enough to believe him, he longs to live. Defy me and he dies next.'

'You could not then marry me,' Deborah cried and regretted her words the moment they left her lips. Miguel struck the priest, who screamed and fell to his knees to beg for mercy.

'He will suffer more—and I'll kill everyone in the village. Every minute you defy me, a man, woman or child shall die for it.' He gestured towards the houses and two soldiers started forward, clearly intending to begin murdering the villagers.

'No!' Deborah cried. 'Enough. I beg you. Do not hurt anyone else. I shall be your wife since you desire it.'

Miguel's eyes gleamed with satisfaction. 'Bring her and the priest!' he muttered. 'We shall have a wedding just as my father wished. As de Vere hangs him, he shall die happy in the knowledge that my sons shall inherit his name and wealth.' He threw back his head and laughed, clearly much amused by his own cleverness.

Deborah was appalled by his behaviour. Surely he had not been this mad before? He had appeared to be in command of his mind during the voyage here, but, hearing his wild laughter, she was shocked beyond measure. What had happened to him in the days when he had disappeared? Was the sickness still upon him? Or had he crossed forever that divide between madness and sanity?

She shuddered, her courage almost deserting her for a moment, but then her head went up and she faced him proudly. She allowed the soldiers to take her inside the church.

From the outside it had looked unremarkable, just a simple village place of worship, but inside there was evidence of great wealth. The altar was decorated with gold leaf and the hangings were of cloth of gold, richly embroidered with semi-precious stones. Don Manola had evidently been a good patron—but what would happen to this place if he did not return?

Deborah feared for the people who lived and worshipped here. With no restraints to hold him back, this madman would do exactly as he pleased—for men would serve him for his gold no matter what he chose to do. His soldiers were thrusting the priest to stand before the altar.

'Marry us!' Miguel commanded. 'Do as I tell you or you die, dog!'

The priest was trembling, obviously unwilling to go through with this unlawful ceremony, yet afraid to disobey. His face was a pasty white as he looked from Miguel to Deborah.

'Do you consent?' he asked her in a croaking whisper. 'Forgive me, lady. You must or he will do as he has threatened. You do not know what he is capable of...' He gave a cry of fear as one of the soldiers hit him in the face and cringed away like some frightened animal.

Deborah hesitated. What choice had she? She must go through with this charade or many would die. Besides, there was no hope of escape now. Nicholas had not come for her. The letter must have been a trick—for how else would Miguel know of their plans? His cruel mind had devised this plot to show her that she was completely at his mercy—and he had succeeded in making her betray herself.

She heard the priest intoning a garbled version of what she supposed must be the wedding ceremony, her eyes fixed on a stained glass window portraying the crucifixion of Christ. When the priest was silent at last, she raised her head, knowing that she must speak now or be the cause of innocent lives lost.

'I do,' she said in a clear voice.

'No!' The words echoed in the stillness of the church. 'By God, you shall not wed that devil while I live.'

Deborah whirled round, a cry of welcome on her lips. He had come. Nicholas had come to save her. There were armed men with him—and a Spaniard. A tall, grey-haired, distinguished man she instinctively knew was Don Manola.

'*Le Diable*...' Miguel cried. His eyes glittered and, before Deborah knew what he intended, he had grabbed hold of her. He twisted her arm up behind her back, making her gasp with pain, using her as a shield. 'Stand back, all of you. I shall kill her if anyone comes near.' He was holding a knife to her throat now, its point pricking her skin. He glanced at the priest. 'Continue, fool.

Marry us or she dies.'

The priest was near to gibbering with terror. He looked from Miguel to the newcomers uncertainly. No one moved as he gabbled incomprehensible words then made a hurried sign of the cross.

He glanced nervously at Miguel. 'She is your wife, *señor*.'

'No!' Nicholas said. 'This is not legal. I can show just cause why they may not be wed. She is in law my wife.'

'Then I shall kill her and you.' Miguel looked at his soldiers, in particular the one who had dragged the priest to the church. 'Take him—but alive. I want to arrange some entertainment for my friend before he dies.'

'No!' Deborah cried. 'No…'

'Let her go. I command it.' Don Manola stepped forward. 'Release the woman, Miguel. She does not belong to you. Let her go and we shall find another more fitting wife for you. This marriage no longer pleases me.'

'No. I want her—and him.' Miguel glared at the soldiers who had made no attempt to obey him and were moving back as if to dissociate themselves now that Don Manola had spoken. It was clear who was the master here. Despite their fear of his son, the men's respect was for the Don. 'We have them both. We shall have revenge for our ships.' Miguel giggled suddenly, sounding like a nervous youth. 'You should be pleased with me, Father. It is all as you said it would be. I have my bride as you commanded. I shall give you the heirs you want…'

The Don moved slowly towards Miguel, his eyes locked to Miguel's in a silent challenge. His face was expressionless, relentless. Miguel blinked and stared at him uncertainly.

'What is it? What do you want of me? Father…'

'Let her go. Come here to me, Mistress Stirling.'

Miguel's hold tightened for a moment as if he would defy his father, the knife seeming to prick her deeper, and then, quite suddenly, he released her. Deborah went quickly to Don Manola, who thrust her behind him without a word, his eyes continuing to hold those of his son.

Miguel was clearly uneasy. He made an odd sound in his throat as if choking and his eyes flicked away, but returned, drawn as if on a string to meet his father's compelling gaze.

'I did not hurt her,' he mumbled, sounding afraid. 'I did not lay a finger on her—tell him, Madonna. Tell him I did not touch you. She is chaste, Father. Just as you said she must be.'

'Good—that is good,' Don Manola said soothingly. His voice held a strange quality, as if he controlled by the power of his will alone. 'Now you must come with me, Miguel.'

'Where are we going?' Miguel's eyes rolled wildly. 'No! Not to that place—not to her! I won't go. I want to stay here and play with my wife. You promised me…' He backed away, the fear clearly in his face for all to see. 'You tricked me. You tricked me.' He held out his hand and the knife gleamed silver in a ray of sunlight flooding in through the high windows. 'I shall kill you. Yes, you shall die. Then I shall be master…' He raised his arm but the shot rang out before he could spring, and he crumpled into a heap at his father's feet, staring up in bewildered surprise from his dead eyes.

'May God forgive me,' Don Manola said and dropped the smoking pistol on the floor. 'I have desecrated His Holy Place. My sins are heavy on my soul.'

He sank to his knees on the tiled floor beside the body of his son, closing the staring eyes. Then he made the sign of the cross on Miguel's forehead.

'God forgive this poor creature who knew not what he did. The sin was mine and mine alone.'

'Come away. Leave him to his penance and his grief.'

Deborah felt the touch of a hand on her arm. She had not dared to move, but now turned gladly to find herself staring at a stranger.

'Nicholas…' she whispered as she saw his cold eyes and harsh stare. 'What is it? Tell me, what is wrong?'

'Come away, madam.'

Deborah felt the grasp of his fingers on her arm. Why had he called her madam in that way? As if she were a stranger—Miguel's wife, in truth. Surely he could not believe she had given her promise to marry the Spaniard willingly? And yet there was no other explanation for his coldness to her. Why was he so willing to believe ill of her?

Henri came to her as she emerged into the heat of the afternoon, which struck her forcefully after the chill of the church. Her head was aching and she felt unwell. Was she dreaming? Henri here? She stared at him in disbelief and then dawning delight as she realized that the fall from his horse had not killed him after all.

'Oh, Henri,' she cried. 'You are alive. I am so very glad. So very glad.'

'My lady,' he said, smiling at her. 'I am happy to see you.'

'I thought you dead when they took me away,' she said, hands outstretched as he came to her. He took them, kissing her cheek. She smiled up at him as relief made her giddy. 'It is so good to know you are alive. I grieved for you, my friend, truly I did.'

'I am glad to find you well,' Henri replied. 'Had you been harmed I should never have forgiven myself.'

Her eyes moved to the body of Carlos Montana, which was still lying in the street, but with his face decently covered. She also noticed that Miguel's soldiers had been forced to lay down their arms and were huddled together, looking at their captors uneasily as if they feared their fate.

'Miguel killed him,' she said on a sob. 'He was trying to help me—and he shot him like a mad dog.' She shuddered, putting a hand to her eyes. Her head was spinning. Henri put an arm about her shoulders as he saw how pale she was. 'Oh, it was terrible…terrible.' She was shivering as he held her protectively, hushing her.

'It is over now, sweet lady. We feared the worst when we discovered Montana lying there, but it seems we were in time.'

'We came here to ransom Don Manola,' Deborah said, blinking as she fought back her tears. She felt so ill, but she must not give way now. She had to explain, to make Nicholas understand and forgive her—because somehow he had misunderstood her reasons for leaving France with the Spaniards. He believed that she had run away with them because she wanted to, when she had done so only in order to save *his* people, because she could not bear to see the home he loved razed to the ground—but he thought her false and faithless! It was because she had tried to run away from him before, of course, because she had broken her word to him the night he caught her at the stables. 'Somehow Miguel had learned of your plans and he got here first. He killed his father's steward and threatened to start killing innocent women and children if I did not agree to marry him.'

'Ah, I understand,' Henri said, smiling as she released herself from his embrace and accepted his kerchief to wipe her cheeks. He glanced towards Nicholas to see if he had heard her explanation, but he had walked away and was speaking to Don Manola, who had just now emerged from the church. 'I knew you must have been forced into this—but why did you not come with me that day when I begged you to ride away?'

She stared in surprise. 'But you know. Surely you know? I was afraid for the others. The château was unprotected while Nicholas was away. I did not wish to be the cause of death and destruction to his people.'

'No—surely you could not have thought that?' Henri frowned. 'You must have known that Nico would not leave you or the others vulnerable to an attack. We had more than enough men to beat off the Spaniards that day. They were hidden, waiting for the signal should an attack come.'

'I did not know that,' Deborah replied. She was feeling so very unwell. Perhaps it was the heat or the strain of the past few days? 'I thought you dead after your horse rolled on you, and I could not bear that others should give their lives for my sake. All I wanted was for the Spaniards to leave Nicholas's people in peace, even if it meant that I must suffer—for I should never have lived as that monster's bride. I should have taken my own life first.' She laid her hand on his arm, giving him a look of appeal. 'Oh, you must believe me. You must! Please do say you believe me, Henri.'

'But of course,' he said and smiled at her. 'I wondered what had happened for I have no memory of those last minutes before I was knocked unconscious. I shall explain to Nicholas...'

Don Manola was coming towards them, clearly in-tending to speak to her, and Nicholas had gone to join Pierre. They were obviously preparing to gather their men to leave. There was no more to be done here.

'Mistress Stirling,' Don Manola said. 'I have come to beg your pardon for what has been done to you in my name. The fault is mine. I insisted on this marriage. I have too many sins to answer for—and I beg your for-giveness, though I may never be absolved in the eyes of God.'

Deborah's heart was wrung with pity as she saw the agony in the Don's eyes and understood his suffering. She had learned something of him from his steward and she knew that he had once been a good and devout Christian. Something had changed him, some secret trag-edy—and he had allowed himself to become obsessed with the one thing he had known was forbidden.

'I am truly sorry for your grief, *señor*. You must have loved your son a great deal…'

The Don took a deep breath and Deborah sensed that what he was about to say was not easy for him, would cost him pain.

'No. I hated him from the moment he was born. Had I had the courage I would have strangled him then. I loved his mother, and because of that love she bore a child—that was my sin. Not hers or her son's. I knew she should never have a child and yet I still went to her. After the birth she became truly insane. I allowed the world to believe she had died of a fever—but she lives even to this day. Shut away and cared for tenderly by nuns. I should have put Miguel away years ago, but I needed an heir. I could not marry, but he could. I meant to have a child with his wife…' At her gasp of horror, he crossed himself, his face contorting with grief and guilt. 'He would never have touched you. I would have spared you that at least.'

It was too horrible! She could bear no more. Deborah felt the vomit in her throat and her senses began to swim. Her head was going round and round in circles and the ground zoomed up to meet her. She moaned and put her hand out to grab at Henri's arm, but the blackness took her mind and she did not know that it was Nicholas who caught her as she fell.

Deborah opened her eyes to find that she was lying in a bed. She glanced around the small room and knew that she was once more in the cabin of the *Siren's Song*. How had she come here? She could remember nothing of the journey to the coast. Her head ached and her mouth tasted bitter, as though she had been ill.

Someone was opening the door. She pushed herself up against the pillows, her heart beating wildly. She felt weak and her limbs were heavy. Surely she must have been ill?

Had Nicholas come to see her? Where was he? She wanted him. She wanted him to hold her in his arms and kiss her—to tell her he loved her and would make her forget the horror she had endured.

'Deborah—my dearest child. Are you feeling better at last? You have had a fever and we were worried about you.'

'Father?' She stared at him, tears springing to her eyes. She felt so weak and Nicholas was not here to comfort her. Was he angry with her? Did he think she had run away from him? Her father was here, but not Nicholas. She held her hand out to Sir Edward. 'Is it really you, Father? How did you come here?'

'I was on board Don Manola's flagship when it was sunk,' he said, moving closer to the bed. 'Oh, my poor daughter. How pale you are. Can you ever forgive me for what has happened to you?'

Deborah slipped her hand into his and he held it to his lips and kissed it. Tears were trickling down her cheek. She felt like a little girl again and wanted him to comfort her.

'It was so frightening,' she confessed. 'When Miguel Cortes took me on his ship…I thought I was lost. He was insane, evil. He frightened me, though I could not let him see it. I would have died rather than wed him, Father.' She clung to his hand. 'You are not angry with me? Please say you are not angry with me.'

'How could I be? You were not to blame,' Sir Edward said, looking at her sadly. 'It was my fault, child. I should have made more inquiries before I considered the marriage.'

'But I disobeyed you. I went walking alone in the mist. Had I not—I might still have been safe at home with you.'

'And perhaps I should have given you to that monster without realizing what I did,' Sir Edward said and crossed himself. 'God forbid! I was wrong to trust Don Manola, Deborah. He is not the man I knew. When I was on his flagship he had me locked below and I might have died there for all he knew or cared. I fought my way out and was knocked into the sea by a mast that came crashing down. I might have drowned had one of de Vere's men not seen me and hauled me out of the wreckage. De Vere himself tended me when I was sick. I have reason to thank him for my life—and yours.'

'Where is he—the marquis?' she asked, brushing away her tears.

'On the *Antoinette*, I believe,' Sir Edward said. 'He has business to conclude and bid me tell you he would visit you in a few weeks' time.'

'In a few weeks?' Deborah stared at her father in distress. 'But…' Pride made her hold back the words she had been about to say. 'Where are we going, Father?'

'I am taking you home,' Sir Edward said. 'You have been through a terrible ordeal, Deborah, and de Vere agrees with me that you need time to recover your health and spirits. He stayed with us until he was sure you would mend and then he transferred to his other ship. I think he was angry with you for running away after you had given him your promise to marry him. Your friend Henri Moreau is taking us home and will escort us.' He smiled and stroked her cheek. 'You will want to see Sarah wed, I dare say?'

'Yes…' Deborah was bleeding inside but she could not let it show. Her wedding was to have been as soon as Nicholas returned from his meeting with the Don— but now she would not see him for weeks. It could only mean that he no longer wanted to marry her. He must believe that she had betrayed him. Surely he could not think that she would willingly have married Miguel Cortes? 'Yes, I had forgotten poor Sarah's wedding. She must be on thorns, wondering what is to happen.'

Sir Edward smiled at her. 'I knew I was right. You feel weak now, my child, but your spirits will return once you are safe in your own home. I am sure it is for the best and everything will seem better when you have had time to reflect. A period of quiet is what you need now.'

'Yes, Father. I expect you are right.'

She did not want to go home. England was no longer her home—she belonged in that open, sunny house in

France where everyone laughed and sang and she had been so happy.

'Sleep peacefully, my dearest,' Sir Edward stood up. 'I shall look after you from now on. Nothing shall be forced on you again. You shall stay with me for as long as you wish. Indeed, I shall be happy if you choose never to marry.'

Deborah closed her eyes as he went out and shut the door softly behind him. He was being so kind and considerate to her—but she did not want to retire from the world and live always with her father. She wanted to be the wife of a man whose kisses made her melt with bliss. She loved Nicholas and would never stop loving him— but he no longer wanted her.

Chapter Fourteen

'What is this I hear, laddie?' King James frowned at Nicholas. 'Some wild tale of abduction? Have ye gone too far this time? Snatched a wench of good family and made away with her? I shall be obliged to see ye hang if the father demands retribution for your crime.' He chuckled as if much amused by the tale, which had been circulating the court for weeks.

'I believe Sir Edward will make no complaint against me,' Nicholas replied, but gave no answering smile.

'Aye, weel, 'tis just as well, since I have use for ye, laddie. *Baby* has begged me to command him home. I suspect 'tis as I feared—these rascally Spanish lawyers have demanded too much and the prince must be brought home. But I must know what is happening. I want the truth of this affair, not some tale concocted to please me. Will ye go?'

'Of course, Sire.' Nicholas did not hesitate, even though he had plans of his own. 'I shall sail at once and place myself at the prince's disposal.'

'Spain will not be pleased if the marriage negotiations have broken down.' James shook his head. 'That they have played us false I dinna doubt. Bring my son back to me, laddie. I canna rest easy in my mind until he is safe home.'

'Yes, of course.' Nicholas frowned as he saw the anxious look in the King's eyes. 'Do you fear war over this business, Sire?'

'I have always tried to make friends with those who would make war on us, but…' The King sighed heavily and shook his head. 'My heart is heavy over this, laddie. I'll not deny it. We must see what comes of this unlucky chance. Once my son is home, we shall know more of the true situation.'

Nicholas bowed, aware that the interview was at an end. 'I shall take the *Antoinette* and leave with the tide.'

James smiled wearily. 'I am thankful I shall not have to hang ye, laddie. The King does not have so many friends that he can spare one to the gallows.'

A faint smile flickered in Nicholas's eyes as he bowed and left the King's private apartments. He had no desire to sail once more for Spain, but a favour had been asked and must be granted. Besides, he must give Deborah time to recover from her ordeal. Nicholas had not wanted to leave her while she was still caught in a fever, but Sir Edward had demanded that he be allowed to take his daughter home, and Nicholas had been forced to give way.

He blamed himself for all she had suffered. He had no right to hold her to the contract she had signed, though it was lawfully binding. If she decided that she would be happier staying at home with her father—or married to someone else—then the contract must somehow be undone.

She was clearly very attached to Henri, had been so from the very beginning. He was her friend and she had shown her joy when they met again outside the church in Spain... Nicholas scowled as he recalled the moment he had heard Deborah promise to wed Miguel Cortes. For a few minutes he had feared she was truly that devil's bride and beyond his reach. After reflection he had realized that such a ceremony could not have been legal, but might still have prevented a true marriage for years while the Papal authorities wrangled over the finer points. Except that he would have made her a widow had the Don not done so first.

A shiver went through Nicholas as he remembered what Henri had revealed to him. How Don Manola could bear the weight of such sins he did not know. He crossed himself. It was a long time since Nicholas had been to confession, but now he felt the need. A blackness had entered his soul after Isabella's murder, festering inside him for too long. He must regain his faith and ask God's forgiveness before he was fit to marry any woman.

He had told Don Manola that the feud between them was at an end. All he wanted now was to take his wife back to France—but did she wish to go with him?

'I am glad to have you back,' Sarah said and hugged her cousin. 'I was afraid you would not be here for my wedding—indeed, I wondered if I should ever see you again.'

'I should not have been happy to miss your wedding, cousin.'

Sarah looked at her uncertainly. Deborah had been home only a few hours, of course, having arrived late the previous evening, and they had not really had much chance to talk, but she seemed subdued, unlike her normal confident self.

'Was it so very terrible?' she said softly. 'You must have been frightened. I think the Marquis de Vere must be very wicked to have snatched you as he did that day. My poor uncle was half out of his mind. I have never seen him so distressed. I think he should petition the King to have the marquis arrested.'

'No! No, you do not understand,' Deborah cried, alarmed at the idea. Her father could not possibly be contemplating such a move, surely? 'The marquis was seeking to protect me from Don Manola's son. Had Father and I sailed for Spain as we intended, it might have been too late. I might have been married before we knew anything was wrong.' She shuddered as she recalled the Don's last words to her. 'You cannot imagine—Don Manola intended...' She shook her head. 'No, I cannot speak of it. Forgive me, Sarah. I must be alone for a while.'

She left her cousin staring after her as she went quickly from the room. Fearing Sarah might follow, she went out into the garden. It was a cool, overcast afternoon, which looked as if it might turn to rain, and she had no cloak, but she did not wish to return to the house to fetch one. She needed to be alone for a while, to have time to sort out her feelings.

Her head down against the wind, she walked quickly towards a small summerhouse where she would be sheltered from the worst of the weather.

It was late September now and the roses had been spoiled by heavy rain. Before long it would be autumn and then the leaves would start to fall—and then it would be winter. Deborah had always loved her home, never minding the isolation that was sometimes forced upon them by severe conditions, when the roads turned to a quagmire and it was impossible to travel, but the thought of long dark evenings alone made her spirits sink. Sarah would be gone, and Sir Edward often spent hours in his library lost to the world. Deborah would be left to her needlework and her thoughts.

Oh, how she wished Nicholas would come to her, but there had been no word from him since they reached England. She had hoped for a letter or a message, just to say he would come as soon as he could—but there was nothing.

Henri had escorted them back to their home, where he would stay for a few days before returning to his ship, in which he intended to sail for France. She wished with all her heart that she could go with him!

Deborah entered the summerhouse and sat down on a wooden bench, her arms wrapped about her as she let her mind drift back to those sunlit days in France when she had danced and Nicholas had made her feel as if she was loved and wanted.

She sat there for almost half an hour, lost in her dreams, deliberately blocking out the other memories—the ones that had begun to haunt her. It was odd how she had felt so strong when she was in Spain, but now, when she was safe, she was haunted by what might have happened.

The sound of booted footsteps made her look up, and in that moment she realized that she had turned cold. She was shivering as she rose to her feet just as Henri entered the summerhouse.

'Your cousin thought I might find you here,' Henri said, looking at her anxiously. He saw how pale she was and took off his cloak to place it about her shoulders. 'You are chilled to the bone, lady. Will you not let me take you back to the house now so that you can warm yourself?'

'Yes, of course I shall come with you.' Deborah smiled at him. 'I was thinking and I did not notice the cold—but I am glad of your cloak, sir, and you are good to give it to me.'

'You were thinking of Nico?' he asked, but did not need to be told the answer.

Deborah met his concerned gaze. 'You know me too well, I think. I had hoped we might have had some word from him before this.'

Henri frowned. 'You are not the only one, mistress. I do not understand him. When you were ill, it was he who sat with you until the fever seemed to abate and he was sure you would recover. I do not know why he did not accompany you home himself. I could have carried any messages he wished to send to London.'

Deborah's voice was caught with emotion. 'I fear he is angry with me. He believes I went willingly with Miguel Cortes—that I was a willing bride.'

'Perhaps he is angry,' Henri replied, looking thoughtful. 'Nico is not always easy to know, my lady. And since Isabella died…' He frowned. 'I know he has suffered agonies of mind—but he should not have hurt you so. You have suffered enough these past weeks.'

'You are so kind…' Her eyes misted as she gazed up at him.

'What may I do to make you smile?' Henri asked. 'Shall I go to London and command him to come to you?'

Deborah shook her head, a sad smile on her lips. 'No, Henri. I would not have you do that. He must come when it pleases him. I would not have him forced—in any way.'

If he wanted to be released from his promise to wed her she would not say him nay, though it broke her heart.

'He is a fool!' Henri said sharply. 'I would not desert you, Mistress Stirling.' An intense longing came into his eyes. 'I know it is not I you love, sweet lady—but I would give my life to serve you. If Nico were fool enough to let you slip through his fingers, I would offer you my heart and name. I do not press my claims above his—but I am here if you need me.'

'Oh, Henri,' she said. 'You are my friend and I love you dearly as my friend, but...' She faltered and could not go on, for she did not wish to give him pain.

Henri took her hand and kissed it. 'I know it is too soon to speak of such matters, but should you ever change your mind you have only to send for me and I shall hasten to your side.'

Deborah nodded but her throat was too tight with emotion to answer for a moment. He was so gentle, so kind, and she wished it was he she had fallen in love with—but it was not. Her heart was breaking for a wicked charming rogue who seemed to have forgotten her.

'We shall speak of other matters,' Henri said. 'Sir Edward has begged me to stay for your cousin's wedding and I have said I will—if you would be pleased to have me stay?'

'Yes, yes, I should,' Deborah replied, having conquered her urgent desire to weep. 'Unless you have pressing business waiting at home?'

'Nothing that would drag me from your side if you have need of me.'

'It is not fair to you,' Deborah replied. 'But I should miss you if you leave us too soon. My cousin does not understand what happened...and my father is consumed with guilt. You are the only one I can talk to about...that day.'

Henri's smile seemed to embrace her. 'You need not fear to speak to me, my lady. If anything troubles you... anything you are afraid to speak of to your father...'

He offered his arm and Deborah laid her hand on his velvet sleeve. 'I have dreams sometimes,' she confessed. 'I dream that Miguel Cortes comes for me.'

'You may rest easy,' Henri said, glancing at her in concern. 'He is truly dead. I made certain of that before we left the village. You are quite safe, my lady. Nico's feud with the Don is at an end. No one will seek to harm you again. I promise you.'

'Thank you.' She blushed. 'I know it is foolish, but I wanted to be certain he was really dead. It all seems like a nightmare. I hardly know what happened that day. I had already begun to feel strange…long before I fainted in the street.'

'You had a fever—perhaps something you ate or merely the heat of the sun. It was a very hot day. After what you had been through, it was scarcely surprising you were ill.' He looked at her intently. 'You are still pale. Are you feeling unwell?'

'Oh, no,' she said and smiled. 'I am truly recovered— and your concern makes me feel so much better. I believe I shall not have bad dreams again now you have reassured me.'

'I am glad I was able to ease your mind.'

Henri frowned as they walked back to the house in silence. Where was Nicholas? It was he who should have been here to comfort Deborah. Why had he abandoned her so cruelly?

Henri felt very angry with his friend. If Nico did not come by the time Mistress Palmer was wed, he would go to France and fetch him!

He was bending over her, his strange, staring eyes feasting on her naked flesh. She felt the touch of his clammy hand, smelled the stench of his unclean body. His flesh was rotting, falling away from the bones of his face...

Deborah gave a cry of fear and woke from the nightmare. She was sweating, trembling as she sat up in bed and looked about her. It was just a dream. She was in her own room and nothing could harm her.

She had not had the dream for three nights, but this time it had been worse than the others had before it and she still felt afraid, even though she knew it was foolish.

She left her bed and went over to the window, staring out at the moonlit garden. How foolish she was to let herself be frightened by a silly dream. Miguel Cortes was dead. She was not his bride.

Where was Nicholas? Why did he not come to her? Three weeks had passed since Henri had brought them home to England and there was still no word from Nicholas.

He could not love her or he would not have stayed away so long. Surely he must know how she longed for him. He was never far from her thoughts, and her heart called out for him. If he cared for her at all, he would surely know how desperately she needed him.

'You look lovely,' Deborah said and kissed her cousin's cheek as she gave her a blue silk garter sewn with pearls. 'Master Henderson is very lucky in his bride—and I hope he knows it.'

'Yes, he does,' Sarah replied and dimpled with pleasure as she hugged her cousin. 'I cannot wait to be his wife—but what of you? Are you feeling better at last, Deborah?'

'Yes.' Deborah smiled. It was now mid-October, almost a month since she had come home, and she was beginning to feel more like her old self. Her grief had begun to turn to anger and she no longer gave way to tears in the privacy of her chamber. She had not had a dream for seven nights now and she believed they might have gone at last. 'I am not as tired now. Besides, I refuse to be miserable today. This is your wedding day and we must all be merry. I want to celebrate my dearest cousin's happiness.'

Deborah had that morning woken with a new determination. She would put her hopes of Nicholas aside and make the most of her life. It would be foolish to spend the rest of her days sighing over a man who clearly did not want her.

He had stayed away because he wanted her to understand that the contract was broken. In France he had thought himself obliged to wed her for honour's sake, because she was under his roof—but now that she was back with her father he had forgotten her.

Well, she had been warned. Marie had told her that it was Isabella he loved, and that once his revenge was complete he would no longer want her. Deborah had not believed her, thinking it was just the other woman's spite—but it seemed she had been right.

It was a cool, crisp day but thankfully there was no sign of the dank mists, which had curled across from the northern moors and made the weather so unpleasant this past week. The sun had decided to shine as if to bless the day and the bride.

Sir Edward was to give Sarah to her husband, and so it was Henri who escorted Deborah to the church. They stood together to watch as the couple took the vows that would bind them for the rest of their lives.

Afterwards, they threw handfuls of dried rose petals

over the bride and groom, and then the guests all trooped back to Sir Edward's house where a feast was waiting.

Sir Edward had spared no expense for his ward's wedding. There were minstrels to entertain them with songs of love, jugglers, and clowns to make them laugh, especially a little fool no higher than Deborah's knees, who ran around with a pig's bladder on a stick, attacking all the biggest men and poking fun at them.

After the sumptuous feast of numerous courses had been served, the musicians set up a merry tune and the bride and groom began the dancing.

'Will you dance, lady?' Henri asked Deborah when the guests began to join the bridal couple in the dance.

'Yes, yes, I shall,' Deborah said as she took his outstretched hand. 'Why not?' Why should she not dance and be happy? She had done nothing for which she ought to feel shame. And if she had noticed that some of the ladies looked at her oddly, she would not let it upset her. Not today of all days!

Soon they were whirling and twirling in a mad romp that had everyone breathless. This was followed by more stately dances, and then yet another wild romp that made Deborah laugh. Her cheeks were flushed with becoming colour and her eyes were shining as she gazed up at her partner.

It was the first time she had felt happy in weeks, and it was so good to cast off her cares for a little time. Henri was her friend and she knew she could trust him, so when he bent his head and kissed her lightly on the mouth she did not push him away.

It meant nothing—just that they were both swept away with the music and laughter, and had perhaps drunk a little more wine than usual.

Watching from the other end of the hall, where he had

been standing unobserved for some minutes, Nicholas scowled. He had been fretting while he was kept kicking his heels waiting the prince's pleasure, and now it seemed he need not have been anxious. Deborah was in no need of comfort—she was clearly quite happy with the situation as it was.

He turned away, leaving the revellers to their amusement. He had ridden hard from London and he was weary. If he spoke to Deborah now, he might say something he would later regret.

Deborah retired to her chamber only after the bride and groom had been properly fêted and conveyed to their marriage bed. To spare Sarah's blushes, Sir Edward had forbidden the guests to enter her chamber, declaring that the old ways were best forgotten.

'I'll not have my niece mortified by outdated customs,' he had declared stoutly. 'We shall see them to the door and then leave them in peace, my friends.'

It was the kindest way, and Deborah was glad her cousin had been spared some of the more vulgar jests that were commonplace at weddings. She kissed Sarah good night and whispered to her, then turned away to her own rooms at once. Now that the laughing and dancing were over, her spirits had begun to sink once more.

Where was Nicholas? Why had he not come to claim her?

Deborah submitted to the ministrations of her maid, an elderly woman who had cared for her since childhood. Jane was a kindly soul but did not make her laugh as Louise had. She dismissed her once she was undressed and sat brushing her own hair by the fire.

She sighed and laid the brush down. She was tired and yet felt unable to sleep. Going over to her window, she looked out and thought how much more inviting the garden was at Chalfont.

The sounds of revelry were dying away now. Some of the guests had already retired, though many of the men had no chamber of their own and would be forced to rest where they could find space. Most of the ladies were sharing a bed with other ladies, as was usual on such occasions. Deborah was relieved that she had not been asked to share or give up her room to guests, as she might have been at another time.

The house was filled to capacity. Had it been just her and her family, Deborah would have gone down to walk alone in the gardens, but she knew that would not be wise while they had so much company. Men had drunk a great deal of wine at the wedding—and a woman with a blemished reputation might find little respect at such a time.

The ladies had not been the only ones to glance at her with speculation in their eyes that night. She had heard no whispers behind her back, but she did not doubt that many believed she had been violated. It was so unfair! She had done nothing to deserve censure, but few would believe her innocent.

There was one escape for her from the life of seclusion that would otherwise be forced on her, she knew. Nicholas might have forgotten her, but Henri was becoming more ardent in his wooing. He was always respectful towards her, but this evening he had taken his chance to give her that brief kiss.

She knew he would speak to her father if she gave him hope. In her heart Deborah believed she was Nicholas's wife. She had given him her promise and her love, and the marriage contracts had been signed. She supposed they could be broken, though it would not be an easy thing to accomplish. Nor did she wish for it, though she had come to believe that Nicholas must. Had it been otherwise, he would surely have sought her out long since.

She refused to weep or continue to break her heart for him. Pride had reasserted itself. She was the daughter of Sir Edward Stirling and a gentlewoman. Let others think what they would of her. She would hold her head high and be damned to them all.

But, oh, she did wish that Nicholas would come!

'Where have you been all this time?' Henri demanded when Nicholas approached him after the bride and groom had gone upstairs. 'I had begun to think something must have happened to you.'

'I had business I could not ignore.'

Nicholas glared at him. The King had sworn him to secrecy over the part he had played in bringing back Prince Charles and the Duke of Buckingham, for he had not merely been a part of the escort but had done what he could to learn the truth of the affair.

'No one must know aught of this, laddie,' James had told him when they spoke privately together at the palace. 'Let history say what it will. And I doubt not that much will be said about this sorry business.'

Nicholas nodded his agreement, knowing the King would not be pleased by what he had to tell. 'I have heard the Spanish marriage contract was signed—and that both the prince and Buckingham agreed the terms. In Spain they expect the marriage of Prince Charles and the Infanta to go ahead at the appointed time. If it does not, they will see this as an insult to both the King and his daughter.'

'Aye, I know it.' The King looked angry. 'I have had

to endure many complaints against the prince and Buckingham—but I canna say what is true and what false.
We shall see what transpires. Yet if I believed what I
have been told, I should say that Buckingham had served
me ill.'

Nicholas wisely held his tongue. James was angry at
his favourite over the failure of their plans—to say nothing of the waste of so much gold and jewellery!—but
he was at times capricious and could be swayed by those
he cared for, right or wrong.

Buckingham and the prince were home again, brought
back to England by an English fleet, of which several
ships belonged to Nicholas, and those courtiers who had
spoken out against the duke while he was away were
not as vociferous now. Everyone knew that the rascal
would likely persuade the King to his side, though his
rash behaviour in seeming to agree to so many of the
Spanish King's demands had brought about a serious
situation. The Papal dispensation had arrived and there
was nothing to stop the wedding taking place by proxy—
except the prince's instructions to his ambassador not to
present them.

On his arrival in England in early October, Prince
Charles had been greeted with scenes of wild joy because the people believed the marriage would not now
take place. It had always been unpopular—and had the
details of what the prince and Buckingham had promised
in King James's name become common knowledge, the
throne itself might have been threatened and James
might have lost his crown. Perhaps the prince had realized this and drawn back because of it at the last moment—though there were whispers that hinted that he
had changed his mind for quite another reason. For the
prince had seen another lady he admired at the French
Court—the Princess Henrietta Maria.

Even if the prince had acted for the best of reasons, James had the right to be nervous. The Spanish had demanded too much, but there was no doubt that the duke and the prince had behaved badly, and the prince's refusal to honour the contract could easily lead to a war between England and Spain.

Nicholas had asked permission to leave the Court as soon as he had completed his mission, by passing on his observations, but James had been in an uncertain mood and had kept him hanging on until the last moment.

'Ye have our leave to go,' he had told Nicholas after he had spent several days chafing at the bit. 'But I want your promise to return within the month. And bring the lassie with you. I would have words with Mistress Stirling and her father.'

Nicholas's patience was almost at an end. He was tired of being at the beck and call of kings and princes. When he was back in France, he would not venture to London again for a long time—nor to the French Court, where he would be welcomed for his father's sake.

He wanted to live peacefully with his wife, and in time their children. But was Deborah still willing to be his life's companion?

Arriving at her home late in the evening to discover it was Mistress Palmer's wedding day, he had kept in the background so that he could observe the celebrations without Deborah being aware of him. He had imagined that she would be in low spirits, uncertain of the future and perhaps missing him a little. It had been both shocking and painful to see her flirting with the man he had thought of as his closest friend.

Henri's words recalled his wandering thoughts with a start. 'Surely your business could not have been of such importance that it kept you from Mistress Stirling all this time? Did you not think she might have need of comfort from you?'

Henri's anger was evident—as was the fact that he was in love with her! He was daring to reprimand Nicholas for neglecting her. Nicholas felt the rage rising inside him. It was all he could do to keep his fists from striking the other man's face.

'It would not appear that she lacked for comfort while I was away,' he said smoothly. His manner was outwardly cool but his tone was sharper than the point of his sword.

'Damn you, Nico!' Henri cried angrily. 'She hath been sore of heart this past month waiting for some word from you. I cannot understand why you abandoned her. Why could you not have taken her to France so that she understood you meant to keep your promise to wed her?'

'Perhaps she does not mean to keep hers.'

Henri looked at him in disgust. 'Has your soul become so warped that you think so ill of her? She was innocent when you took her, Nico. Nothing but God's grace has kept her that way—and I do not speak only of the time she spent with that monster. You yourself came close to seducing her...'

'God's breath!' Nicholas glared at him. 'I could kill you for that!'

'You could try.' Henri's hand went to his hip as if to threaten his willingness to fight, though he had not worn his sword to the wedding.

For some moments the two friends glared at each other, all the warmth and companionship of years as naught. There was a moment when they might have sought to shed each other's blood, but then Henri laughed.

'At least you have some heart left in you,' he said. 'I had begun to think it was buried in Isabella's grave.'

Nicholas stared at him, curled fists gradually uncurling. 'No—did you?' he said and the anger left him as suddenly as it had come. 'I would have wed Isabella for I had no hope of finding the kind of love my father had for my mother. Isabella's death weighed heavy on my soul, for I knew I had caused it.' He held up his hand as Henri would have denied it. 'Yes, it is so, my friend. Deny it if you will, but he killed her because he hated me.'

'But you could not have known what he was—what he truly was.'

'No,' Nicholas admitted. 'I had certainly seen no sign of the sickness that came upon him at the end—but I had sensed there was evil in him. He was a cruel child by all accounts, but I think no one—save perhaps his father—suspected the truth.'

'The face of an angel and the mind of a devil.'

'A dangerous combination,' Nicholas agreed. 'But what kind of a man is Don Manola? I think that perhaps his sins may in truth surpass those of his son.' A flicker of revulsion entered his eyes. 'Think of what might have happened had we not taken her when we did, Henri. The Don would have made certain neither she nor her father saw anything untoward until after the wedding.'

'And then she would truly have been the bride of that devil,' Henri said and he too shuddered.

'Yes.' Nicholas frowned. 'At least we have spared her that. Whatever the future—she has been spared the worst.'

'And now what?' Henri asked. 'Is it your intention to claim her?'

'I think the decision must be hers,' Nicholas replied. 'The King has commanded me to take both Deborah and her father to Court. We shall see what we shall see.'

'You would release her if she asked?'

'I should have no choice,' Nicholas replied. 'I shall have my bride willingly—or not at all.'

'Then we shall shake hands and let the best man win?'

Nicholas laughed. 'A duel between us but without swords. I warn you, Henri. I shall do my best to win her.'

'And I shall do what I must,' Henri replied, a smile on his lips.

Chapter Fifteen

Deborah dressed herself in a simple green gown that morning. It was still early. She imagined many of the guests would still be sleeping off the quantities of wine they had consumed the previous evening. She was too restless to stay indoors, and though there was a hint of rain in the air she would feel better for a walk.

She needed to think carefully about the future. It seemed that Nicholas no longer wanted her. He had never loved her, of course, but for a while it had amused him to court her. Perhaps, at first, he had thought she would be content to be his mistress. She had come very close to letting him seduce her, and her body still tingled when she remembered his kisses and the feel of his hardness pressed against her showing his urgent need.

Deborah allowed herself to think about the night when he had threatened to take her to his bed—or there against the stable wall. What would have happened if he had? Would his honour have demanded that he marry her at once? Or would he still have abandoned her?

She walked, lost in thought, towards the summerhouse where Henri had once found her. The little shelter had become her refuge these past weeks, offering solitude when she could no longer bear Sarah's constant chattering.

She did not grudge her cousin's happiness, but it only made her heart ache the more when she thought of the future. Sarah was married now and would be leaving for her husband's home later that day. How fortunate she was to have found her gentle, caring Master Henderson.

Deborah sighed. It was the fault of her wilful heart. If she had not chosen to fall in love with a charming rogue—yet her heart had chosen for her. She had resisted for as long as she could, but his smile had won her almost from the first.

'Why so sad, my lady?' The teasing voice made her swing round in disbelief, her heart racing like the wind. 'Could it be because you miss me a little?'

Deborah stared at Nicholas. He was laughing at her as he had in France—as if all that had happened since had never been. Her first surge of delight was lost in the tide of anger that immediately followed. How dare he! How could he behave in such a manner?

'So…' she said, her head tilted defiantly at him. 'You have not forgotten us after all, sir. I had begun to think you could not tear yourself from the pleasures of Court.'

'It was hard to do so,' Nicholas replied. 'But I decided it was time I came. I trust you have recovered from your fever?'

'Yes, I thank you. It is more than a month since I was ill, and it was but a trifling thing.'

'Ah, yes, now that you remind me, I believe it is almost a month.'

Deborah was seething. Oh, he was a mocking devil! He deserved to be roasted alive—or that she should show him she was indifferent.

'A pity you were not here yesterday,' she said. 'It was my cousin's wedding.'

'Yes, Henri told me so,' he replied. 'I shall send Mistress Henderson a gift.'

'I am sure she will be pleased.'

'Mistress Palmer was never difficult to please, I think?'

Deborah glared at him. Was he saying she was? She refused to respond to his baiting. She would be cool and dignified, forcing him to treat her with respect.

'When did you arrive, sir?'

'Oh, not long ago,' Nicholas replied vaguely.

'And for how many days shall we have the pleasure of your company?'

'Not more than two or three, I fear.'

'I suppose you have more urgent business?' Her eyes glinted with the annoyance she could not hide. 'Pray do not let us detain you, sir.'

'The King commands me to return soon,' Nicholas replied. 'He also desires to speak with you and your father, Mistress Stirling.'

'With me?' Deborah looked at him in surprise. 'He did not so much as notice me when we were there earlier in the summer. What can he want of me?'

'Perhaps to hear your opinion of whether I should hang,' Nicholas said. 'Kidnap is a serious offence, punishable by death. You might dance at my funeral, mistress.'

Deborah's eyes smouldered. 'You are pleased to jest, sir. Your levity is unbecoming. Have a care. I may well complain of you to His Majesty.'

Nicholas swept his hat off and bowed to her. 'I am entirely at your mercy, mistress.'

She gave him a fulminating glance, her good intentions flown. What was she supposed to answer? He was impossible! Did he mean to claim her for his own or not?

'Have you seen my father yet?'

'A few moments ago. He was not best pleased by the summons—but he will obey. Your father is a wise man, Mistress Stirling. He knows that kings can be capricious.'

'Kings and men!' Deborah muttered beneath her breath.

'What was that you said, Mistress Stirling? I did not quite hear you.'

She itched to strike him, but that would be beneath her dignity. If he imagined she would fly to his arms the moment he arrived, he should be taught the error of his thinking.

He had used her most ill, indeed he had. Snatching her and carrying her off to his home. Oh, that lovely sunlit house! How she longed to be there again with him—but he must show her that he truly wanted her as his wife.

She would not be won lightly. If he had been here when she needed him so badly it would have been different, but he had put his business first. Now he must dangle on her string. He must court her if he would wed her.

'I said that kings must be obeyed,' she lied and lifted her chin proudly. 'Besides, I shall not be sorry to spend a little time at Court. It will soon be November and winter can be very dull here in the North. I like to dance and laugh. Yes, it will suit me very well to go to London.' She smiled at him. 'Tell me, sir—does Henri go with us?'

'If you invite him, I dare say he may.' Nicholas frowned as he saw her eyes spark. What mischief was this? Was she merely playing him at his own game? Or had she given her affections to Henri these past weeks?

'Then I shall,' Deborah said serenely. 'Henri has been a great comfort since we came home—both to my father and to me.'

'I am glad to hear it,' Nicholas said. He smiled too, but this time it did not reach his eyes. 'You must naturally ask him if he would care to accompany us.'

Oh, the wretch! Deborah had meant to provoke him, hoping he might take her in his arms and kiss her as he had when they had argued before.

'I turn cold,' she said. 'Perhaps we should go in. I would not wish to take a chill before we leave for London.'

Nicholas glanced at her and could not quite hide his concern. 'You must learn to take more care of yourself,' he said. 'You were unwell not so long ago.'

'It was merely a touch of the sun,' she replied, and turned away before he could read her eyes. She did not want him to pity her.

'You were fortunate it was nothing more,' Nicholas said more harshly than he intended. 'I warned you not to stray too far from the château while I was gone. Why could you not have obeyed me?'

Tears stung her eyes but she blinked them away. He blamed her as she had known he would!

She began to walk away, towards the house, refusing to answer. He was unkind. She could not accept his blame because she already felt her guilt too keenly.

'Deborah…'

She refused to look back. It was too cruel! She had suffered enough for her foolishness. She had wanted him to hold her, to kiss away her fears—and all he did was scold her. Henri was so much kinder!

'Deborah, I did not mean to hurt you,' Nicholas said, but it was said so softly that she did not hear.

She had hoped he might come after her as he had once before, but he made no attempt and it hurt her that he could let her go. Would he never forgive her for what she had done? Would he never try to understand?

Nicholas watched her go into the house. He was half inclined to go after her and reason with her—but if he did he would end by taking her in his arms and kissing her until she surrendered to him as she so nearly had once before. Yet if he did that he would never be quite sure.

She must choose. If she would be happier with Henri then she must have her way. He had given her no choice the last time and he had been tormented by his doubts. He wanted her to come to him of her own free will.

Nothing less would do!

He saw her disappear into the house, then turned away. He had been a fool to quarrel with her. If he wanted to win her heart, he must be gentle—and give her a reason to want to leave behind her home for him.

Yet she had been happy in France. He knew she loved Chalfont as he did. If only he could be certain that she loved its master.

Deborah dressed herself in the youth's clothing she had sometimes worn for her fencing lessons with her father. She was restless and felt the need to ride alone. In her disguise, with her hair tucked beneath a cap, she would not be noticed and could easily slip back into the house before anyone was about. She had done it often enough in the past without detection.

She ran down the stairs and let herself out of a side entrance, heading for the stables. The grooms would not be stirring yet, though they had seen her dressed this way when she had ridden out with Sir Edward and would not be surprised. They were all fiercely loyal to her, and she did not believe they would betray her by loose talk.

She reached the stable yard, making straight for the stall that housed her favourite gelding. The horse came to her at once as she opened the split door and called its name, snickering as she offered the apple she had saved for him from supper the previous night.

'Good fellow,' she said, patting its nose and rubbing her face against the warm soft hair of its neck. She fetched a bridle, slipping the reins over the noble head as it tossed as if to show agreement with this escapade. 'You need the exercise as much as I do, don't you, sweetheart?'

'Not running away again, I hope?'

Deborah whirled round as she heard the mocking tones of the marquis's voice. 'Did you follow me?' she demanded. 'How did you know it was me?'

'I was not certain until you spoke to the horse,' Nicholas said, his eyes bright with challenge. 'I saw someone leaving the house in a furtive manner and decided to investigate.'

'I was not furtive! I merely wished to leave without being seen.'

Nicholas laughed. 'Is there a difference? I apologize, mistress. I thought you might be a thief about to rob my host.'

'As you see, you were wrong. You may go about your business, sir, and leave me to mine.'

'But your business is also mine.'

Deborah's heart jerked. What was he saying?

'I do not know what you mean, sir.'

'Do you not?' His brows lifted. 'Why, what should I mean but that I also wished to ride while it is early.' He smiled oddly. 'Could you not sleep, Deborah?'

'I often ride early,' she said, turning away. She was not going to admit that she had been unable to rest, knowing that he was sleeping in the room that had been Sarah's and was close by her own.

'But not always attired thus, I think?' His wicked eyes went over her, bringing a flush to her cheeks. 'You make a pretty youth, my lady—but I prefer you as a woman.'

Deborah could not look at him as she went to fetch her saddle, but Nicholas followed and took it from her.

'You will allow me to help you?'

'If you wish, though I have done it before.'

'I do not doubt it,' he replied, amused. 'Tell me, lady, what more is there to know of you? I confess I am intrigued.'

Deborah raised her head, meeting his dark gaze in a spirit of defiance. 'My father had me educated as though I were his son—and that included fencing lessons. I wore these clothes for my lessons and sometimes to ride with my father—if we wished to ride hard, as we sometimes did.'

'Ah, that explains much,' Nicholas said. 'You are fierce in defence of your independence, Deborah. I have seldom met a woman with such spirit.'

Deborah blushed. 'Perhaps you would wish me to be more maidenly, sir?'

'I have no complaints.' He met her searching gaze. 'I merely seek to understand you. Will you allow me to accompany you on your ride—or do you wish to go alone?'

'There is no reason why we should not go together.'

'It is a pleasing pastime,' he said. 'I enjoyed our excursions when you were my guest, Mistress Stirling.'

Deborah almost retorted that she had been his prisoner, but she knew how it felt to truly be a prisoner now
and realized that he had always treated her as his guest.
Indeed, he had been a courteous host, doing all he could
to ensure her comfort.

'I—I found my visit to your home pleasant in many
ways, sir.'

'I am happy to hear it,' he replied, a little smile quirk-
ing the corners of his mouth. 'Come, let me help you to
mount. It will take but a moment to saddle my horse.'

She allowed him to help her, sitting astride her horse
as she watched him prepare his own. It was a mettlesome
creature, but not as fine or as wild as Nero.

'You may show me your father's estate,' Nicholas invited. 'I saw very little as I rode here for it was in darkness.'

'It is quite small compared to your own,' she said.
'We have tenant farmers, but my father's land is broken
into parcels scattered here and there. We do not have
your vineyards or such pleasant surroundings. As you
must have observed, we are close to the moors, which
can seem inhospitable in winter.'

'Yes, I suppose so. I believe the winter is severe here
in the North?'

'Sometimes the roads are impassable and we spend
days and weeks with no company. That is why…' She
hesitated and then continued, 'I found your friends entertaining, my lord. I wanted them to think well of me.'

'And why should they not?' Nicholas asked. 'You are
a lovely, intelligent woman, Deborah. My friends had no
cause to think ill of you.'

'There are some that do. I have seen it in their eyes—
in the way they look at me.'

Nicholas frowned. 'Then they should think shame on themselves. You may hold your head high. You have naught to blush for, Deborah.'

She smiled but made no reply, merely allowing her horse to trot from the yard with Nicholas riding at her side.

Deborah enjoyed her ride that morning. She had found Nicholas a pleasant and entertaining companion. Somehow as they rode and talked she had realized the tension was easing out of her. She was no longer angry with him for abandoning her. It was the beginning of a new relationship. His smiles were sometimes mocking, sometimes almost tender. She suspected that he meant to court her—which must mean he still wanted her for his wife.

As the day progressed, Deborah became aware that there was an amicable rivalry between Nicholas and Henri. They both sought to engage her attention at every opportunity, fetching her wine and sweetmeats as they and her father sat together that evening in the parlour. Nicholas sang a song of love for her, and Henri told them a story about witches and wizards and King Arthur's knights.

Deborah played a pretty piece on the virginals and Sir Edward accompanied her on his flute. He had not touched the instrument since his wife died, and Deborah was surprised and pleased to see how relaxed he seemed.

'It is a pity we cannot have more evenings like this,' he told her when she kissed him good night later. 'Unfortunately, a request from His Majesty is tantamount to a command. We must leave by the day after tomorrow at the latest. However, the marquis has invited us to stay with him at Chalfont this winter, and our baggage is to be sent on to his ship so that we need not return here after our visit to Court.'

'We are going to France?' Deborah stared at him, her heart beating faster.

'I have promised that we shall,' Sir Edward said. 'I would like to get to know de Vere better. He seems a well-educated, intelligent man, Deborah. I think it will be pleasant to escape the worst of the winter. I confess the cold eats into my bones these days, and France has a milder climate than our own, I believe.'

'Chalfont is very beautiful,' she said. 'I am sure you will like it, Father.'

'Yes, I am sure I shall.' He smiled at her. 'Sleep well, Deborah.'

She was thoughtful as she went to her chamber. What did that look mean in her father's eyes? Was he beginning to plan another wedding?

A little smile touched her mouth as she allowed her maid to undress her. She was happier than she had been for many weeks.

The journey to London had been made more difficult by the rain of the past two days. In places there had been ruts so deep that it would have been almost impossible for a heavy travelling carriage to pass. Deborah had ridden with the others, preferring a little dampness to being jolted until she was black and blue.

They had stopped often at inns along the way so as not to tire her, and it was three days before they reached their lodgings in London. Nicholas had taken a large, impressive house near the river and everything was prepared for their arrival.

'I thought it convenient for us to remain together,' he told her. 'I trust the arrangement is to your satisfaction, Deborah?'

'Yes, of course,' she said and smiled. She had begun to feel more and more at ease with him these past few days. 'It will be much nicer this way, all of us together as we have been.'

'You should find all that you need in your chamber, but should you need anything you have only to ask. My pleasure is to serve you, my lady.'

She blushed faintly and thanked him, feeling butterflies of joy spreading their wings deep inside her. When she went to her chamber, Deborah discovered several gowns had been laid out for her approval. She touched the fine material, recognizing some of it as that which she had chosen to be made up for her by the seamstress at Chalfont. Nicholas must have arranged for them to be brought over for her use.

She chose a pale blue silk for her audience with His Majesty that morning, dressing with care. The pearls Nicholas had given her were amongst her things and also a handsome brooch set with precious stones—but there was no sign of the betrothal ring he had given her.

Why had he provided so much, but not the ring?

The thought brought a frown to her brow, but she put it from her mind as she went downstairs to meet her father and Nicholas.

Nicholas was standing at the foot of the stairs, gazing up as she walked down dressed in her finery. His eyes were warm with approval, and he took her hand as she reached him, lifting it to kiss her fingertips.

'You look beautiful,' he said. 'I have never seen you more lovely.'

'I thank you, sir.' She dimpled with pleasure. She could not doubt now that he was courting her and the knowledge made her heart sing for pure joy.

'A chair awaits you, my lady. We should leave at once. His Majesty does not care to be kept waiting.' His look was wicked. 'I do hope I shall not find myself a guest in the Tower by this evening?'

Deborah laughed. 'Oh, I do not think it, sir,' she replied. 'But we shall see.'

She smiled at him as he helped her into her chair, then he and her father walked beside her as she was carried through the streets towards the palace. She recalled thinking once how safe she would feel with Nicholas as her escort. Glancing at him now, she felt proud and pleased. This man was soon to be her husband. She was convinced of it and the thought made her happy.

Always when her father had taken her to the palace before, Deborah had been made aware that they were provincial nobodies and tolerated merely because of her father's wealth. This morning, however, they were greeted by a deferential footman who conducted them to a luxuriously appointed chamber, which was clearly a part of His Majesty's private apartments.

Deborah was aware of a fluttering sensation in her stomach. She had never spoken to the King before, and having heard of his capricious nature, was anxious to make the right impression.

'Do not worry,' Nicholas said. 'He will be charmed with you, Deborah.'

She smiled shyly, but just as she was about to reply the door opened and King James entered the room. A little flustered because he had not been announced, she sank into a deep curtsy.

'Stand up, stand up,' James said. 'Let me look at you, lassie. Aye, I see why the rogue snatched you. She's a bonny lassie, Nicholas. You are to be congratulated on your taste. When is the wedding?'

Nicholas frowned. 'It has not been decided, sir.'

'Not decided?' The King looked at him hard. 'This will not do, sir. A marriage between you is imperative. Ye canna ruin a young woman's reputation and not marry her. You *will* marry her—and I'll give a banquet for ye here. 'Tis the least I can do.' He turned his attention to Deborah, eyes bright with mischief. 'There, lassie—is honour satisfied? You'll not ask me to hang the rogue? He'll make you a fine husband. A dozen ladies of the Court will testify to it, I've no doubt.' He nodded to himself, obviously pleased with the outcome.

'I—I do not want you to hang the marquis,' Deborah said, her voice little more than a whisper. 'But—but I do not wish for this marriage.'

'Not wish for it?' The King looked startled. 'You have no choice, mistress. You must be wed—or retire to a nunnery. There is no alternative for a lady of your birth.' He frowned. 'Nay, you've no heart for the life of a nun, I'll be bound. You are angry with the rogue—but he shall wed you. I am sure Sir Edward agrees with me.'

'My wish is to see my daughter happy, Sire.'

'Aye, weel, that's as may be,' grunted the King, looking somewhat disgruntled that his generosity had not been received as he'd expected. He looked at Nicholas again, his brows lowered. 'You will oblige me, sir? I have a wish to see ye settled. No more ado. We'll have the wedding tomorrow and be done with it.'

Nicholas inclined his head. 'How can I refuse your most generous offer, Sire? When I said the wedding was not decided, I meant only the day and the hour. Tomorrow is as good as any day.'

Deborah shot a reproachful look at him. How could he agree to the King's outrageous demand so easily? But of course—he had *known* this was going to happen! It had probably been agreed before he left London to come to her. No doubt His Majesty had sent him to her.

A surge of anger rose in her. Why did men always imagine they had the right to dictate these things? Was she to have no say in the matter?

'This evening there is to be a masque,' the King went on. 'Ye shall all attend. It is our wish to see our friends make merry. Leave us now, Mistress Stirling—Sir Edward. You'll stay, Nicholas. I would have private talk with ye.'

'As you wish, Sire.' Nicholas turned to Deborah. 'Go with your father, my lady. I shall see you later.'

Deborah gave him a speaking look. Oh, but she would have much to say to him when they were alone! For now she could only curtsy to His Majesty and accompany her father from the room.

Sir Edward looked at her anxiously as they left the palace. 'You did not mean what you said just now, daughter? I believed you were happy to wed de Vere. You had already given him your promise, had you not?'

'In France—yes,' she replied. She stared at her father in frustration. 'But that was before… I do not wish to be married because King James commands it.'

'Is that all?' Sir Edward smiled. 'I think de Vere was not best pleased by His Majesty's interference in the matter—but the intention was always there. He spoke to me on the morning after his arrival at our home.'

'But not to me,' Deborah said, though her voice was so muffled that it did not reach her father who was summoning a chair for her. 'Oh, why did he not tell me?'

She was torn between vexation and disappointment. Only a few hours ago she had been utterly convinced that Nicholas loved her. Now she was uncertain again. Was he marrying her because he truly wanted her—or because honour demanded that he do so?

Chapter Sixteen

Deborah stared in surprise as she entered the house and saw trunks being carried through the hall. What was going on?

'I thought our larger trunks were being taken straight to the ship?' she said, turning to her father.

'These are not yours, Mistress Stirling.' A young footman approached Deborah and bowed his head to her. 'Forgive me for interrupting, but perhaps you were not expecting Mistress Trevern?'

Deborah was surprised. 'Mistress Trevern! The marquis's cousin is here?'

'She arrived not twenty minutes ago,' the footman replied. 'I believe she has been made comfortable.'

'What's this?' Sir Edward asked. 'The marquis's cousin? You knew nothing of this, Deborah?' He frowned as she shook her head. 'How unfortunate that no one was here to receive her. You must go to her at once, my dear. Make certain she has been looked after properly and has all she needs.'

Deborah had been thinking the same. Although she knew that Marie disliked her, she was in some sense the hostess here while Nicholas was absent.

'I shall go up to her at once.' She smiled at the footman as she passed him. 'Thank you for telling me.'

The door to the guest chamber Marie had been given was open, and Deborah could hear her sharp voice complaining loudly as she approached.

'No! Not there, you clumsy dolt. I'll have you thrashed if you...' Marie broke off mid-sentence as she turned and saw Deborah in the doorway. 'So—I thought I should find you here.' Her wrathful eyes fell on the footman who had deposited her trunk. 'Very well, that will do. You may go and return in a few minutes.' She closed the door with a snap after him.

'I came to make sure you are comfortable here—and that you have all you need,' Deborah said. 'Should you wish for anything you have only to ask, as I am sure you know.'

Marie's eyes narrowed to jealous slits. 'What makes you mistress here? I understood this was my cousin's house.'

'Yes, the marquis has leased it for a time and was good enough to offer my father and I his hospitality so that we might all stay together—but as we are soon to be married, I felt it my duty to make certain you had not been neglected.'

'So—he is still determined to marry you,' Marie muttered, her mouth thin with disapproval. She had apparently lost none of her hostility towards Deborah. 'I imagined he would have had the sense to end the affair after you ran away with his enemy and caused him so much trouble to fetch you back.'

'I did not run away.' Deborah looked at her proudly. 'I was taken without my consent. I believed I had no choice but to do as they wished.'

Marie glared at her, barely able to contain her hatred.

'That is not my understanding of the affair. I suppose you have convinced my cousin of your innocence. Men are such fools where they love. Well, it is naught to me. If Nicholas believes himself bound to wed you, he must do so and repine at leisure. I did not come here to dance at your wedding.'

'Does the marquis expect you?' Deborah asked. 'He made no mention of your visit.'

'I have Nicholas's assurance that I am always welcome in his house,' Marie said. 'When he sent for your things, I had them packed and then, a day or so later, decided to follow. I have something I wish to discuss privately with him.' Her gaze narrowed. 'I was told he was with you at the palace—has he not returned?'

'No, not immediately,' Deborah replied. 'He stayed to discuss some business with His Majesty. I believe he will not be long in coming.'

Marie nodded. 'Then I must be patient.'

'May I help you in any way?' Deborah made a determined effort to make friends with Nicholas's cousin since they were to be family and might meet in the future. 'I do not wish to quarrel with you, Mistress Trevern.'

'I shall order a light repast in my chamber,' Marie replied. 'I mean to make only a short stay in London before I return to France.'

Deborah lifted her head proudly. 'You will stay for our wedding, I hope? We go to a masque at Court this evening—would you care to come with us?'

'When is your wedding?'

'Tomorrow. The King gives a banquet for us.'

'Then perhaps I shall—and I may as well join you this evening.' She gave Deborah a grudging smile that did not reach her eyes. 'Thank you for your invitation.'

'You will be very welcome,' Deborah said. She smiled at Marie. 'Now, if I cannot do anything for you, I shall leave you to rest.'

'Nicholas is fickle,' his cousin said suddenly. 'He is only marrying you because he feels it his duty. I would not care to be wed for such a cause. Jean is in love with me. I have come here to ask Nicholas to give me his consent and blessing.'

'You are to be married?' Deborah was surprised and pleased. 'I am so glad, Mistress Trevern. Truly I am. I do most sincerely wish you happy.'

'I do not want your good wishes,' Marie said 'I have consented because I do not care to live under Nicholas's roof once he has a wife. This marriage was the best I could hope for.'

'You do not love Jean?'

'I love Nicholas,' Marie said. Her eyes blazed suddenly. 'And I hate you, Mistress Stirling. I wish that the Spaniard had killed you when he had you.'

Deborah felt the force of her hatred. The look in Marie's eyes sent shivers down her spine. For a moment she could not speak, then she inclined her head.

'I am sorry you do not love Jean,' she said and turned away.

It was sad that Marie was so unhappy. At least Deborah loved the man she was to marry—even if he was the most impossible, infuriating man she had ever met!

All that afternoon Deborah stayed in her room and waited for Nicholas to send word that he wished to see her. She did not go down, because she wished to avoid another confrontation with Marie. She longed to see Nicholas, because she needed to speak with him about their marriage privately, but she waited in vain. He had still not arrived by the time it was necessary to leave for the Court masque. Henri and Sir Edward had promised to escort the ladies, and they would take two stout footmen with them for there were footpads and beggars, and it could be dangerous to walk through the streets after dark.

Marie had used the afternoon to good effect it seemed, being so charming to Sir Edward that he was completely taken with her and told Deborah he was delighted she would have a female companion for a few days.

'I know you must miss Sarah,' he said. 'It is good that you have Mistress Trevern to talk to about the things ladies like to discuss in private—the kind of things no man could ever hope to understand.' He smiled at her indulgently.

'Yes, Father.' She returned his smile. 'I do miss Sarah, of course.'

She had told him nothing of Marie's bitter words; there was no point in distressing him and it would only make things more uncomfortable while Marie was staying in the house.

'But I am quite happy with just you for company—and Nicholas.'

Sir Edward nodded. 'Have you calmed down after your little show of temper, child? I knew you would after some quiet reflection. You could not find a better husband, you know. I like de Vere—and I respect him.'

'You were used to call him a rogue, Father.'

'I have come to know him better,' her father replied. 'When I called him a pirate I did not understand why he attacked those ships. I think had I suffered as he did, I might have sought revenge for the wrong done me. Don Manola deceived me. He was not the man I once knew. It was a sorry business, Deborah, and we may be thankful that de Vere was there to prevent worse.'

'Yes, I know. I know I have much to thank Nicholas for, but...' She sighed. 'Where do you think he is, Father? What kept him from coming back to us this afternoon as he promised?'

'I cannot tell you,' Sir Edward replied, giving her a rather strange look. 'But I dare say it was business. You cannot expect to tie such a man to your apron strings, Deborah. You have always had your own way with me—but I may have indulged you too much for your own good. Your husband will expect you to comply with his wishes.'

'Yes, Father.' Deborah's spirit rebelled though she did not answer her father back. Why should it be that way? Why must a woman always obey? Why could a man and a woman not love equally?

She knew that her thoughts were shocking and would meet with no sympathy. She would on the morrow be forced to wed the marquis whether she wished it or not, and that could not please her. She wanted to be loved! To be the most important thing in the whole world to her husband—but perhaps that was wishing for the moon. Oh, but she did want to marry Nicholas. Why must everything be spoiled by the whim of a capricious king?

Deborah had danced several times with Henri, and once with her father, refusing all other offers. She did not like the way some of the courtiers eyed her so lasciviously—as though speculating whether or not she was ripe for seduction! So she stood watching the dancing for much of the evening, wondering where Nicholas was and why he had not attended the masque.

'Mistress Stirling?' She turned as the footman approached and made her a respectful bow. He held a small packet out to her. 'I was asked to deliver this note to you.'

'A letter—from whom?' she asked, immediately suspicious.

'I do not know the sender,' the man replied. 'I am merely the bearer, mistress.'

'Thank you,' Deborah said. 'I have no money with me, but my father is by the window and will reward you.'

'I have been paid, mistress. Excuse me.'

Deborah watched as he walked away, then took her letter closer to a branch of beeswax tapers so that she might read it more carefully. She did not recognize the hand and wondered who would choose to send her a letter at such a time. She broke the seal and began to read carefully.

If you care for the Marquis de Vere, come at once to the courtyard by the river. If you fail you will never see him again. Tell no one of this letter or he will disappear forever.

The note was unsigned. Deborah gave a gasp of fear and glanced round for the man who had delivered the message. Where had he gone? She must know who had paid him to carry the letter!

She saw him leaving the banqueting hall and decided to follow. There was no time to speak to her father— besides, he was dancing with Marie Trevern. Deborah threw a despairing glance his way, then hurried after the footman. However, by the time she had managed to thread her way through the throng of merrymakers, some of whom sought to delay her, there was no sight of her quarry.

She paused for a moment. What ought she to do? The letter might be some kind of trick. Supposing she was being lured into a trap? Marie hated her. She might have paid someone to attack or kidnap Deborah.

Surely she was letting her imagination run away with her? Her instincts warned her that she should return to the masque and speak to her father or Henri—but supposing the message was genuine? She could not risk the threat that, if she told anyone, Nicholas would disappear forever.

What was her life if Nicholas was dead?

She was sure she knew which courtyard the note mentioned, for they had used it earlier that day. It led down to a stretch of grass by the riverbank and was a favourite spot for the courtiers to stroll on a summer's afternoon. She would go there. Whatever the sacrifice demanded of her, she would pay it. Yes, even if Don Manola had taken Nicholas hostage and the price she must pay was heavy. There was nothing left for her without the man she loved.

She ran through the dark, draughty outer passages of the palace, away from the lights and the music of the reception rooms, through a walled garden, down a flight of steps and into the courtyard. Here there was no light except for a sprinkling of stars in the sky, but she was not afraid. Only Nicholas mattered!

She could see nothing—no sign of anyone.

'Where are you?' she called. 'I am here. Where is the marquis? What have you done to—?'

She heard a sound behind her, but before she could turn round something was thrown over her head. Not a suffocating blanket this time, but a cloak of velvet that smelled of a familiar scent—not a woman's perfume, but the scent of a man.

It was Nicholas's cloak, she knew that instinctively.

'Who are you?' she said, making no attempt to resist as she was swung off the ground into a man's strong arms. 'Where are you taking me? Where is Nicholas?'

A soft laugh was the only answer she received, but it was enough. Every instinct told her that it was Nicholas himself who had captured her. Her heart was beating wildly as her mind raced. It must have been Nicholas who had sent her that letter—but why?

She knew when he carried her down some steps into the boat and deposited her gently on the wooden bench. He had still not spoken a word to her, neither had he removed the velvet cloak that loosely covered her head and shoulders, but the arm that held her was not imprisoning and she could have removed it herself had she wished. She made no move to do so, nor did she try to escape. There was no need to be afraid, for she knew where he was taking her.

As the boat began to pull away from the bank, the cloak was removed and placed about her shoulders. Still she did not move or speak one word of protest.

'Do you not wish to know where you are going, Deborah?' Nicholas asked. 'I expected a scolding. It is not like you to be so accepting.'

'I know where we are going,' she said with a demure smile. 'You are taking me on board the *Siren's Song* and from there we shall sail for France.'

'How did you know it was me?'

'You used your cloak,' Deborah replied. 'It carries the scent of you. I did think the letter might be a trick at first—but the cloak gave you away.'

'You complained of the filthy blanket the last time,' he reminded her.

'And should do so again!' she replied with a flash of spirit. 'Indeed, I must ask you to explain yourself, sir. Why have you chosen to carry me off without a by-your-leave?'

'Ah, that is better. I had begun to wonder if I had kidnapped the wrong woman.'

'You are pleased to mock me, sir. I hope you have a good reason for almost frightening me to death with that terrible letter. I thought your life in danger.'

'Were you frightened for me, Deborah?'

'Foolishly, yes. I ask again, why have you abducted me?'

'Since you made no attempt to escape, would you not rather call it an elopement?' His voice was soft, seductive, touching a chord within her. 'The answer is simple—I thought it would please you, my lady.'

'Please me?' Deborah turned her head, straining to see his face in the darkness. She was pretending to be angry, but it was false, for she knew what lay behind this mad plan of his. 'You take too much for granted, sir. I have not yet said I shall marry you.'

'I have not yet asked you,' he replied. 'As I recall, I told you we would be wed the first time—and now King James has done the same. It occurred to me that you might find that a little irksome?'

'It made me very angry,' she replied truthfully, and she was smiling inside though she would not let him see it yet. He had known that she was vexed by the King's commands, and that she did not care to be told who she must marry—even if it was what she wanted with all her heart. Truth be told, she did not mind that he had abducted her one little bit. 'Why is it that women are always expected to obey? Do you not think men and women should be on equal terms—at least in love?'

'I have observed that in many cases it is the woman who commands,' Nicholas murmured, a hint of laughter in his voice. 'If she is clever, she can bend the man who desires her to her will.'

A little smile touched Deborah's lips. 'But the man would have to desire her very much—would he not?'

'Very much.'

'Would he also love her?'

'With his heart, his mind, his body—his very soul.'

'A woman loved in that way would not need to command,' Deborah said softly and her heart was beginning to sing for joy. 'She would know herself blessed and would want to give back as much love as she received.'

'Then her lover would be a fortunate man.'

'Her lover—not her husband?'

'Oh, certainly her lover,' Nicholas said wickedly. 'Men marry for fortune or position—is that not so?'

'Yes, it is often the case,' Deborah agreed. She was enjoying this verbal fencing! He played a strange game with her, but his nearness was making her heart behave foolishly. 'I had several such offers from gentlemen when I first attended the Court—but I believe not one of them loved me. It was my father's fortune they coveted.'

'Surely not all were so base?'

'There was one offer that did not concern my father's wealth—but I do not think it was of marriage,' she murmured, a hint of laughter in her voice.

Nicholas laughed out loud, clearly much amused. 'I recall something—but we were speaking of lovers. Shall I make you my mistress, Deborah?'

'You have me in your power, sir. I am your prisoner. You may do with me as you will.'

'Oh, I think not,' he murmured. 'But if you will not consent to be my wife, what am I to do with you? I cannot send you back to your father again. I believe King James would hang me then.'

'I might consent to wed you…if I decided it would suit me to be your wife.'

'And what would help you decide? I wonder…' He pretended to consider. 'A necklace of emeralds, perhaps?'

'Oh, you wretch!' Deborah turned on him and beat against his chest with her fists. 'How dare you tease me so wickedly! You discuss our marriage with my father. You agree to His Majesty's command that we marry…'

'But disobeyed him, at some considerable risk—since he will not be pleased with me. Why should I do that? Unless it was to please a wilful lady. You did not truly wish to be married by royal command—did you, Deborah?'

'You know I did not,' she retorted. 'Will you never ask me, you devil? How can you be so—so infuriating and yet so charming?'

She knew he was laughing, even though he sought to hold it inside.

'Will you marry me, Deborah?'

'I might,' she replied, still holding out. 'It depends upon why you want to marry me, sir.'

'Because I covet your father's estate? Is that reason enough?'

'I hate you!'

'Because the King will hang me if I don't?'

'You are detestable!'

'Because I love you more than life itself and would rather die than let you go?' he said softly, his lips close to her ear. 'Because I cannot sleep for thinking of you.

Because I remember how it felt to hold you in my arms and know I never have and never shall feel such true happiness again unless I have you always near me.'

She touched her fingers to his lips in wonder. 'Do you truly love me so much, Nicholas? More than you love Isabella?'

'I never loved Isabella. She was a good, gentle woman. I respected and liked her. I hoped love might come when we were wed. And after she died I felt guilty, because I had helped bring about her death. Miguel killed her because of his hatred for me.'

'You were blameless. He was insane.'

'I know it now. I did not then.' He smiled at her, touching her cheek with his fingertips. 'But I knew from the first moment I kissed you that you were my soulmate.'

'Oh, Nicholas.' She sighed and leaned her head against him. 'Why did you never tell me this before?'

'At first I could not admit it even to myself—and then, oh, so many things prevented me,' he murmured, his mouth against her hair. 'Anger, guilt, fear—and jealousy. I saw you kiss Henri on the night of your cousin's wedding. I wondered then if I had lost you.'

'Henri kissed me, not I him.'

'But you did not repulse him.'

'He is my friend—and it was a friend's kiss, given on impulse on a night of celebration.'

'Henri loves you.'

'Yes—but he knows that I love you,' Deborah said. 'He offered to wed me if you did not come for me...' She gazed up at him, wishing she could see his eyes and read his expression. 'Why did you stay away? Why did you leave me while I was ill?'

'It was not my wish,' Nicholas said. 'Your father demanded that you be allowed time to recover from your ordeal in Spain. What could I do? I had no right to refuse him. Had I not put you into danger... I have had nightmares thinking of what might have happened on that ship. Had I come only a day later...'

'You saved me,' she whispered softly, touching her lips to his to hush him. 'I was stubborn and refused to listen to your warnings.' A shudder went through her and his arms tightened about her. 'Had my father and I gone to Spain as agreed, I might have been married to Miguel... You know what Don Manola planned for me? He meant to get a child with me himself, because he could not marry.'

'Yes, I know. He was obsessed by his need for an heir to replace the son he knew was insane. I think he will be punished for his sins by a higher authority, Deborah. He is at heart a good Catholic and he is haunted by what he has done. Perhaps we should pity him.'

'Yes, perhaps we should,' she agreed. She smiled as he drew her against him, content to lay her head against his shoulder. She felt safe, protected. 'You will not leave me again? You will not sail as a privateer again?'

'Never.' He smiled and stroked her cheek tenderly. 'I swear it. I shall stay at home and spend my life making you happy, Deborah. I have done with the caprice of kings and princes.'

'The King will be angry because we ran away. Will he seek to punish you for disobeying him?'

Nicholas looked at her confidently. 'Do not fear, my love. I doubt he will send an army to arrest me, for it would cost him money he would not care to waste in such a cause. I have been a good friend to James. Besides, he has other problems. England may soon be at war with Spain over the breakdown of the marriage contracts.'

She looked up at him in sudden alarm. 'You will not go to war? Oh, please, Nicholas, promise me!'

Nicholas kissed the top of her head. 'You must find a way to keep me at home, Deborah,' he said and the wickedness in his voice sent a thrill of desire winging through her.

Chapter Seventeen

It was late when they went on board the *Siren's Song* as she lay at Greenwich. The sky was a velvety black, lit only by a sprinkling of stars, the sound of the water lapping against the boat a gentle swell as the tide that would take them to France began to turn.

Nicholas escorted Deborah to her cabin, then went back on deck to give the order to weigh anchor. She laid his cloak over the back of the captain's chair, then sat down on the edge of the bed to wait. Her whole being throbbed with anticipation. Would he come to her—or would he remain on deck until they reached France?

Her heart began to thump wildly as she heard the sound of his footsteps and then the cabin door opened. He stood on the threshold smiling at her, and, as she saw the look in his eyes, her body tingled with longing and desire.

'You were expecting me?' he asked huskily.

'I hoped you would come.' She held out her hand to him invitingly, a naughty smile on her lips. 'You have not yet kissed me, my lord. Is it not the custom to kiss a lady after she has accepted your proposal?'

'Would you have had me ravish you before the boatmen?' he asked, eyes alight with wicked mischief. 'Do you imagine that I could kiss you now and walk away? I am not a saint, Deborah. I have wanted you, burned for you too long. I shall not answer for the consequences if you continue to look at me like that.'

'How do I look at you, Nicholas?' she asked softly.

'As if you longed for me to make love to you.'

'The way you did that night in the stable yard?' She raised her head, the shine in her eyes bright enough to blind a man. 'You almost had me then. I could not have denied you had you persisted—you know that I think?'

'I wanted more than your body, Deborah. I wanted your heart and soul…all of you.'

'You have me,' she replied and then gave him a teasing look. 'I think we have each other, sir, and it must be for the future to see who will command.'

'You may command me in anything,' he declared passionately as he drew her close to him, his arms holding her pressed hard against him so that she could feel the throb of his passion.

'Then I command you to make love to me,' she whispered as her own desire became a flame that would meet and match his own fire. 'Make me yours, Nicholas. Make it now…'

He bent his head, his mouth taking hungry possession of hers in a kiss that seemed to draw the very soul from her body. She felt as if she were dissolving into him, becoming one being, a part of a living, breathing flame of desire that was consuming them both.

'Oh, my love. I have dreamed of you so often…' he murmured huskily, lips against her throat. 'Dreamed, desired…needed you. I never ceased to think of you when we were parted.'

'And I of you.'

Deborah released the ties of her overdress, letting it slide to the floor, then her bodice and silken petticoat. Nicholas ripped away the fine linen of her shift to reveal the soft, rose-tipped mounds of her breasts to his fevered gaze. He bent his head to lick the buds delicately with his tongue before taking them into his mouth to gently nuzzle at her. She moaned with pleasure as he slid to his knees before her, burying his head against her femininity as if to breathe her in and absorb her into himself.

She shuddered as the waves of desire began to break over her, so much more strongly than she had yet experienced, shaking her with their force. She was swept along on a tide of sensual pleasure as he lifted her in his arms and carried her to the bed. He laid her down gently, then hastily stripped away his own clothes, casting them to the floor. Naked, he laid down next to her, thigh to thigh, gazing into her eyes.

His warm breath on her skin made her tingle as he began to explore her body intimately, caressing and delighting every piece of her as he slowly lingered over her, enjoying, savouring, anticipating the moment when they came together.

When at last she felt his throbbing manhood thrusting at her, seeking entrance to the warm, willing centre of her, she was already wandering on the plains of an unknown heaven and scarcely felt the loss of her maidenhead, a sharp pain kissed away in seconds by his mouth on hers and then a return to the pleasure that had her writhing beneath him and calling his name over and over again in her joy.

Never could she have imagined the pleasure Nicholas was giving her, and she him. Their bodies moved in a slow dance of sensual delight, matching each other perfectly so that when the tide of desire finally swept them both to that far shore it was so powerful that neither could speak for some time afterwards.

When they did it was the foolish, tender talk of lovers satiated and content, bodies still intertwined and minds attuned.

They slept and woke and made love again, this time with a hungry passion that devoured them both in its intensity.

'I am cruel to use you so,' Nicholas whispered remorsefully against her ear. 'You will hurt tomorrow. I should have given you space to heal after the first time.'

'I did not wish for time,' Deborah whispered as she snuggled against him, contented and at peace. 'Do not leave me, Nicholas. Hold me until we reach France.'

'I shall hold you forever,' he murmured, drawing her into him so that their bodies fit together as one. 'I love you, my angel.'

She slept peacefully in his arms, waking to find she was alone and it was morning. They were anchored in the bay off Chalfont and, as she rose to dress, she felt a tingle of anticipation. She was home again!

'Oh, it is so good to have you home again, my lady,' Louise cried as soon as she saw Deborah. 'I was so frightened when they told us you 'ad been captured by that wicked man. I think I never see you again and I am sad.'

Deborah embraced her. 'Thank you, Louise. You did not believe that I had gone willingly?'

'Of a surety, no!' Louise cried, laughing naughtily. 'You love the marquis, yes? And 'e love you. Why should you go? You 'ave everything your 'eart desires 'ere, no?'

'Yes. Yes, everything,' Deborah said and sighed with

contentment as she moved about the room she now thought of as her own. 'I am so happy here.'

'And so much in love.' Louise looked at her knowingly. Deborah was no longer a child, she had become a woman who had known passion. 'It is all settled between you now—yes?'

Deborah laughed. 'You are a wicked girl, Louise— but I missed you when I was in England. No one has ever looked after me as well as you do.'

'I should 'ope not,' Louise said with a shrug of her shoulders, but the look in her eyes showed that she was pleased with her mistress's praise. 'And now I prepare your bath, yes?'

'Oh, of all things that is what I should most like,' Deborah cried. 'Yes, please… Oh, Louise…' she called the girl back. 'You have not seen my betrothal ring? Some of my things were sent to England, but my ring was not amongst them.'

'It was 'ere,' Louise said and frowned. 'Mistress Trevern—she pack your pearls 'erself. I pack only your gowns.'

'Then I must ask Mistress Trevern,' Deborah said. 'Thank you, Louise. I shall enjoy a warm bath before I go down to join the marquis.'

As Louise went away to prepare the water, Deborah made a brief search for her ring. She knew where she had laid it down on that fateful day, but it was not there, nor had it fallen beneath the table.

Marie must have taken it deliberately! Deborah felt vexed. It had not fitted her well, but Nicholas would have had it altered to fit her finger.

There was no point in looking for the ring any longer. Louise had returned to tell her the bath was ready and to help her undress. She slipped into the deliciously warm, scented water and sat back with her eyes closed. How good it felt.

She had experienced a little soreness in that tender place Nicholas had lavished so much attention on the previous night, but the warmth—and perhaps some healing balm Louise had put into the water—was easing away the slight pain she had felt as they rode to the château earlier.

A smile touched Deborah's mouth as she compared this homecoming to the first time she had visited Chalfont. She had said such foolish things to Nicholas! And all the time she had been falling hopelessly in love with him. She had been a naïve girl then, but he had taught her all that was needful to become a woman.

'Why do you smile, my lady?'

His husky tones made her open her eyes with a start of surprise. 'I did not hear you enter,' she said, feeling a little shy that he had found her bathing. She glanced behind her—the door from her chamber had not opened. 'How…?'

'Through the curtain yonder.' He grinned teasingly. 'Did you never wonder what lay beyond it?'

'Your chamber?' she cried and was prompted to laugh but would not. Every night she had been at the château he had been so much closer to her than she had ever guessed. 'You are a rogue, sir! You might have walked into my bedchamber at any moment.'

'You know not how tempted I have been,' Nicholas replied, his eyes challenging her. 'I have watched you sleep and longed to take you in my arms.'

'Watched while I slept? You are no gentleman, sir!'

'I fear I cannot be,' he murmured wickedly. 'For I should not be here this moment—but I do not wish to leave. Do you bathe often, Deborah? Is that why you always smell so sweet? Why your skin is so soft?'

'My lord!' she protested, her cheeks aflame. 'It is the middle of the day. Such talk is not seemly.'

'Would you have me come to you only when it is dark?' He smiled and knelt down beside the bath. His hand strayed towards her shoulder, his fingers caressing the silk of her wet skin. 'I do not think I can wait so long—yet I know I must. We should not make love again so soon.'

'I want to be with you,' Deborah said, all pretense at outrage gone. She stood up, her lovely, slender body revealed in all its glory. 'Dry me, my lord. Let us pleasure each other.'

'Yes, I shall pleasure you,' Nicholas said, 'though I shall not take my ease of you again so soon. You are too precious to me, my love. I would not cause you a moment's pain.'

He wrapped her about with the sheet, patting her dry and then discarding the damp bathing sheet so that she was naked in his arms as he carried her to the bed.

Nicholas began by kissing her feet and the hollow in her ankle. His lips moved tantalizingly slowly upwards to the inner softness of her thigh—and then to that part of her that ached for his touch. She had thought the pleasure he had given her the previous night might never be repeated, for surely such joy could not always be a part of loving, but the warmth of his lips and tongue set her spiralling to dizzy heights. She was shaken by the force of the spasms of sensual delight his unselfish loving brought to her.

Afterwards, as he lay with his head against her breast, she sensed that he still hungered and yet would not take his ease of her for fear of hurting her. Greatly daring, she pushed him so that he rolled over on his back and lay staring up at her as she raised herself above him.

'May I not pleasure you as you did me, my lord?'

'Do you wish to?' he asked. 'I would not ask anything you did not wish to give, my love.'

Deborah smiled and bent her head, kissing first the hollows at his shoulder and then his chest, little teasing flicks of her tongue that followed a narrow trail of dark hair downward towards the sensitive centre of his need. She lingered artfully until she had him groaning, moving lower and lower until she reached the object of their mutual desire.

Afterwards, when they lay in each other's arms, satiated, content and happy, Nicholas remembered why he had come to her as she was bathing. He rose and sought for the small velvet pouch amongst his clothing, then brought it back to her and tipped its contents into the palm of his hand. She saw it was a magnificent emerald ring, which he proceeded to slip onto her betrothal finger.

It fitted perfectly and she knew it had been made for her. 'It is lovely,' she told him. 'The ring you gave me on the day of our betrothal has been mislaid. I left it on the dressing board when I went riding for fear that I might lose it.'

'Have you asked Louise if she has seen it?'

'She said Marie packed my personal things. She had seen it earlier. Marie must have packed it, I suppose—though I did not see it in London.'

'I wondered why you did not wear it.' Nicholas frowned. 'I shall ask Marie if she has put it somewhere for you when she returns.'

'Is she to return?'

'Until her wedding. I have given her a dowry—it is the least I could do.'

'You saw her that afternoon in London?' Deborah asked.

'Yes. I did not disturb you because Marie said you had complained of a headache earlier—and I had in any case decided that we should elope.'

'I did not complain of a headache. It was my heart that ached when you did not come to me as you promised.'

Nicholas nodded. 'Your heart does not ache now?'

'No—you know that I am happy, Nicholas.'

Nicholas looked serious. 'I do not think Marie is happy. We must try to be kind to her, Deborah. Not everyone is as fortunate as we are.'

'Yes, I know.' She smiled at him lovingly. 'I must get up. You should go away, my lord, and leave me to dress.'

'I would lie with you all day,' Nicholas replied. 'But I have been from home some little time and I have things to do. We shall be alone this evening—but tomorrow your father and our guests arrive. The following day we shall be married.'

'Go, then,' Deborah bid him. 'For I know you must have much to do.'

'We shall dine together,' Nicholas said. 'And tonight I shall come to you.'

'Yes.' Deborah caught his hand and kissed it. 'We must never be apart again.'

'Never while we both live,' he vowed and then he left her.

He was standing over her, his red eyes fearful to behold. She could feel his hot breath on her and she cried out to Nicholas to save her. He was going to force her to become his bride…

'Hush, my love,' Nicholas said, rocking her in his arms. 'It was but a dream. He can never hurt you now. He is dead and I am here with you. I shall always be with you.'

'Yes, I know,' she said and clung to him. 'I am foolish to have these dreams now. It is all behind me. I am safe with you.'

'Did you have dreams before?'

'Not always the same,' she confessed. 'I thought it was because I feared to lose you—but I have no need to fear that now.'

'You will not lose me,' Nicholas said and found her lips.

He kissed her tenderly and she turned into his body, snuggling up to him like a trusting kitten. 'Take no notice of my foolishness, dearest. I love you. Just love me and all will be well.'

Nicholas made love to her tenderly, and then they fell asleep in each other's arms.

Deborah had been walking in the gardens, picking herbs she intended to use in her simples. It was still warm despite the fact that it was now almost winter. Not as hot as it had been in the summer, but pleasant enough to enjoy being in her garden.

'Forgive me for disturbing you, my lady.' One of the servants had come up to her. 'You asked to be told when Sir Edward Stirling and Mistress Trevern arrived.'

'Are they here?' She smiled at him. 'Thank you. I shall come at once.'

She walked into the house and, after giving her basket to a servant, ran straight up to the chamber that had been prepared for her father.

'You are here,' she said as he opened his door to her knock. 'How pleased I am to see you, dearest Father.'

Sir Edward looked into her eyes, then nodded and smiled. 'You are happy,' he said. 'It is in your eyes, Deborah. I wondered how you would feel when de Vere told me he planned to elope with you—but I see it has served.'

'Yes.' She went to kiss his cheek. 'I love him—and he loves me. I know that now.'

'Of course he loves you—did you doubt it?' She nodded and he chuckled as if much amused. 'Foolish girl. A blind man would have known it, but love is often blind.' He frowned then. 'I had thought I might marry once you were wed, child—but since I have been told to regard this house as my second home, I see no reason for it. No, I shall keep your mother's memory sacred and find my happiness in you and your children.'

Deborah felt a sense of relief. She had wondered if her father had been attracted to Nicholas's cousin, but it seemed his heart remained his own.

She kissed his cheek. 'I knew that Nicholas had told you this is your home. You must stay with us as often as you wish, Father. I would be happy if you made your home with us, and I know Nicholas would also, for the house is so large and he loves to fill it with his friends. And now I must see that Mistress Trevern has all she needs.'

'Be careful,' her father warned. 'I did not see it at first—but I have discovered that she hates you, Deborah.'

'Yes, I know,' Deborah replied. 'It has been that way from the very beginning. She had hoped that Nicholas would marry her and she has been unkind on several occasions—but I have tried to ignore it. She is Nicholas's cousin.'

'Yes—but I still say be careful.'

'I shall,' she promised, kissed him and went on her way.

Pausing outside Marie's room, Deborah took a deep breath. Mistress Trevern had made her hostility known from the outset, but it could not harm her now. She knew that Nicholas loved her and Marie's spite could not change that or damage her happiness.

She knocked and was invited to enter. Marie had been looking at something, and hid her hand quickly behind her back. Her defensive manner was so marked that it made Deborah suspicious, and she was sure she knew what the other woman was hiding.

'What are you concealing?' she asked. 'Is it my betrothal ring, Marie? I know you took it. It was in my room when you helped Louise pack my things, yet it was not amongst the things that were sent to me in London.'

'How dare you?' Marie's eyes flashed with anger. 'Are you calling me a thief?'

'I know you did not steal it for its value,' Deborah said. 'You thought Nicholas would believe I had been careless and lost it. You wanted to cause trouble between us—did you not?'

'He is a fool to love you!' Marie said viciously. 'I would have given him everything. Everything! You could never love him as much as I do!'

'I do love him, perhaps more than you could ever know,' Deborah said, remaining calm despite the other's show of passion. 'And he loves me. You cannot change that, Marie. Whatever you do. Nothing and no one can come between us.'

'It was his ring. I wanted something of him! Why must you have it all? Why am I to have nothing?' Marie suddenly hurled the ring at her. It cut Deborah's cheek. She touched the wound and found a trace of blood on her fingertips. 'I wish it had killed you!' Marie cried. 'Yes, you should die. If you were dead, Nicholas would turn to me. He loved me until you came…'

Before Deborah had realized what she intended, Marie darted forward and snatched something from the top of her travelling trunk. Deborah saw a flash of silver and sensed that it was a knife. One of the footmen must have left it there after cutting the ropes that had bound the trunk. She gave a scream and put out her hands to protect herself as Marie lifted her arm threateningly.

However, even as Marie launched herself, someone thrust Deborah aside and put himself between them. Deborah watched the struggle, which was brief and over very suddenly. Nicholas was too strong for Marie and within seconds the knife went flying through the air—to be picked up by Sir Edward.

'I was anxious,' he said to Deborah, as she looked at him white-faced and shocked. 'I knew she would harm you if she could—and I told Nicholas what I suspected.'

Marie was sobbing bitterly. She sank to her knees at her cousin's feet, clutching his legs as her grief poured out.

'Why did you bring her here?' she wailed. 'We were so happy without her. Send her away, Nicholas, and we can be happy again.'

'Deborah is the woman I love,' he said harshly. 'You are the one who shall leave, Marie.' He wrenched away from her clinging arms and walked to Deborah's side, his arm about her. 'Tomorrow I shall wed this woman. You leave this house within the hour. You have your dowry—take it to a nunnery and spend your life in repentance.'

'Forgive me,' Marie begged, weeping bitterly as she remained on her knees. 'I lost my mind for a moment. I did not truly mean to kill her.'

'Had I not come in time, I doubt not you would have done your best to take Deborah's life.' Nicholas could barely contain his fury. 'I shall tell Jean what kind of a woman you are, cousin. I do not think he would wish to have you as his wife if he knew the truth. No, you shall be taken to a nunnery.'

'You are so cruel,' Marie sobbed. 'I did not think you could be so cruel to me. At least let me return to England—with the dowry you gave me. I may find a husband there.'

'You deserve no consideration from me!'

Deborah laid her hand on his arm. 'Let Marie go to England,' she said. 'It would be too harsh to force her to life in a nunnery. She does not love Jean—but she might find happiness with someone else.'

Nicholas stared at her and then at Marie, who had now risen to her feet. He hesitated for a few moments, then nodded. 'Is that what you truly want, cousin?'

Marie glared at Deborah as if she would refuse the favour because it came from her, then her eyes dropped and she seemed to sag as if all the fight had gone out of her.

'I am sorry, Marie,' Deborah said. 'It was never my intention to hurt you.'

'Forgive me…' The words were muffled and indistinct but Deborah heard them.

'Of course,' she said. 'You must try to forgive yourself.'

Nicholas took Deborah's arm and led her from the room. 'You are too forgiving,' he said. 'She would have been out of harm's way, unable to cause trouble for herself or others.'

'It would have been too cruel,' Deborah murmured. 'We are both so fortunate, Nicholas. We ought to be able to show mercy to your cousin. She deserves a chance of happiness.'

'Yes, I suppose she does,' Nicholas said. 'I was angry because I feared for you—just as I was when I saw you being married to that monster in Spain.' He gave her a rueful look. 'I was harsh to you that day—and then you turned to Henri. When I returned from the King's business, I believed I had lost you. And again I was angry. You must teach me to be kinder, my love.'

'You will not need to be angry in the future,' Deborah said and reached up to kiss his cheek. 'You will never need to doubt my love for you—nor I yours for me.'

Chapter Eighteen

The rays of a wintry sun shone through the high windows of Nicholas's private chapel, setting rainbows of colour dancing on the ancient flagstones. The building had been closed since his father's death, but now a priest had blessed the chapel and was waiting to perform the wedding ceremony.

Nicholas turned his head to watch as his bride came down the aisle on her father's arm. She looked so serene and beautiful that his heart contracted with love for her. He had indeed been blessed. He knew himself unworthy of the love she bore him, but he would strive to deserve it for the rest of their lives.

Deborah was walking in a dream, so happy that it all seemed unreal. Unaware of her groom's thoughts, she saw only his smile as she reached his side.

She was wearing a gown of cream velvet with trimmings of heavy gold embroidery over a petticoat of white silk. Louise had dressed her hair with white flowers, leaving it to flow loosely on her shoulders. She wore a long string of creamy pearls and a choker of magnificent emeralds and precious diamonds about her slender throat. Matching earbobs hung from her lobes, and she had a bangle of gold set with emeralds and pearls on her wrist.

She was dressed in a manner befitting the much-loved wife of a wealthy man, but the light in her eyes outshone any jewels as she gazed up at her husband-to-be.

Deborah listened carefully to the priest as he solemnly intoned the words that gave her to Nicholas, making her responses in a clear sure voice.

'You are man and wife in God's law,' the priest said, smiling at them. 'You may kiss your wife, sir.'

Nicholas's kiss was soft and brief, but his eyes promised so much more. Then they were leaving the chapel and being congratulated by their friends.

'You are happy, my lady,' Henri said, and it was not a question for her happiness was in her eyes. 'I am content. I shall not see you for some months—but I shall return one day, I promise.'

'We shall always be glad to see you.'

Henri had stood up with Nicholas as his best man. She knew that any differences had been settled between them, and she was glad. It would have hurt her to know she was the cause of a breach of their friendship.

'Do not fear,' Henri replied. 'I love you both dearly. I always knew you belonged to Nico.'

Madame Dubois came to wish Deborah happy. 'It is so good to have you back with us, madame. Nicholas told me what happened—how brave you were.'

'Thank you,' Deborah said. 'You must call me by my given name. We shall be close friends now. I want you to come often to our home, Jeanne.'

'But of course,' Jeanne cried and kissed her. 'We shall gossip and drive our husbands wild—but we shall be happy, no?'

'Yes. We shall all be happy.'

Deborah's eyes followed her husband about the room as he greeted his guests. She enjoyed being fêted as a bride, but in her heart she longed for the moment when they would be alone.

'I love my friends dearly, but they are apt sometimes to overstay their welcome,' Nicholas said much, much later that night. Louise had dressed Deborah in a filmy nightgown and she was sitting at her dressing table when he entered. She had been brushing her hair and turned with a smile as he came to take the brush from her. 'Let me do that...'

Deborah was content to let him brush her hair. 'You were a long time in coming.'

'I had great difficulty in preventing them from accompanying me here,' he replied with a rueful smile. 'Fortunately, your father forbade it.'

'I knew he would,' she said. 'How soothing it is to have one's hair brushed.'

'Are you soothed enough?' Nicholas asked. 'Or are you too tired to make love tonight? It has been a tiring day.'

'I am not tired,' she said and stood up, turning to face him with a smile on her face. 'I have been waiting for this moment all day. Pray take me to bed, my love.'

'You wish is my command, lady,' he said, then bent down to sweep her up in his arms. Depositing her carefully on the bed, he knelt beside her, gazing down at her loveliness. 'You are so beautiful, my beloved. I know I am not worthy of you—but I beg you will never cease to love me as you do now.'

'I could no more stop loving you than cease to breathe,' she said and held her hand out to him. 'Why do you say you are not worthy, Nicholas? I know you to be generous, honest and loving—why do you not value yourself?'

'I have done things of which I am now ashamed,' he replied. 'The Spanish called me *Le Diable* and I fear I deserved the name.'

'My father believes you had just cause.'

'I am grateful for his understanding—but can you forget that I was once no better than a pirate?'

'I should never have called you that—what you did was not for private gain or greed.'

'I gave away the gold I took—to my men, King James and others. I wanted nothing except revenge, but revenge is cold and empty. It destroys the soul. I learned that when you brought me back to a sense of goodness and I remembered what it was like to live and be happy.'

'Then you have only to make your peace with God—for I have already forgotten that there was ever a time I thought ill of you.'

'I have made my confession and received absolution.'

'Then think of it no more,' Deborah said. She flashed him a wicked smile. 'Indeed, sometimes I have thought you a wicked devil—but I am your wife. No matter what you do, I shall always love you.'

Nicholas smiled and bent to kiss her lips. Any shadows that had lingered in his soul were swept away as he took her in his arms.

'The Devil's bride,' he murmured. 'Yes, you are mine. And I shall never release you though my namesake comes himself to claim me. We are bound for all eternity, Deborah.'

'I am content that it shall be so.' Her eyes danced with wickedness. 'And now it is my wish that you waste no more time in talk, my lord.'

Nicholas's laughter rang out strong and sure.
'I am at your command, my lady,' he said.
And he was—and she at his.

* * * * *

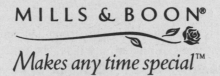

MILLS & BOON®

Makes any time special™

Mills & Boon publish 29 new titles every month. Select from...

Modern Romance™   Tender Romance™

Sensual Romance™

Medical Romance™ Historical Romance™

MAT2

A Perfect Family

An enthralling family saga by bestselling author

PENNY JORDAN

Published 20th July

*Available at branches of WH Smith, Tesco,
Martins, RS McCall, Forbuoys, Borders, Easons,
Sainsbury, Woolworth and most good paperback bookshops*

MIRANDA LEE

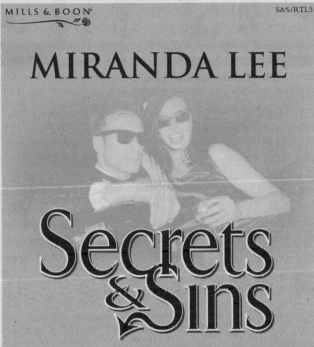

Secrets & Sins

Passion, sensuality and scandal
set amongst Australia's rich and famous

A compelling six-part linked family saga.

Book 5 - Scandals & Secrets

Available from 3rd August

Available at branches of WH Smith, Tesco,
Martins, RS McCall, Forbuoys, Borders, Easons,
Volume One/James Thin and most good paperback bookshops

2FREE

books and a surprise gift!

We would like to take this opportunity to thank you for reading this Mills & Boon® book by offering you the chance to take TWO more specially selected titles from the Historical Romance™ series absolutely FREE! We're also making this offer to introduce you to the benefits of the Reader Service™—

- ★ FREE home delivery
- ★ FREE gifts and competitions
- ★ FREE monthly Newsletter
- ★ Exclusive Reader Service discounts
- ★ Books available before they're in the shops

Accepting these FREE books and gift places you under no obligation to buy, you may cancel at any time, even after receiving your free shipment. Simply complete your details below and return the entire page to the address below. *You don't even need a stamp!*

YES! Please send me 2 free Historical Romance books and a surprise gift. I understand that unless you hear from me, I will receive 4 superb new titles every month for just £2.99 each, postage and packing free. I am under no obligation to purchase any books and may cancel my subscription at any time. The free books and gift will be mine to keep in any case.

H1ZEA

Ms/Mrs/Miss/Mr ....Initials......................................
                                                          BLOCK CAPITALS PLEASE

Surname ....

Address ....

....

....Postcode.................................

Send this whole page to:
UK: FREEPOST CN81, Croydon, CR9 3WZ
EIRE: PO Box 4546, Kilcock, County Kildare (stamp required)